"I kne **ki** **from t** **I set**

Jared explained. "I

She was touched
been so hard for him to make. Jared reached out
for her and she went to him at once. He breathed
a warm kiss onto her lips.

Dellie gathered the courage to touch him, loos-
ening the silk of his white tie. Had not the cards
told her that he would come? *Trust in the cards,* a
voice inside urged her.

"It was meant to be," she said.

Jared needed no further encouragement. In one
swift move, he untied the sash at her waist. Her
robe draped open, baring her body to his gaze . . .

Magic Nights

Laurel Collins

DIAMOND BOOKS, NEW YORK

MAGIC NIGHTS

A Diamond Book / published by arrangement with
the author

PRINTING HISTORY
Diamond edition / November 1991

ISBN: 1-55773-614-6

Diamond Books are published by The Berkley Publishing Group,
200 Madison Avenue, New York, New York 10016.
The name "DIAMOND" and its logo are trademarks
belonging to Charter Communications, Inc.

PRINTED IN THE UNITED STATES OF AMERICA

10 9 8 7 6 5 4 3 2 1

To my two daughters,
Melissa and Amanda,
with love and thanks for
understanding that even mothers
need time to dream.

Magic Nights

CHAPTER
1

St. Gervais, 1840

A round, yellow moon hung low over the cane fields that filled the landscape just beyond the veranda. Mademoiselle Louise Chandelle Marie-Thérèse Valmont (a ponderous name for a child of only seven years) pushed open the French doors of her plantation home and stepped out to get a better view. The rhythmic beating of the Rada drums that had roused her from her sleep continued still, and now there was chanting as well: some French words and some that were foreign to her . . . *Damballah* . . . *Legba* . . . *Erzulie*. . . . Mesmerized, she left the veranda and walked out behind the house, following the sound. A playful tropic breeze tossed the ringlets of her fair hair back over her shoulders and fluttered the nightgown at her ankles. She wriggled her bare toes in the dust of the narrow path that wound back into the jungle and pressed on fearlessly.

There was no dread of the darkness in her. She had been born on this island, in the big, white house called Belle Terre, and she knew each plant and tree of the exotic tropical jungle. Mama Tess had taught her. And she was not ignorant of the chant resounding in the distance. She had heard it often enough, this primal sound that echoed through the still night air, and when she grew old enough to ask its origin, Mama Tess had regarded her with a grim visage. "Voodoo," she had told her but would say no more.

And so Chandelle (for this was the special name by which she was known to her beloved Mama Tess) decided that tonight she would follow the sound of the drums, deep into the forest behind the slave quarters, determined to see for herself about this "voodoo."

In a clearing near the river a bonfire blazed, and round it the black men and women whirled in a frenzied dance. Protected by the foliage, Chandelle drew nearer, listening to the chants that called forth their gods. Not far from the trio of drummers stood a most unusual-looking woman, dressed in white and wearing a tignon that covered her hair. She held a large rattle in her hand that she shook in rhythm with the drumbeats, and a large brown snake was draped over her shoulders like a shawl. Her skin was a warm cinnamon color, her looks exotic, and the child surmised that the woman was the leader of this band of writhing savages.

She could not believe that these were the same docile field hands who tended Papa's cane fields, and for the first time she felt afraid. The increasing cadence of the drums matched her heartbeat, and when she would have turned and run, a newcomer approached the group. He was a tall boy of about sixteen years and fair-skinned in contrast to the rest. He took the snake from the woman's shoulders, placed it upon his own, and said in French: "*Damballah Wedo,* behold your children! *Aida Wedo,* here are your children! Behold your children, *Damballah!* Here are your children!"

The others had joined in the chant, and at length he raised a hand to silence them. "We call upon the *loas* to aid us. *Ogoun Balandjo,* punish those who would enslave us. The day of vengeance is here!"

The boy looked up then, and Chandelle was certain that his black eyes met hers. She was transfixed as his lip curled into an evil smile. And then, quite suddenly, a hand closed over her mouth and she was pulled away from the scene.

"This is no place for you, child!" Mama Tess chided in a hushed voice as she lifted Chandelle into her arms and held her against her ample bosom. "Come now. I will put you in your bed, and this time you stay, *n'est-ce pas?*"

"*Oui, maman,*" the child replied in a small voice.

And it was not the last time that Tess would have to protect the life of her charge that night.

Chandelle sat cross-legged upon her quilt beneath the great drape of mosquito *barre,* and by the light of the chamberstick on the night table, she examined her treasure. The silver box was a present from Papa. It had come all the way from France, and the lid was chased with her initials: *LCV.* Within were the cards, the "tarot," as Mama Tess called them. They had belonged to Chandelle's mother, who had been a renowned cartomancer in the French court. Chandelle liked to hear Papa tell the story of how he traveled across the ocean to find a wife, and of how one night at a party there was the most beautiful woman he had ever seen telling fortunes for her friends. He arranged an introduction and asked her to read the cards for him. He thought it only a game, but she told him many things that were true, and he was intrigued. After they were wed, Mama said to him that the cards had told her that very night that she would be his wife.

And so each night Chandelle took them out of the silver box and listened to them, but they never spoke a word. She liked to look at the pictures all the same, and read the strange names: the Magician, the Moon, Death, the Tower, and the Knight of Swords. . . .

She laid them out, one beside another, all in a row. The Magician had a kind face, like Papa's, and she decided that she liked him, but the crayfish crawling up out of the water on the Moon card, the animated skeleton called Death, and the lightning-struck Tower frightened her. Last was the Knight, riding upon a charger and brandishing his sword. He was just as she imagined the heroes to be in the fairy tales that Papa read to her sometimes. She decided to like him as well.

Mama Tess knew the secret of the cards. She had been lady's maid to Chandelle's mother before her death, and Madame Valmont had taught her how to read them. Mama Tess promised that soon she would teach Chandelle, and the child decided that she would remind her of that in the morning.

The warm breeze that fluttered the lace curtains of the long window and made the candle gutter low carried on it an acrid smell. Smoke!

It was not time to burn the cane, and curious, Chandelle pushed aside the netting and went to the window. The night sky glowed orange, and billows of thick, gray smoke rolled in like storm clouds. Dark figures bearing torches crisscrossed the road, and new fires sprang up in their wake. She thought of her papa. Surely he would know what all this was about. He must be home by now. She went to her door, but when she opened it, she was met instead by Mama Tess.

Tess swept into the room, her heart hammering in her breast. Without a word the child pointed to the window. Tess followed the small finger and gazed out on the landscape. Fire was everywhere. And from this height she could see the figures running in the darkness. "*Mon*

Dieu!" she whispered under her breath, hoping the child had not heard. "They gonna burn the house!"

"Where is Papa?" Chandelle inquired.

"At the mill. Don't you worry none, child."

But Tess was worried herself. Monsieur Valmont was at the mill, and them crazy field hands was between him and his house, setting fire to the cane fields. She ought to have guessed when she heard them voodoo drums that there'd be trouble this night.

Tess turned away from the hopeless situation outside, and then she saw the cards on the bed. Five of them, all in a neat row. She examined each one carefully. This was not a good sign.

"Who laid them cards, child?" she asked.

"It was me," Chandelle admitted, and seeing the concern on Tess's face, she added: "But it was only a game. That's all."

"*Ma pauvre petite,*" Tess replied, gathering up the cards and returning them to the silver case.

What was to be done? She had heard tell of slave revolts on other islands, and of the terrible, bloody things that came to pass. Tess looked down upon the fair-haired child she had raised from infancy. Her papa could not save her now, poor little one. The red glow on the horizon told her that the mill was already ablaze. If they'd found him there, he might be dead by now. Tess crossed herself at the thought. It was left to her to save her sweet Chandelle.

Tess moved quickly, dressing the child in only a mended cotton shift so that there would be nothing to draw attention to her. Then she took the colorful kerchief from her own throat and wound Chandelle's blond locks into a turban. She lay another kerchief on the bureau, and in it she emptied the contents of Chandelle's jewel case and the silver card case, then wrapped it all securely.

Not daring to breathe, she led the child down the back

stairs and heard the shouts of the approaching men; they
were so much nearer now. She thought of the money box
full of gold coins in Monsieur's study, but there was no
time to retrieve it. They paused at the kitchen hearth only
long enough for Tess to gather up a handful of ashes to
smear upon the child's face and arms and legs. Perhaps
if they mistook her for Tess's own child, she would be
spared.

There were footsteps on the veranda now. Time had run
out. Tess crossed herself once more, and with the child's
small hand in one of hers and the knotted kerchief in the
other, Tess hurried into the black depths of the jungle.

"Are we going to France?" Chandelle asked her. "Will
Papa meet us there?"

Mama Tess shook her head. "Not to France, *ma petite,*"
she told her, "but we must leave the island. It is not safe
for us here."

And then Chandelle began to sing softly, to herself, the
lullaby about a little lost child that Papa would sing to
her whenever she was frightened and could not sleep at
night. "Ere you reach the mountains blue, tarry on the
windward shore. There beneath the golden hill, I shall
wait, my little one.

"Do not fear the dark-as-night, nor the garden made
of stone. I shall light you on your way. There you'll find
me, little one."

Mama Tess had not told her, but Chandelle knew just
the same that she would never see Papa nor the island
again. Tears blurred her eyes and ran onto her smudged
cheek, but she turned her face away so Mama Tess would
not see.

CHAPTER
2

St. Louis, Missouri, 1853

Lucien Valmont leaned on the bar and peered through the haze of smoke to a nearby table of the riverboat saloon, where sat the object of his interest: a tall young man with sandy-colored hair, dressed in the gambler's uniform—a black frock coat and trousers and a fancy silk brocade waistcoat. His grim face was hidden by a wide-brimmed hat with a silver band, but Valmont recognized him just the same. He watched him toy with a fresh pack of cards, spreading them easily and then shuffling them with a smooth hand. The stranger did not look particularly dangerous from this vantage point, though Valmont did not miss the bulge of the bowie knife that was thrust in his boot, nor the holstered Colt revolver at his hip.

The gambler had his eye on another table, where two coarse-looking fellows were browbeating a nervous young gentleman into a game of poker. All at once he drew himself up and approached the group.

"Looks as though you're short a hand," Valmont heard him say as he promptly took the empty chair for himself.

The burly, bearded man shot a quick glance to his part-

ner—a gangling lad in rough homespun who was handling
the cards—and both turned cold eyes upon the newcomer.

"Surely you won't deny me a place at your table," the
gambler said to the pair. "You seemed eager enough for
this gentleman's company."

"Suit yourself, mister," the lad shuffling the cards replied, trying to effect a casual air.

The pale young gentleman put out his hand. "I'm Timothy Wescott," he said to the gambler, "from Cincinnati."

"Best play your cards close to the vest, Mr. Wescott,"
Valmont heard him reply.

The odd group was soon engaged in their game, and
during the first few uneventful hands, Valmont found himself with the perfect opportunity to study the man who'd
captured his interest.

"What did you learn, Burke?" Valmont asked his aide,
who drew up beside him now. His eyes, though, were still
focused on the table nearby.

"You was right, Mr. Valmont, sir. His name's
Durant . . . Jared Durant. Keeps to himself mostly, but
I found a man in Battle Row—claims he served under him
in the Mexican War. He told me that Durant was decorated for bravery at Monterrey, said he weren't a man to
be taken lightly, either. Something must've happened to
him down there. They say he came back with a death
wish—"

"*Vraiment,*" Valmont replied absently, "one can see it
in his eyes.

"There's always talk about his sort. A man on the edge,
that's what I'd call him," Burke observed. "Appears to
be a gambler by trade; the men on the docks say as how
he'll take on any challenge if the stakes are high enough."

Timothy Wescott pulled at his stiff shirt collar now. He
was losing, by the looks of it. Reaching into his waistcoat

pocket, he unhooked his watch and tossed it into the center of the table.

"There," he said. "It's worth five dollars at least."

The burly man leaned forward, though, and flicked a stubby finger at the pocket watch. "Now, what would I do with the likes of that? Don't need no fancy timepiece. If you ain't got cash money—"

In one swift move Jared Durant reached across the table and grabbed the man by the shirtfront. "I'll cover the bet," he growled. "Now, play your cards."

He fairly threw the man back into his chair. "And mind you," he added, "the ones in your hand, not the two in your cuff."

"You callin' me a cheat?" the big man retorted, and Valmont could see Wescott flinch at the sound of chairs scraping the floor as the men on either side of him prepared to rise.

"There isn't a man on the levee hasn't heard tell of you, Jack Stephens, and your friend here," Durant shot back. "Subtlety hasn't been your style thus far. Now, I can see that Mr. Wescott is anxious to get on with the game, so I'll ignore your lack of manners. If you're still looking to defend your good name, though, I'll be happy to oblige you after the hand is played."

Valmont seemed pleased at the scene playing itself out not far away. His hand slipped into the pocket of his frock coat, and he impatiently fingered the brooch that lay there. "Tell me, Burke," he said. "Where does this fellow Durant come from?"

"The man who served with him down in Mexico told me he's a Virginian . . . said he'd heard a couple of officers talkin' once 'bout how his daddy gambled away the family plantation. You reckon that's why he's so anxious to raise cash, so's he can buy it back again?"

The Frenchman took in all that his companion said but was too busy formulating his own plans to reply.

At the table nearby Wescott had come out a winner, and after retrieving his watch and pocketing his winnings, he beat a hasty retreat.

Durant let out a hearty laugh as he pulled himself out of his chair, but was taken quite by surprise as the younger of the misbegotten pair at the table suddenly charged at him, knocking him flat on his back. Durant kept on laughing, though, until he saw the glint from the blade of his own knife, which the boy had appropriated.

"The way I figure it, mister, you owe us fifty dollars," the lad standing over him said. He was full of bravado now as he waved the knife before Durant's face. "Countin' up what we lost and what we coulda made off of that fella. He'd have been an easy mark, if not for your interferin'."

Silence filled the room; everyone stopped what they were doing and watched to see what would happen next. Jack Stephens drew nearer. "Ain't so funny now, are you, mister? I'd say you'd best pay up, before my partner here gets tired of waitin' and commences carvin' you up like a Christmas turkey."

At the bar Burke made a move to go to Durant's aid, but Valmont reached out and put a hand on his arm to stop him. "Wait," he ordered, his voice hushed.

Durant showed no fear. He lifted his chin, baring his throat for the knife's blade, and he glared up at his attacker. "Do it!" he spat. "Do it, boy, and you'll do us both a favor!"

But the lad had not anticipated such a response. His hands began to shake, and when he realized that he could not meet the challenge in Durant's eyes, he dropped the knife and ran off, with Stephens close upon his heels.

Jared Durant rose up and dusted himself off, as if what had just transpired was of no great import. Then he went back to the table he'd first occupied, took out his deck of cards, and absently began to shuffle it again.

"Mr. Valmont, sir," Burke put in. "Don't see why you need bother with this fellow. Any one of us who works for you would gladly handle the job, whatever it be, no questions asked."

"I appreciate your loyalty, *mon ami,*" Valmont replied, "but for the special task I have in mind, I need a man with particular qualifications. You have done well. Expect a bonus in your pay envelope this month."

"Thank you kindly, sir."

Yes, Valmont decided, his instincts had not been wrong. This Durant fellow was just what he was looking for.

Jared Durant struck a match on the underside of the table to light his cheroot and pretended not to notice the man who approached him with a whiskey bottle in one hand and two glasses in the other.

His dark frock coat was of an expensive cut, and the black waistcoat was embroidered in rich gold thread. His striped cravat was held in place with a gold stickpin, stamped with the fleur-de-lis and a wreath of laurel leaves around it—a rich Creole come upriver on business, Jared surmised, or perhaps a European on holiday. The man walked with a pronounced limp and had a long scar that ran down the side of his face and tugged at the corner of his right eye.

"Monsieur?" he said in a cultured French accent. "May I join you?"

"By all means," Jared replied and waved a hand toward an empty chair.

The Frenchman sat down, then poured a generous amount from the whiskey bottle into each of the glasses. He took one for himself and handed one to Jared, who took the glass and unceremoniously downed the amber liquid, all the while tapping the deck of cards on the table with his other hand. What did this man want?

His gaze settled on the cards, and Jared's mouth curved into a smile as he retrieved his cigar. "Do you play?" he asked.

The Frenchman nodded. "But I wonder, *mon ami,* why it is that *you* play when the cards are the cause of all your misfortune?"

Jared regarded him cautiously. "Have we met, sir?"

"No, but I shall remedy that promptly. I am Lucien Valmont, the owner of this vessel."

Jared studied the man for a long while before he met the shrewd, gray eyes at last. "It would appear that you already know who I am."

"*C'est vrai,* Monsieur Durant." I have been watching you. I have seen you at my tables many times. I was told that your father was a gambler—" Seeing the dark look that came over Durant, Valmont amended his statement. "But I was, perhaps, misinformed."

Jared took a long draw on the cheroot and eyed the whiskey bottle at Valmont's elbow. "No, indeed, sir. But my father's unfortunate experience has not left me with an aversion to gambling . . . only to losing."

Valmont laughed at this, pouring another drink, which Jared gratefully accepted.

Jared did not know what to make of the man who sat beside him, chatting as easily as if they were two old friends. His nerves were still somewhat jangled from his encounter with the sorry pair of cardsharps, and he wondered if Valmont had witnessed it. He could feel quite distinctly the tension that hung on the air, much like the curling smoke that rose from the cigar balanced in the crook of his finger. Valmont was no fool. What was he after?

"I am certain, Mr. Valmont," Jared told him, "that you have not come here only to discuss my family history."

"You are quite right, monsieur. I have sought you out because I understand that you will take on certain 'tasks' for the right price. I have such a task—"

Jared's chair scraped the floor as he stood up and stubbed out the cheroot. "I don't know what you've heard, mister, but I don't kill a man without my own reasons, and money isn't one of them!"

Valmont paled, and for the first time his composure slipped. He ran an unsteady hand through his dark hair, which was threaded with silver. "Monsieur Durant, *s'il vous plaît*. Sit down, have another drink. You misunderstand. I was told that you have been employed by Mr. Allan Pinkerton in Chicago . . . as a detective."

Jared's eyes narrowed. Valmont looked older to him now and tired. "I was in his employ," Jared replied, "for a time. But we have since parted company, so I'm afraid that I can be of no help to you—"

"Please, Monsieur Durant," the Frenchman pleaded, "it is my only child, my daughter—"

Jared could see by his expression how difficult it was for a man like Lucien Valmont to beg. He was not used to being dependent upon others, and so Jared decided to sit down again and listen to him.

"I have told no one else here in St. Louis of my past," Valmont began. "It has always been too painful for me to speak on it, but now I find that I must. I come from the island of St. Gervais in the West Indies. My father and his father before him were planters. We farmed a vast acreage in sugarcane. It was a good life, Monsieur Durant. I had no more aspirations than to raise a family and live out my life on the island. But there is no telling what fate has in store for us, is there?

"My wife died giving birth to our daughter, and I swore

then that the light was gone forever from my life. Friends tried to console me, telling me that I must let the infant child be my candle, and so it was that I gave her the name 'Chandelle'—Louise Chandelle Marie-Thérèse Valmont. And she was so full of life, monsieur. She grew to be as lovely as any of the exotic flowers on our island and as bright as any child could be. She was always questioning me, 'Why is that, Papa?' or 'Tell me more, Papa.' "

Valmont paused to draw an uneven breath, and Jared could not miss the fact that his eyes were bright with tears. Then the Frenchman poured them yet another drink and downed his own swiftly.

When he continued, his gray eyes seemed vacant. "It was thirteen years ago, just before the emancipation of the slaves by the French, and my Louise was seven years old. I'd sent her to bed and gone to meet my overseer about a problem at the mill. How could I have known? There was a revolt of the slaves on the island that night. I was beaten and left to die when the mill was set ablaze. They burned it all, all of my Belle Terre: the mill and the fields . . . and my home."

He squeezed his eyes shut and pressed a fist, knuckles whitened, against his forehead. "I swear by all that is holy, monsieur, I would not have left her had I known."

Jared looked on helplessly while the man agonized over his past.

"By God's mercy, I was spared, rescued by some of those men still loyal to me. They carried me away to a neighboring island for my own safety. When I had recovered from my injuries, I was told that my house had been burned to the ground, Monsieur Durant. Charred timbers and ashes were all that remained. I searched for my child among those who had fled the island, but she was not to be found.

"As soon as I was able, I returned to St. Gervais, with

two of my trusted servants, to look for Louise. The isle
was in chaos. The French troops from the fort had yet to
restore order to the city, and so I kept my identity hidden.
The sugar mill, my home, my fields—all were destroyed,
just as I had been told. For days we searched, but to no
avail. At last I was forced to admit that my daughter had
died in the fires which had consumed our home."

"I don't understand, sir," Jared put in. "Of what help
can I be if the child is . . . dead?"

Valmont did not reply at once. The muscle in his jaw
knotted, and he withdrew into himself. At length he
seemed to regain some of his strength. "I left the island,"
he continued, "vowing never to set foot on its soil again.
I went as far away as I could, here to St. Louis. I became
a man very much like you yourself, monsieur, a man who
courts death. Ah, but she can be an elusive mistress, *non?*"

Clearly Valmont thought he'd found in Jared a kindred
spirit, and perhaps it was true, but Jared still could not
discern what the man wanted of him.

"Two days ago," Valmont went on to explain, "one of
my dealers came to me with a piece of jewelry, a brooch,
that someone wished to use to ante a bet. I recognized that
brooch at once; it was a distinctive design, a circlet of dia-
monds which had belonged to my wife and which I had
put into my daughter's keeping. I have no doubt that it
was in her jewelry case, on her bureau, on the night of the
fire."

Valmont drew the brooch from the pocket of his frock
coat and laid it on the table before Jared. "Yes, it may
somehow have survived the fire. Yes, someone may have
stolen it from the ashes . . . but, monsieur, if it were your
child, what would you do?"

Jared picked up the brooch and turned it over in his
hand so that the lamplight overhead caught it and re-

flected off of it. "Do you believe it possible that someone helped your daughter to escape the fire, Mr. Valmont?"

"There were several servants in the house that night. Who can tell? But I cannot rest until I know for certain if my daughter still lives. If I were half the man that I was before this tragedy, nothing would stop me from finding her if she is out there somewhere. But the years have not been kind to me. I am a broken man and in poor health."

"You must have a hundred men in your employ. Why not enlist one of them . . . or hire Pinkerton himself? Why me?"

"You are here now," Valmont explained. "I cannot wait, and I need someone who will answer to me alone. I know from what I have learned that you are a man who understands honor. You have the skills and the determination to take on this task. I believe that you are much the man that I was—before all of this. I would trust no one less with the safety of my most precious possession. I will pay any price, Monsieur Durant, whatever you ask. Only tell me if my daughter lives."

Jared nudged the drunken man, who lay curled in the stairwell, with the toe of his boot. There was no response, so he stepped over him and went up to the second floor of the boardinghouse.

Battle Row was the dumping ground for the dregs of St. Louis society, and this was only one of the many ill-constructed, vermin-infested structures in that infamous section of town. The raucous sounds coming from the saloon downstairs were not loud enough to drown out the skittering noises that echoed through the darkened hallway, raising the hackles on Jared's neck. Instinct moved his right hand closer to his holstered revolver as he knocked on the door as he'd been instructed to do.

It opened a crack, and a face that looked garish in the half-light peered out. "Yeah?"

"Maggie? Sam Patterson sent me," Jared told her.

She threw open the door, and he stepped in, shutting it behind him. The room was rank with the smell of sweat and cheap perfume, and Jared wished he'd had the foresight to have one more drink before coming up. He needed it now. Damnation! How had he let Valmont talk him into this? What was the use in this exercise? The trail had gone cold more than thirteen years ago.

"Put your money on the bureau," the girl standing before him said.

She wore a knitted shawl over a cheap cotton chemise and petticoats, and though she couldn't have been more than sixteen years old, her expression was jaded.

Jared pulled a money clip out of his double-breasted shirt, peeled off one of Valmont's bills, and laid it on the bureau.

Maggie slipped off her shawl, and Jared held up a hand to stop her. "I'm after information, that's all."

The girl dropped onto the bed. "You're the best thing's walked through that door in months, mister. It'll be my pleasure. Come here," she said, patting the mattress with her hand, "and I'll make you forget your troubles."

"That's a tall order," Jared replied, "and more than you can fill, I'm afraid. Now, sit up and talk to me."

He adjusted his stance, and the hard look in his topaz eyes left no room for argument.

"What do you want to know?" she asked, pouting her rouged mouth as she sat on the edge of the bed.

Jared reached into the pocket of his buckskin coat and drew out the diamond brooch. "You recognize this?"

He held it out to her, and she edged away with fear in her eyes. "I didn't steal it, mister. I ain't no thief, no matter what Patterson told you. He makes me pay him. I didn't have the money, so I gave him the brooch."

"I'm not accusing you of anything, Maggie. Just tell me how you came by such a piece of jewelry."

She regarded him nervously. "It was a gift. There's this deckhand, Tom Skinner, who comes by regular. He wants to marry me, but I like my freedom, you know," she said, lifting her chin as if she were a highborn lady. "And he didn't steal it, neither," she added, anticipating Jared's next question. "He told me how he won it in a poker game."

"I see," Jared said, pulling on his beard-stubbled chin. "And do you happen to know the name of the riverboat your friend works on?"

"The *A. B. Chalmers,*" she said and bent to retrieve her shawl, having lost interest in the conversation.

Jared turned to leave, but laying a hand on the door-knob, he hesitated. "If I were you," he told her without turning back into the shabby room, "I'd seriously reconsider Mr. Skinner's proposal."

Durant left the row of squalid frame buildings and walked back to the levee and the line of riverboats, their twin black smokestacks silhouetted against a dark sky.

Valmont had set aside a stateroom for him on the *Marietta,* a well-appointed side-wheeler, and Jared was impressed with it. It was the grandest lodging he'd had in months, complete with a porcelain knob and oil picture on the cabin door. It reminded him of a life-style that was buried in his past, though, and left him unsettled and craving a drink.

He tossed his jacket on the bunk, stripped off his shirt, and preparing to shave, he examined the haggard face that stared back at him from the mirror on the washstand. The reflection was disturbing; Jared barely recognized this grim-faced stranger, and the sight made him hear again the last words that Allan Pinkerton had said to him before he'd been dismissed: "You've done your job well—too well, in fact. We've taught you to disguise yourself as a gambler and a drunkard so that you might fit in with the rougher elements, as our investigations require. Now you mix easily with these people, but it's no longer a disguise you're wearing. You've become one of them."

The razor slipped at his throat, and Jared cut himself. He dabbed at the blood with a towel, then rinsed the remains of the lather from his face as he studied his reflection again, trying to deny Pinkerton's words and wishing that he could as easily wash away the memories of Battle Row and a hundred other places like it.

But it was true, God help him, every word of it. Much as Jared wanted to believe that he was a better man than his father, who had gambled away everything and then taken his own life, when the responsibility fell to him, he, too, had proved a disappointment to his family.

What was it that Valmont had said to him? That he was a "man of honor, with skill and determination"? If he only knew the truth. Jared considered then why he had let Valmont talk him into this at all. It was a damned fool's errand, that much was for certain. It wasn't the money. Though the Frenchman had been more than generous thus far, money was easy enough to come by. Jared decided finally that he empathized with Valmont's longing to find his daughter and put things back the way they were, and he wondered if it was too late for him to do the same.

CHAPTER
3

New Orleans

From the balcony of her room behind Celestine's on the rue Gallatin, Dellie could look out on the levee and watch the bustle of traffic on the river. It was an invigorating scene but one that often left her sad of late, for she could not stare out upon the aggregation of steamships and sailing vessels, riverboats and coastal packets, without wondering where they were bound. A ship could leave this port for New York or the Indies or even California, and the riverboats headed north every day for Natchez, Vicksburg, Memphis, and St. Louis. Year after year Dellie had watched their comings and goings with an impassive air, but lately the sight of them made her long for escape.

The wind chimes that hung from the scrollwork of the wrought-iron balcony supports tinkled as she brushed by them, and she smiled at the sound. It called up memories of the chimes Mama Tess had once helped her to make from seashells when she was just a child. They'd hung them out on the veranda of her island home to catch the ocean breezes. It was all so very long ago. Why, Dellie wondered, did these memories plague her more and more as the days passed?

The sound of hammering below her caught her attention, and leaning over the railing, Dellie spotted Jonas, Madame Celestine's black giant of a servant. He was repairing a broken shutter.

"*Bonjour,* Jonas," she called down to him.

He stepped back and squinted his eyes against the brilliant morning sun to see her.

"You'd best pin up your hair an' put on your shawl, Miz Dellie," he warned, shaking his hammer at her, " 'fore some drunken sailor fella comes by an' gits de idea dat you be one of Miz Celestine's 'fancy' ladies."

"Have you tried the liniment I sent down?" she asked, ignoring his censures.

"Surely did, Miz Dellie, an' I thank you kindly. Now, get yourself inside 'fore I calls Mama Tess to come an' tan your hide for runnin' about in your chemise wid your hair all loose."

Dellie laughed at his warning but did as he told her, for just then a closed carriage appeared in the alley below and stopped near the stairs that led up to her balcony. Someone was coming.

Dellie went inside, closed the shutters, and drew aside the drape that separated her bedroom alcove from the rest of the room. She put on a skirt and then sat down on the stool before a watery looking glass to coil and pin her thick blond tresses beneath a tignon of dark fabric. With a sigh, she gathered up her shawl, pulled the drape, and went to the table, where the cards lay in their silver box.

When the knock came at last, Dellie struck a match to the candle on the table and put on a sober demeanor, as was expected of her. "*Entrez,* " she called out.

A young lady entered in a froth of crinoline skirts. Her features were obscured by a heavily veiled bonnet, and she wore a plain, dark cloak, which the warm September weather did not warrant. Dellie was not surprised, though. Whenever young ladies were brave enough to come here, they would disguise themselves, for no lady would be seen on the rue Gallatin.

"Mademoiselle," Dellie acknowledged and waved a hand to the chair opposite.

No sooner had the woman taken the seat than she slipped out of her cloak and threw back her veils, revealing a pale, heart-shaped face framed by dark curls.

"Mademoiselle LeBreton?"

"Quelle bonne surprise, non?" the woman responded.

"Why, yes," Dellie admitted, "but you were here only last week."

"Ah, but this is a special visit to my special friend," the lovely Creole explained, her black eyes alight with mischief.

"Merci, mademoiselle," Dellie said to her.

"And I have told you that you must call me Solange. Subservience does not suit you, *mon amie.* Now, put on a pot of tea for us, and I will tell you why I am here."

Dellie went down to the kitchen to put the kettle on the stove. When she came back to the table, Solange LeBreton had removed her gloves and folded her delicate hands neatly in her lap.

"My parents are giving a party in celebration of my eighteenth birthday," Solange announced, "and I should like you to attend."

Dellie could not hide her astonishment. *"Moi? Ce n'est pas possible.* Your parents would never allow such a thing . . . me, the Witch of Gallatin Street, in their gracious Creole mansion."

"You are no such thing," Solange retorted hotly. "When first I came here to have my fortune told, it was on a dare . . . to prove to my friends that I was not afraid.

I expected that I should find an evil, toothless old hag in these rooms, but instead I found you, Dellie. You are no witch, only someone with a special talent. All this talk of witches and evil on Gallatin Street is just nonsense used to frighten the children."

Dellie leaned forward, regarding the pretty, dark-haired girl with a serious countenance. "You must take care, my friend Solange. Believe what you have heard about this place. The worst kind of men come here. They come to drink and play at cards at Madame Celestine's and establishments like it up and down the rue Gallatin, and then— well, perhaps you do not know what goes on upstairs at Madame's place, but I know. I have lived here above her kitchen, just across the courtyard from her house, since I was a child, and I have seen many things, not all of them pleasant. These streets are dangerous, even in the daylight. I am lucky to have friends who know me here. They are not the right sort of friends to have, perhaps, but they keep me safe, and so does the tale of the Witch of Gallatin Street. You would be surprised to learn how superstitious even the hardened people who frequent these streets are."

Solange took up Dellie's hands in her own. "You do not belong in this place, *mon amie.*"

"But this is where Fate has put me," Dellie replied as she got up to fetch their tea.

Dellie took her time in the kitchen as she prepared the tray. Mama Tess was not there to question her behavior, and so she tarried, arranging a sliver of Mama Tess's gingerbread on a plate to go with Solange's tea and allowing her mind to think on this proposal her friend had just made. She could not seriously consider accepting the invitation, of course, but it was exciting nonetheless to imagine herself socializing with the *haut monde* of New Orleans.

Dellie was not eager to rejoin her friend waiting upstairs. Solange LeBreton was an only child, whose every whim had been indulged by her doting parents. She was accustomed to having her own way of things, and indeed, when Dellie finally returned, she could see that Solange had lost none of her resolve. "So you will come to my party, *non?*"

Dellie put down the tray as she took her place at the table once more. "I cannot. Wherever did you get such an idea?"

"Why, from you, of course," Solange replied as she took the cup Dellie held out to her. "The story you told me of how your parents met was so romantic, and I thought to myself: Why should Dellie not have this same kind of chance for happiness?"

Dellie smiled at her friend's kindness. Solange had so carefully planned all of this and solely for Dellie's benefit.

"You *must* come," Solange insisted. "I will tell Mama that you are an acquaintance of mine, from school in Paris. I shall say that you are the daughter of a French planter from the Indies, and that you are in town and staying with friends. All of this is true, is it not? You will come to my party, and you will laugh and dance and amuse everyone with your fortune-telling, and perhaps you will catch a gentleman's eye, and he will fall desperately in love with you."

Dellie stared into her teacup, not for a moment carried away by this fantasy. "And when this gentleman learns my address?"

A frown creased Solange's dark brow. "Don't spoil things," she said, pouting.

The two sipped at their tea in silence, and after Solange had eaten the last crumb of her gingerbread, she stood up and slipped on her cloak, then pulled an envelope from her reticule. "Here is your invitation," she said and laid it on the table. "I shall send my driver for you on Friday next at eight o'clock."

Dellie let go an exasperated sigh. "I shall only send him away."

"Do come, Dellie," Solange entreated. Replacing her veil, she went out the door and down the stairs into her waiting carriage.

Dellie stared hard at the envelope lying on the table beside her silver card box, then pushed it aside. She took out the tarot cards, and her brow creased as she concentrated. After riffling them, she set one card down in the center of the table and crossed the next over it, continuing until ten cards lay in the usual spread.

Her eyes scanned the pictures that were now as familiar to her as old friends. They came to rest upon the card in the uppermost right position . . . the Knight of Swords.

"Again," she muttered.

He came to her more often lately, as if a harbinger of events soon to unfold, and he left her uneasy and afraid.

"What do the cards say this fine morning?" Mama Tess called as she came up the back stairs from Celestine's kitchen with coffee and the fried rice cakes that were called calas for Dellie.

"Come and see," Dellie told her and waved a hand toward the table, her bracelets jangling.

Mama Tess set aside the breakfast tray and went to stand at Dellie's elbow.

"Who is he, Mama?" Dellie asked, unable to hide her distress.

The black woman nodded her head slowly as she studied the spread and then gave a gentle pat to Dellie's arm. "The cards will tell—when the time is right," she replied cryptically. "Don't you worry yourself none."

Dellie reached out a hand and swept the cards out of place. "I want to go home to Belle Terre," she said, as though she sensed impending disaster. "Please, Mama Tess. Can't we go home?"

At first Dellie had been content to be wherever Mama Tess was, and her memories of life on St. Gervais had been clouded by nightmarish recollections of that fateful evening when her whole world had gone up in flames. But as she grew older, Dellie's memories of the night of destruction began to fade, leaving her to remember all the good things: the joys of her childhood and the wonders of the island itself, the lush, green rain forests and high volcanic peaks that stretched up to the sky, the miles of white sand beaches and sharp limestone cliffs that rose up in places along the shore like great stone fortresses. . . .

Papa told her once that St. Gervais had been home to the Valmonts for more than two centuries. Two centuries! And now she, the last of the Valmont line, was destined to live in exile from her homeland, for whenever she brought the subject to Mama Tess, the old woman would hear none of it. She would not even contemplate returning to the island, and Dellie could not think to go without her.

"I've been saving some of the money I've earned reading the cards," Dellie went on, determined to convince her this time. "It's not much now, but soon I hope to have enough to pay the passage for both of us."

Mama Tess shook her head, her expression grim. "No matter. Belle Terre is no more. Naught for us there but bad memories. New Orleans is our home now."

Losing patience, Dellie tapped her foot on the floor as she gathered her cards into a pile and shuffled them. "You've always cared for me as best you can, Mama, but lately I've begun to feel like the tropical bird that Madame Celestine tried to keep in a cage in her parlor. You remember the one? It could not bear being caged and so dashed itself against the bars again and again, trying to get out . . . until finally it died."

Mama Tess regarded her, disapproval in her sharp, black eyes. "Such a tale! You are restless, my mamzelle, that is all that ails you."

Spying the envelope on the table, Tess picked it up. She drew out the invitation and examined it. "What's this?" she asked Dellie, for while Tess was a wise woman in many ways, she could not read.

"Only a letter from Mademoiselle LeBreton," Dellie replied, too quickly.

It was the first time in all of her life that Dellie had lied to Mama Tess, and guilt swept over her all at once. She could not even say why she'd done it. She had no intention of accepting the invitation to Solange's party.

"A beautiful young miss," Tess observed, "but bound for trouble, that one."

With that there came a knocking at the back stairs door, and when Mama Tess tossed the invitation on the table and went to the door, Dellie seized the opportunity to take it up and hide it in the waistband of her skirt.

Mama Tess opened the door for Emma, one of Madame Celestine's girls. Her dark hair was piled high on her head, and she wore a wrapper of red Chinese silk.

"Good mornin' to you, Miss Dellie. Have you any more of that miracle medicine you made up for Madame? Her cough was awful bad last night."

"It's no miracle, Emma," Dellie said to the girl, who was not much older than herself, "only syrup of nettle, wild cherry bark, and blackberry root, mixed with a little brandy and sugar."

Dellie went to the bureau at the far corner of the room, where she kept her medicines. The bureau top was covered with vials, bottles, and jars, and she sorted through them until she found what she was looking for and then began to filter a thick liquid from one of the jars into a small bottle. "Tell Madame Celestine to take a spoonful of this as she needs. It should ease the cough, but if she cannot sleep again tonight, you must send for Dr. Fortier. Do you understand?"

Emma took the bottle and nodded. "You're an angel, miss, an angel with a gift for healin'. I just don't know what we'd all do without you. There's not one of us girls you ain't helped out at one time or another."

"You are kind to say it," Dellie told her, "but now you'd best take that syrup down to Madame."

Dellie closed the door after Emma had gone down, then turned back to Mama Tess, who'd been silent throughout their exchange. Tess's heavy arms were folded over her bosom, and though she was no longer taller than Dellie, her bearing made her still seem so in Dellie's eyes.

"You see?" Tess said, shaking a finger at her. "You see how they need you here? Where you're needed, that's where your home ought to be, no use in arguin' 'bout that. You been blessed with a special gift, child—"

Dellie felt overpowered. The bars that were closing in around her were no less real than those that had ensnared Madame Celestine's exotic bird. She found it hard to draw breath. "I have no special gift," Dellie insisted. "It was your teaching, and the books you bought for me so that I could learn more about medicines."

Tears filled Dellie's eyes as she went on. "Do not be angry with me, Mama, but I do not belong here."

Mama Tess gently folded her arms around her "mamzelle" the way she had when Dellie was only a tiny thing. "Child, ain't nobody born what thinks he belongs in a place like this. Misfortune, that's what brings them here. Lord knows you seen enough of that in your young life. You was born to be a lady, and that seems to be somethin' you can't never forget. I feared as much when it was left to me to raise you. Maybe I done wrong by you, maybe

I ought to have taken you to the convent, where the good Sisters could have cared for you better."

"No, Mama!" Dellie cried, patting Tess's broad back. "Don't say such things! You are my family, all that I have in this world."

"Look at what a life I've made for you here. You say yourself that you don't belong in this place—with these people, and Lord knows it's the truth. But there weren't no choosin' one way or another, Dellie. The people in these United States still keep black slaves. How could I just sashay up to one of them fine mansions on the rue Esplanade to ask for work? People who got themselves a houseful of slaves don't got much call to be hirin' no free-born Negroes.

"I don't got yellow skin like them pretty quadroons, so weren't a chance that any of those highborn Creole ladies were gonna hire me as maid or hairdresser. About all I would have been good for was to cook in the kitchens of one of them upriver plantation homes, and then you, my child, you would be left all on your own. When Madame Celestine offered to take us in, my prayers they were answered."

"I'm sorry, Mama. I know it was hard for you, but soon now I will take you home, to St. Gervais. You can rest easy, and I will care for you."

The old woman drew back from Dellie and patted her hand. "You are a good child," she said, "but we can't never go back. I tell you there is more evil on St. Gervais than in the whole city of New Orleans. Come now, we will see what the tarot says. You must trust in the cards, like your sweet mama done, rest her soul, and things are gonna come out right."

Tess and Dellie went to sit before the table. Mama Tess handled the cards this time, but Dellie cut them three times before Tess laid them out: five cards, side by side, and he was there again, the Knight of Swords. Dellie was not afraid of him now, though. He was coming for her soon, and she would put her future in his hands.

CHAPTER

4

Jared Durant stepped out from under the portico of the elegant building called the Cabildo, which housed the New Orleans city hall. He mopped his brow with his handkerchief, then replaced his black slouch hat as he headed for the shade of the sycamore trees that bordered Jackson Square.

Three weeks he had spent in this city, his eye captured by every young woman of just the right age, just the right coloring, but he was no closer to finding Louise Valmont than he had been at the outset. With the help of Valmont's business associate, Antoine Bredou, who resided in the Vieux Carré, Jared had made inquiries amongst the old guard Creole families, but without success thus far. He had spent the whole of the day yesterday in a fruitless search, poring over marriage and death certificates in this very building, but not today, he'd decided all at once. Today he would walk the city streets and expend some of his pent-up energies.

The chances of finding Lucien Valmont's lost daughter now were slim, Jared had to admit, and yet he continued

31

to say to himself, "Just one more day." He was surprised
at his own tenacity.

It had been an easy enough job at first. He'd traced
down the captain of the packet ship, who, but for the diamond circlet brooch he'd been given in payment for passage, might not have remembered the black woman and
fair-headed child that he'd brought from the isle of St.
Gervais in the West Indies to the dock at New Orleans.
Valmont had been so pleased by this news. Thirteen years
ago, when she'd stepped onto the levee in this city, Louise
Valmont was alive and well—but now, who could say?

Jared walked the length of the square and passed
through the iron gate with no particular destination in
mind, crossing Levee Street in a direction that would take
him away from the St. Louis Hotel, where he was lodged.
Before him he could see a forest of ships' masts and clouds
of dark smoke that belched forth from the twin stacks of
the riverboats. The levee was piled high with cotton bales,
crates, and hogsheads, and the iron-wheeled drays rolled
between the tall rows carrying yet more of the goods that
had been unloaded from the ships.

Continuing on this tack, Jared came to the French Market. The long arcade, its massive pillars supporting a slate
roof, was teeming with activity. There was squawking and
wing-flapping from fowl in their cages. Vendors and cus-
tomers haggled over price, ladies discussed their pur-
chases with Negro *domestiques,* friends met and shared
gossip, and all of this in a Babel of different tongues.

The stalls themselves displayed an array of colorful and
exotic fare: the bright greens and yellows and reds and oranges of the fruits and vegetables, sacks of coffee beans
piled high, tables laden with unusual assortments of herbs
and spices.

Jared found his nostrils assailed at every turn: the floral
perfume that wafted on the air around the cart of a qua-

droon, who was cheerily dispensing carnations, Spanish jessamine, and violets; the pungent odor of shellfish; and the enticing aroma of freshly brewed coffee that he could not resist, despite the heat.

At last his eyes came to rest on the Choctaw squaws who sat on the side pavements, selling their woven baskets and herbal concoctions. They seemed no more out of place here than any of the rest of the citizens who paraded the flagstone banquettes.

In the midst of all of this confusion it was a wonder that he even noticed her at all, deep in conversation with one of the Indian women. They seemed to be discussing the merits of one of the noxious-looking herbs that the latter was purveying. The woman who'd caught his eye wore the headscarf that was called a tignon in these parts. Like a turban, it was wrapped around her head, covering her hair completely, but rather than the usual madras print, her tignon was of a dark, Oriental fabric. Her skin was very fair, else he might have mistaken her for a quadroon, for her looks were exotic, marked by high cheekbones and eyes with a sensual slant. As he drew nearer, he could see that those eyes were blue—not the pallid blue of a robin's egg, but the deep, clear color of a sapphire. She wore large gold hoops in her ears and a number of bracelets on each slender wrist. It was indeed a fetching picture she made, standing there with her basket on her arm, clutching a shawl to her breast with one hand, while the other was animated with the conversation, as the French were wont to do.

Leaning back against a pillar, Jared sipped at his coffee and watched her from beneath the wide brim of his hat. She made her purchase and continued on her way, pausing nearby to examine the produce in one of the stalls.

But now the girl selling flowers drew Jared's attention. "Some pretty flowers for your lady today, monsieur?"

On impulse Jared purchased a small bouquet of violets, but when he looked for the woman he'd been watching, she was gone. His eyes scanned the busy scene until he spotted her again—at the far end of the market shed. A rough-looking sailor had grabbed her arm, upsetting her basket. No one else in the crowded marketplace seemed to notice, though.

Jared wound his way through the tangle of humanity, bent on her rescue, but when finally he reached her, the scene which met him was quite different than what he'd expected to see. From the folds of her skirt the woman had drawn a wicked-looking knife with a slender blade. She now had it pressed close against the man's throat, a drop of blood appearing at its tip as she berated him in French, in a flurry of words that Jared could not understand. The sailor promptly threw up his hands and made a hasty retreat.

At once Jared went to pick up her basket and retrieve her packages, his mouth twisting in an amused smile. "Are you all right, mamzelle?" he asked as he returned her basket. She turned those sapphire eyes on him, and he felt himself suddenly drowning in their depths. God, but she was beautiful!

"Do you wish me to escort you home?" he offered.

"Non, merci. Ce n'est pas nécessaire," she said, and then, as if she realized that he did not speak French, she added, "No, thank you, I can manage, monsieur."

The woman looked off in the direction in which the sailor had fled, and her full mouth curved into a smile. "He won't be back."

The knife disappeared again within the folds of her skirts, and she left him without another word, heading for the banquette that bordered the narrow street beyond.

Jared tried to guess at exactly what she might have said to the sailor and wished now that he'd not forgotten so

much of the French he'd learned at school. He wanted to
know more of her, but when he looked up again, she was
gone.

Leaving the market, Jared crossed the street. He had
reached an impasse in his search for Mademoiselle Valmont, and like a rudderless ship, he was drifting. Surely
Valmont would understand his need for a day's respite,
and tomorrow—yes, tomorrow he would begin the search
for Louise Valmont anew.

There was no confusing Gallatin Street with any other
in the Vieux Carré; it was more of an alley, really, where
congregated the rougher elements of the city. It seemed
a harmless enough place in the daylight, but still not an
inviting one. Here the buildings were as unkempt as their
inhabitants: peeling paint, windows with smeary, cracked
panes, broken stairs, and overgrown *parterres*. Gallatin
Street could compare with any of the dozens of hellholes
Jared had haunted in the past and which now haunted
him. The shriek of female laughter from within one of the
buildings cut through the quiet, shattering Jared's peace
of mind. He ought to get away from this place. It was too
like the many memories that he wanted to erase from his
life, but still he kept walking until he found himself standing before a weather-beaten structure, two stories tall,
with a name painted over the door: Celestine's.

It was a spacious establishment. The double doors were
opened out, and the chink of glasses within beckoned him.
One drink couldn't hurt. He stepped in out of the morning
sun, and when his eyes had adjusted to the change of light,
his face split with an amused grin. Celestine's was a gambling house.

There was a keno table and roulette wheel near the bar
for the more pedestrian clientele, but in an adjoining
room, mirrors and painted landscapes decorated the walls,
and there were baize tables for poker. It was all, he noticed

upon closer inspection, slightly threadbare but succeeded still in its attempt to imitate the finer gambling parlors that operated in the better sections of the city. Along the wall were damask-covered armchairs where, even at this hour, reclined those young ladies only too eager to share their charms with a man—for the right price.

The tables would be filled in a few more hours, but it was early yet. Only a few patrons were scattered around the room. Jared stopped at the bar for a bottle of whiskey and a fresh pack of cards, and as luck would have it, he found a poker game and settled down to prove himself . . . one more time.

Dellie inhaled deeply, savoring the aroma of baking bread as she came into the kitchen and set her basket on the table.

"Mama?" she called. "I'm back from the market."

Mama Tess emerged from the pantry, wiping her floured hands on her apron. "That's a good child. Did you get my oranges?"

"Yes," Dellie told her and began to take a verbal inventory as she unpacked the basket and set the items on the table one by one, "and the filé and potatoes and coffee and even a sack of roasted peanuts."

"And what's that I see?" Tess inquired as Dellie drew out a small bouquet of violets.

This was strange, indeed. Dellie examined the flowers. She had made no such purchase. Where had they come from?

And then she recalled the man who'd come to her aid in the market. He must have put the violets in the basket when he repacked it for her. Dellie tried then to remember his face but found, to her surprise, that she could not.

"There was a drunken sailor in the market this morning," she started to explain. "He grabbed my arm and upset my basket. Everything tumbled out—"

Tess's dark eyes grew wide with concern. "He did not harm you . . . ?"

Dellie breathed in the sweet fragrance of the violets and shook her head. "I had my knife," she said. "I ought to have cut out his tongue for what he said to me, but I only had to threaten him with a colorful curse on his manhood, and that frightened him off quickly enough."

"And the flowers?"

"A gentleman helped repack my basket. He must have put them there."

"What sort of gentleman?" Tess asked, still wary.

"He was well dressed but with a fancy waistcoat like a riverboat gambler. Honestly, I cannot recall anything else about him."

"Keep away from gamblers, Dellie. They'll only bring you sorrow. Ask Madame Celestine, she'll tell you how things are."

"Don't worry about me, Mama. Madame has warned me many times. I can deal with this gambler . . . and any other man who stands in my way."

Later, when she returned to her room, Dellie put the flowers into a glass of water and set them in the center of her table, where she could admire them.

Despite the bold face she'd put on for Mama Tess, Dellie could not seem to rid herself of the memory of the sailor who'd accosted her: the florid complexion, mottled from drink, the rotted teeth and foul breath. His very touch had made her feel dirty.

How much longer would it take until she could save enough for the passage home? A long time probably, and after that she'd still have to convince Tess that they should go. Dellie wondered how she could escape from this life, even for a little while, and then she remembered Solange's invitation. What would it be like if *la sorcière de la rue Gallatin* could disappear for one night so that Mademoiselle Louise Chandelle Marie-Thérèse might live again— as she was meant to? Dellie was too old for fairy tales, though, and knew full well that such musings were nonsense. Louise Valmont may as well have died in the fire that night on St. Gervais, for there was no place at all for her here.

Celestine's had no shortage of women, and several of them might even have been called attractive. More than one had appeared at Jared's elbow throughout the afternoon as he'd played at cards, especially when he'd held the winning hand, but as he listened to the two gentlemen at the bar discussing the merits of a particularly fetching lass, he felt sure that she was none of those here present.

"She carries herself like she were a highborn lady," the younger fellow said. "Ain't never seen a pair of eyes so blue nor skin so white on Gallatin Street, I can tell you that. Most of these gals been handled so much that whatever color they might've started out, by now it's done rubbed off."

"So you don't think she's been 'handled' much? That's right hard to believe, Webster. I passed her on the street the other day, and she smiled pretty enough."

Jared recognized the second, more skeptical fellow. He was Silas Crane, a fellow gambling man, who regularly worked the river between St. Louis and New Orleans. His poundage attested to the fact that he invariably spent his winnings in the finest restaurants in New Orleans. His dark beard, in fact, was still flecked with crumbs from his breakfast.

"You'd best hope a smile's all you get from her," Webster retorted. "They say she learned her some black magic from them voodoo people. That there's somethin' you don't want to mess with, and I hear she stabbed a fella a few months back for gettin' too friendly."

"A regular little spitfire, eh? But I'd be willing to wager that a man of your talents could get her into his bed."

Webster downed his drink and ran a hand through his lank yellow hair. "How much?" he asked.

"A hundred dollars."

"I may be crazy, mister, but I ain't no fool. My life's worth more than that."

By now Jared's interest was piqued. He could not resist the challenge, especially if it meant besting Silas Crane, and so with his bottle in hand, he approached the pair. "Make that five hundred, Silas, and I'll take your bet."

"Well, well, if it isn't Jared Durant, come all the way down from St. Louis to try and separate me from my money. Hank Webster, meet the only man fool enough to take on a wager before he knows all the particulars."

"I know all I need to know, Silas. How difficult could it be to bed one of the ladies in this district? All you need is cash money."

"You don't know what you got yourself in for this time," Webster told him, shaking his head. "They call this one the Witch of Gallatin Street. She tells fortunes and casts spells."

"Ah, but then the challenge will make the victory that much more enjoyable," Jared replied, still confident.

Crane was laughing. "All right, Durant. I'll give you a week. The lady in question resides near here, in the building across the courtyard, on the second floor. You get yourself invited into her room for the night, and you've won the bet."

"And how will you know if I've done that?"

"One of Celestine's girls is a special friend of mine. I'll have her keep an eye out for me."

Jared shook Silas Crane's hand to seal the bet, chuckling to himself all the while. Maybe this trip to New Orleans would be a profitable one, after all.

When Jared stepped out of Celestine's and onto the banquette, the sun was already casting long shadows. He strode briskly around the building and through the alleyway. Staring past the gate that led into the courtyard, he could see that there was indeed a dilapidated building there behind Madame Celestine's establishment. It was a tall structure of brick, covered in crumbling stucco, with a roof that resembled a carpenter's chisel. Many houses in the Vieux Carré had such an arrangement, with the kitchen and servants' quarters set apart from the house itself. Jared looked up at the tiered balconies and smiled, certain that he'd found the lodgings of the Witch of Gallatin Street.

Within the courtyard was a fragrant garden, where blossomed tall wands of yellow flowers amid banana trees and palmettos with their graceful, fanlike fronds. Its exotic perfume was carried on the breeze, and Jared breathed in deeply, filling his lungs with the heady scent. The garden was more of a jungle, really. It was lush and green and had overgrown its bounds. Clinging to the stuccoed walls were vines with blooms that resembled scarlet trumpets, and a carpet of blue lobelia covered the ground between the flagstones. Amid the decay and desolation of this neighborhood, Jared was surprised to find such beauty hidden away here behind the courtyard walls. Was it all the result of a witch's spell? he mused.

He climbed the stairs to the uppermost balcony, where hung a wind chime made up of dozens of tiny brass bells. Reaching out to brush it with his fingertips, he listened to the light chiming that rang out on the air. She must have heard the sound, too, for when Jared looked up, the woman he'd come in search of was standing there in the doorway. The sleeve of her cambric blouse had slipped to reveal a soft white shoulder, and she was wiping her hands upon her apron.

Jared had to fight to keep his jaw from dropping in astonishment. This was the same woman he'd seen earlier in the French Market, the one who'd been brandishing a knife. Perhaps Webster hadn't been exaggerating when he said she'd stabbed a man for getting too close. Jared's brow creased in thought as he considered his approach, no longer so certain of success.

When Dellie saw the tall man on her balcony, she recognized him at once. This was the same man who'd come to her aid in the market this morning. He was clad in a dark frock coat and trousers, but with a waistcoat of rich burgundy satin and silver brocade, like so many of the riverboat gamblers who frequented Celestine's. She had been warned time and again to avoid the company of such men, yet curiosity made her linger.

As he removed his wide-brimmed hat and toyed with the silver band, Dellie took a moment to study his features, which had managed to elude her memory earlier. He had an intelligent brow and a face that was not unmarred by experience. There was a hardened look about him, in fact, that cautioned her to be wary, but still she was intrigued. His eyes were the color of topaz. Cat's eyes, she thought.

"So, it is you, monsieur," she said carefully. "You wish me to read the cards for you? Or perhaps a charm to bring back your luck?"

He summoned a charming smile for her then. "No, mamzelle. The cards have already been very kind to me this evening. I've come here in search of pleasant company."

Dellie had to admit that she was disarmed by the deep baritone voice with a gentle Virginia drawl, but reason had not abandoned her entirely. She felt a stab of disappointment to realize what he was after.

"Ah," she said wisely and took an unconscious step backward, "then I think you have gone astray. If you will go back down the way you came and across the courtyard, I'm certain that one of Madame Celestine's girls will be happy to oblige you."

She moved to shut the door, only to find that the gambler had stepped onto the threshold and was now very close to her. "No other will do. 'Tis you I want."

Dellie's heart was beating frantically. She met his golden eyes, careful to keep her emotions in check.

"That is quite impossible," she replied, trying to decide whether it would be wiser to reach for her knife or to shout down for Jonas. "Now, if you will excuse me, monsieur—"

Again she stepped back, intending to put the door between them, but his arm snaked around her waist to capture her, and he drew her against the hard length of his body. Dellie's breath left her in a rush.

"I am a man used to having what he wants," he whispered against her ear. "You have only to name your price, mamzelle."

At this, Dellie promptly reached out and slapped his face. "*Diable!*" she spat.

He drew back at once, throwing up his hands. And then he laughed, while leveling his sharp eyes on her. "I've never needed to force myself where I'm not wanted," he said. "It was just a friendly invitation, that's all."

"I think you ought to leave now, monsieur," she told him.

A smile twisted on his lips. "I do love a challenge, though," he said as he walked away.

Dellie slammed the door and pressed herself against it as if to keep out the devil himself. Then she threw the bolt.

Madame Celestine was right. There was no trusting a gambler. And again the thought came to her; she did not belong here on Gallatin Street. Somehow she had to escape from this place.

CHAPTER
5

The following morning, as the sun climbed into a cloudless sky, Dellie left the house to do some errands as a favor to Madame Celestine. She carried with her an empty basket and a shopping list, intending to make the rounds of the shops on Canal Street and return before lunch. As soon as she came out of the courtyard gate, though, she saw the gambler with the cat's eyes waiting there for her. She froze in her steps. He approached contritely and presented her with a handful of fragile pink flowers.

"I've come to apologize," he said. "I assumed that all Madame Celestine's tenants plied the same trade. I was wrong. It was an honest mistake, you must admit."

Dellie could not argue with his logic. She accepted the flowers but still eyed him cautiously.

"I should like it very much, mamzelle," he continued, "if you would dine with me this evening."

"You realize, monsieur, that we have not been properly introduced. I could not think of going anywhere with you."

He stepped back and bowed with great flourish. Dellie

44

had to stifle an amused smile. "Jared Durant, at your service, mamzelle . . . and you?"

"My name is Dellie," she told him and then started down the banquette before this man caused her to neglect her errands.

"Only Dellie?" he wondered as he tagged along beside her.

She cast a sidelong glance his way. Mama Tess had taught her, from the time they'd first come here, never to offer too much information to strangers, and this man was most definitely still a stranger. "That's enough," she replied.

"Now that we have the formalities taken care of, will you accept my invitation?"

Dellie had to admit that Jared Durant was a more agreeable fellow this morning, but no matter how charming he seemed to her now, he was not to be trusted. She'd seen that much already. It was likely a man just such as he who had broken Madame Celestine's heart so long ago, she reminded herself.

"I am sorry, monsieur," she told him. "I think not."

He was surprisingly patient in the face of this latest rejection. "Aren't you going to thank me for the flowers, at least?"

"I shall thank you for the violets you put in my basket yesterday, but as for these, I shall have to thank Madame Celestine, as they came from her garden."

"A beautiful lady should always have flowers," he replied, as if he'd not heard her clever retort at all.

Much as Dellie would have liked to take the compliment in stride, she felt her cheeks flush, giving her away. This was her Achilles' heel, and he must have seen it at once. Dellie had received precious few compliments in her lifetime, and though she wished she could deal him another witty reply, the words would not come.

When she was only a child, Dellie had often watched from her secret hiding places as Madame Celestine's girls plied their charms on the men in the gambling rooms, but it seemed that she had learned little of value, for now her tongue was tied up in knots. And when Jared Durant was bold enough to take her arm as she dodged the traffic to cross the rue Royal, it unsettled her still further.

"Surely a lady as lovely as yourself must receive many such tokens of affection from her admirers," Durant said, aware of her discomfort.

Dellie shook her head. "The men who happen across my path generally do not have your polished manner, monsieur."

"The sailor in the market yesterday?"

"Oui, c'est ça."

As much as she tried to remain indifferent to him, Dellie could not deny that her senses were full of the tall man who walked so close beside her now. The air about him was redolent of bay rum and cheroot; she found it a pleasant combination. Jared Durant was lean, but the flexed muscle of the arm enfolding hers was hard and well formed. His moves were graceful, and Dellie could not help but compare him to the sleek, golden cat that sometimes slept under the arbor in Madame Celestine's courtyard.

"It was kind of you to come to my aid," Dellie admitted when she'd found her voice again.

"But hardly necessary. You managed the situation easily enough."

"I have lived on Gallatin Street for many years now. One learns how to survive but still never grows accustomed to it."

There was a long silence, and Dellie wondered if perhaps she had misjudged this man. He regarded her now, asking about her life as if there were no subject on earth that he'd rather discuss.

"How did you come to live at Madame Celestine's?" he wanted to know.

"Mama Tess first brought me to live here when I was only a child," Dellie explained. "She came to cook for Madame Celestine, and at first I shared her room downstairs by the kitchen, but then Madame said I was old enough to have my own. She's been very kind to us."

"And to me as well," he put in. "I cleared a tidy profit at her tables last evening. The boys were all caught up in eyeing Madame's fine ladies. Luckily for me, that left them no time at all to watch their cards."

With this the spell was broken. All the while they'd been walking, Jared Durant had been a gentleman, polite and engaging, but now he was the gambler again—thinking only in terms of gain. Dellie was sorely disappointed. Of course, he'd only been toying with her.

By this time they had reached the doors of Harper's Emporium, and she withdrew her arm from his, pretending to concentrate her attentions on the display in the shop window. "Thank you for walking with me, monsieur," she said, dismissing him.

"It's such a fine day for walking. I could help you with your shopping, if you like."

And then she turned on him. "I'm certain, Monsieur Durant, that you have more important matters requiring your attention. There is yet money to be made, *n'est-ce pas?* Farmers to be fleeced? Travelers to be swindled? I would not dream of keeping you from such important work."

Durant's brow arched in surprise at the sudden change in her. "I take it that this means you won't reconsider my invitation for dinner?"

"Good day, monsieur."

Dellie took refuge inside the shop, focusing all her attention on finding those items on Madame Celestine's shopping list in order to keep her mind off of Monsieur Jared Durant. A length of yellow ribbon, a packet of hairpins, half a dozen linen handkerchiefs, and a bottle of carnation-pink perfume. . . .

All at once she heard a voice, speaking just above a whisper. "Why, Dellie Valmont, you never told me you had a beau!"

Dellie followed the voice back behind one of the tall shelves that separated the shop into two halves, and there she found her friend, Mademoiselle LeBreton. "Solange, have you been spying on me?"

"Shhh! My maid's just over there. She'll hear us. And I don't have to spy. You've been walking down the rue Canal on your gentleman's arm, as bold as brass."

"He's not *my* gentleman," Dellie protested.

"Who is he, then? And why have you never mentioned him before?"

"His name is Jared Durant. I met him only yesterday in the French Market. He's asked me to have dinner with him."

Solange kneaded her gloved hands gleefully. "How romantic!" she exclaimed and began to set the scene. "He admires your beauty from afar and simply must meet you. He invites you to dine at a quiet restaurant, where you can be alone—" She hesitated then, noticing the impatient look on Dellie's face. "You accepted, of course."

"It wasn't like that at all," Dellie replied, "and of course I did not. He's a gambler, Solange."

"All the more exciting. Gamblers have money, you know, lots of money."

"Gamblers never have money for long," Dellie retorted. "There's always another game waiting. They will use you if it suits their purpose and then be done with you without a second thought."

"That's Madame Celestine talking," Solange observed. "Not you. Everyone in New Orleans has heard the story of how she gave up a comfortable life as the mistress of an upriver gentleman when she fell in love with a gambling man, and then how he left her before the year was out, making off with all her jewels. But you cannot let her convince you that all men—not even all gambling men— are evil, Dellie. You must have a life of your own. And how often does a handsome gentleman appear on your doorstep, asking you to dine?"

Jared Durant was not a man who gave up easily. That evening, after the sun had crossed over the river and slipped down to gild the horizon, Dellie heard a knocking on her door.

"Who's there?" she called.

She waited several minutes, but there was no reply. Cautiously she unlatched the bolt and peered out from behind the door to see Jared Durant there, leaning against the jamb.

"There's still time to change your mind," he said. "Dine with me tonight, Dellie. Will you?"

Why was Jared Durant wasting his time on her when she'd already made it clear that there was no winning in this game? Dellie's placid expression belied the turmoil of her thoughts. It was not wise to accept such an invitation, she knew that, but as Solange had said to her, How often did a handsome gentleman appear at one's door asking one to dine?

It was fortunate that Mama Tess was busy downstairs, preparing a supper for Madame Celestine's special guests, for she'd have turned him away without a second thought. Dellie, however, hesitated. If Jared Durant's intentions were solely dishonorable, certainly he'd have made his move by now. What harm would it do to accept his invitation?

"*Merci,* monsieur," she replied at long last. "I shall go take off this apron and fetch my shawl."

When Dellie disappeared inside, Jared went to look out over the balcony rail, grinning to himself at his good fortune. Perhap he'd yet win that bet he'd made with Silas Crane. But with that thought, a wave of guilt washed over him. Was the winning all that he wanted?

The daylight was waning now. In the distance beyond Celestine's he could make out the levee and beyond that the traffic on the river. Billowing clouds of dark smoke from the steamboat docks were silhouetted against the warm pastels of the evening sky, as, too, were the bare masts of the sailing ships. As twilight settled in, flecks of light began to appear all across the great crescent of the city. New Orleans had a way of getting in a man's blood, like a fever. This Witch of Gallatin Street had the same effect on him. He'd not done Valmont's work for two days now but had instead spent the time pursuing Dellie—and, he admitted to himself at last, it wasn't for the money nor the wager. She made him feel more alive than he had in years.

When Dellie returned, Jared took her arm, and they left the shelter of Celestine's courtyard. As they crossed Levee Street, Jared turned back to look at the collection of ramshackle buildings whence they'd come. The sun slipped under the horizon, and like magic, Gallatin Street came to life. Lively music and shrieks of boisterous laughter could be heard from within the boardinghouses and taverns.

Jared's gaze settled on Dellie, her bright blue eyes alight with anticipation. How could she have lived in such a place for so many years without being affected by it? She may have learned to survive but, unlike many others, her beauty had not been marred by the experience. Bitterness welled in him as he realized how the same years had changed him. Perhaps, even now, she was looking at him with disdain for the man he'd become.

"Why do you stay here?" he wondered. "There must be a hundred other places for you to live where you would not be subjected to the treatment I witnessed yesterday."

"This place is home to Mama Tess now. She will not leave, and I cannot leave her."

"Tell me more about your life," Jared prompted. "Can you really see the future?"

Dellie was still unsure of him, but for tonight, at least, she was determined to enjoy herself, and she discovered that she was more at ease when she talked of familiar things.

"It was Mama Tess who taught me all about the tarot. She says I have the gift. People come from all over the city to have me read the cards for them . . . and for the medicine. Mama knows everything about herbs, and she taught me how to make medicines, too. Once I'd learned all that she had to teach, she bought me books so I might learn more."

"Ah," Jared said to her then, "so that is why they call you a witch."

Dellie stiffened, staring hard at the toes of her shoes for a very long time. She knew well enough what the people here called her. In this city where Marie LaVeau, the voodoo queen, still reigned supreme from her tumbledown cottage on St. Ann Street, the people were a superstitious lot. Voodoo and witchcraft might be part and parcel of their everyday lives, but Dellie did not want any part of it herself, and for some reason she did not want Jared Durant to believe it.

"I like to help people, Monsieur Durant, that's all. It

is true that sometimes I make for them charms and spells, if it is what they wish. It is the way of the people here, and it is all harmless enough."

Durant laid a hand over hers, which was resting on his arm, to calm her. There was a warm amber light in his eyes. "I didn't mean to offend you, Dellie. I know, as well as anyone, that sometimes it's wiser to let people believe we are something that we are not."

As they strolled along the banquette in silence, Dellie contemplated his words. Durant stopped all at once and released her arm as a serious expression came over him. "Now, Mamzelle Dellie, that I have heard all of your dark secrets, I feel obliged to tell you some of mine. Promise me that you shall not be too disappointed, though."

One corner of his mouth turned up, giving him away, and Dellie nodded, going along with the game.

He swept the hat from his head and stepped to put himself before her. "I do confess that I am a gambler and an unrepentant one at that. Does this shock you? I can see that it does. Perhaps it would aid my cause to add that I win more often than I lose. And while I do have something of a reputation in St. Louis, I will tell you, in all honesty, that I have never been put off a riverboat on account of my vocation, nor can any man claim that I have cheated him. I live my life, as they say, by the luck of the draw."

His discourse was so animated, so designed to amuse, that Dellie could not help but laugh at him.

"And so, mamzelle, having heard the sort of man I am, do you still wish to dine with me?"

Dellie hesitated. Solange was right. She had to live her own life. She slipped her arm back through his in the way of a reply. "But, of course, monsieur. How can I resist the charms of the one honest gambler in all of New Orleans?"

And so Jared Durant took her to a restaurant on Chartres Street frequented by the genteel folk of the city.

Dellie was surprised to find that on his arm she did not feel the least bit inadequate. They dined on shrimp gumbo and baked redfish, served with fine French wine, and for dessert there were currant tarts. It had been a long time since she'd felt so indulged.

She came to see that Jared Durant was like no other man she'd chanced to meet, and certainly not like any gambler. His manners were impeccable, his conversation witty and amusing, though he never spoke in great detail about his life or made mention of his past. They had a pleasant enough time, though, talking of trivial matters and events of the day. He made her forget about Gallatin Street, and for the first time in months Dellie's thoughts did not turn to the island for escape.

Following dinner, Jared took her for a long walk through the streets of the Vieux Carré. Dellie stared unashamedly at the treasures in the shop windows: bonnets trimmed in flowers and ribbons and lace, ivory-handled silk parasols, gloves and shawls and folding fans. She had never had use for such things before, but now she found herself imagining how her life would be if she were a lady like Solange LeBreton.

When they neared Gallatin Street once more, it seemed to Dellie that Jared's grip on her arm became possessive. More than once his sharp gaze had threatened passersby whose eyes had lingered over her too long. This pleased her somehow. Dellie was suddenly anxious to know more of this man, and she wondered how much she could learn about him if he'd let her read the tarot cards for him.

"You're a pensive sort, mamzelle," Jared told her after they'd walked a long block in silence.

"I don't mean to be poor company," Dellie apologized.

"Have more confidence in your charms, Dellie. Any man would consider himself damned fortunate to spend time with you, conversation or no. I was only curious to know if there was something particular on your mind."

"I was thinking that I'd like to read the cards for you, if you'd let me."

They had reached Madame Celestine's now, and Jared led her through the courtyard gate and up the stairs to her balcony, where he turned to her and slipped his hands about her waist. "Another time, perhaps," he said. "If they showed you something awful, you might not forgive me, and I want nothing to spoil this evening."

He was so close that Dellie could feel his heart beating against hers. She pulled in a tremulous breath, afraid to meet his eyes, not knowing what to expect next. Her shawl slipped down to rest in the crook of her arm, tugging on her sleeve and baring one shoulder, and as Jared moved to replace it, his hard fingers lightly brushed along the length of her arm, sending shivers through her. He toyed with the fabric for a moment, but thinking better of it, he bent to press a warm kiss against the bare shoulder, and then another upon the column of her throat. When at last he brushed his lips over hers, ever so lightly, Dellie gasped in surprise.

A strange excitement was bubbling up within her. The breeze from the river had died away suddenly, and the night air was heavy and still and full of the sound of her own labored breathing. A droplet of perspiration that had formed at her temple trickled downward now across her cheek to the hollow of her throat and then slipped between her breasts.

Dellie had never been this close to any man; she turned her eyes up to Jared, hoping that he would understand, but his face was well hidden in the shadow of the wide-brimmed hat he wore, making it hard to read his expression.

"I've never met a woman quite like you before, Dellie," he said, his voice a hoarse whisper.

Dellie was not certain how to reply. She feared that very soon he would find her inexperience tiresome. Next to this man who was gifted with all of the grace of a cat, Dellie felt clumsy.

Durant met her next with a kiss that was deep and intimate. He tasted of rich wine and a mingling of spices, and soon Dellie began to relax in his arms, not at all averse to the flush that spread through her as a result of his kiss. Shyly she reached for him, her small hands sliding beneath his frock coat and over the smooth satin of his waistcoat to rest in the small of his back.

She pressed closer against the warm, hard length of his body as his open mouth trailed along her jawline, and he whispered her name into her ear. Dellie was beyond hearing him. Her thoughts were centered on his hands, deftly moving upward from where they'd been resting on her hips to cup her breasts as he bent to kiss the valley between them. And then he looked up at her as he began to fumble with the ribbon tied at the low neckline of her blouse. Even in the darkness she could read the question in his golden eyes.

"Dellie?"

The color drained from her face all at once when she realized what he was asking.

"Non," she said to him, drawing back and responding in a flurry of her native French. *"Je ne puis pas. Jared, s'il vous plaît—J'ai peur. Je n'ai jamais—"*

Jared tried to clear the fog that had settled in his brain. What was it she was saying to him? He struggled with the translation. "I cannot . . . I'm afraid . . . I've never—"

"You don't have to be afraid of me, Dellie," he told her. But his words did not convince her. She regarded him, her eyes wide and childlike, pleading with him to understand.

"I'm sorry," she said to him then as she stepped over the threshold and put her door between them. *"Bonsoir, mon ami."*

Jared sat for a long time at the bottom of the stairs, watching Dellie's window up above. He did not understand her, this puzzling woman-child. Just yesterday he'd watched her hold a burly sailor at knifepoint, and yet tonight she'd fled from him like a frightened little girl. Could Dellie truly have lived so many years in this place and still be an innocent?

CHAPTER
6

Dellie knelt on a paving stone before the herb garden Madame Celestine let her keep in a *parterre* in the courtyard and brushed the damp earth from a chicory root before she thrust it into the pocket of her apron. With a small clasp knife, she cut a flowering stem of tansy and put it in the opposite pocket.

The morning sun was warm on her back, and the waves of heat that coursed through her brought back vivid memories of Jared Durant and her experience of the night before, despite all her best efforts to forget. Dellie had never imagined a man could have such power over her senses; it was a frightening realization.

The years she'd spent observing life from her room behind Madame Celestine's had led Dellie to believe that the relations between a man and a woman were no more than a commercial transaction, but last night she'd learned that it wasn't so. Last night the handsome riverboat gambler had awakened such feelings in her that she'd nearly lost control, and she knew it must never happen again, not if she truly wanted to escape Gallatin Street.

Jared Durant was a gambler, he'd admitted as much. Even if he was a man she could trust, he still was at home in places like Madame Celestine's, as Dellie could never be, and as she'd learned last night, he had the power to tie her here and to this way of life. She'd known it from the first moment that he touched her.

Dellie got to her feet, wiping her hands on her apron, and as she passed the open French doors of Madame Celestine's parlor, the woman called to her.

"Dellie, the coffee is hot. Come share a cup with me."

"But I've been digging in the garden, madame—" Dellie protested.

"There is hot water in the basin in my room. Wash your hands and come sit beside me, *ma chère.*"

Dellie did as she was told, disappearing into the shadows of Celestine's shuttered bedchamber to wash up and remove her soiled apron. When she returned, she stopped to admire Celestine, who was now pouring the coffee.

The woman wore a dressing gown of rose-colored silk, edged in the finest Brussels lace, and her dark hair, uncoiffed, hung in heavy, dark waves to her shoulders. Her *café au lait* complexion was mottled, though, by her illness, and her gray-green eyes dulled by lack of sleep. Consumption had taken its toll on her, but her proud bearing was evidence enough that Celestine Balfour had once been the most beautiful quadroon in all of New Orleans.

"How are you feeling this morning, madame?" Dellie asked her as she sat down beside her on the settee.

"*Bien, merci.* Your magic potion does wonders."

"Not magic, madame," Dellie insisted.

"Perhaps not like Marie LaVeau's magic," Celestine said, handing Dellie a steaming cup, "but magic just the same to ease such a cough as mine that I might rest."

"I shall write a receipt of the ingredients for you so you can have the 'magic potion' always."

"You talk as though you will be leaving us soon."

"I must return home one day, madame," Dellie replied. "I must!"

Celestine's full mouth curved into a thoughtful smile. "And what of our Tess?"

Dellie's confidence crumbled at this, and she stared at the cup and saucer resting on her knees. She did not know how she would ever convince Tess to come home with her to St. Gervais, but she returned Madame Celestine's smile just the same. "I will take her with me, of course. The island is her home as well."

Celestine touched Dellie's shoulder lightly. "You have grown into quite a young woman, *ma chère,*" she said and then paused for breath. Dellie could see that the conversation was tiring her.

"You are so kind to me, madame, but you must rest now. I will leave you."

"No," Celestine replied quickly and put a hand on Dellie's arm to keep her in her place. "First you must listen."

She hesitated, drawing a raspy breath, then drank of her hot coffee, which seemed to help.

"I think sometimes," she began, "that Tess would keep you a child forever, but it cannot be so. Perhaps this was not the best place for you to grow up—perhaps we ought to have sent you to the convent to live with the Sisters—but it would have broken Tess's heart."

Dellie regarded her, puzzled. "Madame?"

"You have grown into a beautiful young woman, but beauty is a dangerous thing, *ma chère.* It draws men to you but not always the right sort of men."

Now Dellie understood. Someone must have seen her in the company of the gambler Jared Durant and informed Madame Celestine.

Dellie drank her coffee and set the cup on the low table before them. "Do not worry yourself, Madame. I may be young yet, but I am strong, too. And there is no room in my heart but for Belle Terre and St. Gervais. Had you ever been there, you would know why. It is the most beautiful place in all the world. The ocean breeze is warm and scented with flowers. The sun shines every day, and the jungle is green and alive with the singing of birds. No black smoke from the riverboats in the air, no stench of filth in the streets, no drunken sailors lying in wait around every corner or in the shadows of the alleyway. All of the Valmonts for the past two hundred years have lived and died on the island of St. Gervais. Mama is buried there, and Papa . . . somewhere in the ashes. . . . I shall save money enough for the passage: mine and Mama Tess's as well. I *will* return and soon, too. The cards tell me so."

Celestine stared out of the French doors. As Dellie continued, she seemed to concentrate on the shrubbery in the courtyard but nodded at intervals to indicate that she was, indeed, listening.

"I understand that Mademoiselle LeBreton visited you again and that she has invited you to attend a party," Celestine said, changing the subject.

"Yes," Dellie replied, surprised, "but how could you know this?"

"Tess told me."

"But she could not read the invitation, and I did not tell her—"

"Perhaps not, but Tess was your mother's maid for enough years to recognize an invitation when she sees one."

So Mama Tess had known all along about the invitation. Dellie was ashamed. She could not even say why she'd lied to her, except that lately Dellie had felt as though Mama Tess were smothering her. Perhaps Madame Celestine was right—perhaps Mama Tess wanted to keep her a child forever.

"You will attend this party?" Madame Celestine inquired.

"I cannot possibly."

Celestine took a purse from within the folds of her gown and put it into Dellie's hands. "Take this to Madame Hélène."

"The dressmaker?"

The older woman nodded. "She will make for you a proper gown for such an occasion."

"Madame, you are too kind, but I cannot accept this money—"

Celestine held up her hand and drew a long, uneven breath. "Not another word. You will go to this party, Mademoiselle Louise Chandelle Marie-Thérèse Valmont, and meet the right sort of people for once."

"But you are the right sort . . . and Mama Tess . . . and Jonas. . . ."

"Not the sort your family would have wanted for you. Those aristocrats who live in their mansions on the rue Esplanade—they are your people. Given the opportunity, Fate might yet right the wrong done you."

Dellie stared at the money purse in her lap. "Mama Tess will not be pleased."

"She knows what must be."

"*Merci, madame,*" Dellie said. Excitement welled in her, and she embraced her benefactress, "*mille fois, merci.*"

Madame Celestine disentangled herself, and rising gracefully, she went to her desk to fetch a velvet-covered box. Then she returned to sit beside Dellie once more. "These belonged to my mother. She gave them to me when I attended my first quadroon ball. They are the only jewels which 'he' did not take from me when he left. I want you to have them, *ma chère,* to wear to Mademoiselle LeBreton's party."

Celestine handed the box to Dellie, who opened it carefully. Resting on a bed of black velvet was a delicate necklace, made up of a dozen sapphire teardrops, with earrings to match.

Tears filled Dellie's eyes and flooded over. "Madame, I cannot—"

"But you must! I insist."

"*Merci*, madame," Dellie said, embracing Celestine, and then she got to her feet. "I must speak to Mama Tess. Is she in the kitchen still, do you think?"

Dellie wiped away the tears with the back of one hand.

"Yes, child. You go and see your Mama Tess," Celestine said as Dellie headed for the door, "*et bonne chance, ma chère!*"

"Here, gentlemen, is the hand you've paid so dearly to see: three fair ladies and a pair of aces."

"Damnedest luck I've ever seen," the young man across the table said as he threw down his cards.

"Comfort yourself with the knowledge," his companion noted, "that a man who is lucky at cards is seldom as fortunate in other aspects of his life."

"True enough," Jared Durant replied as he pocketed his winnings. "None of the ladies in this pack can keep a man warm at night."

A ship's officer, wearing a blue coat, tapped Jared on the shoulder. "The captain will see you now, sir."

"Thank you," Jared said and, rising, tossed a gold half eagle to each of the fellows at the table. "Never take a man's last dollar," he told them. And to the man who'd spoken first, he said, "Take home flowers tonight to that new bride you've told us of, sir, and think kindly on this poor soul who has taken your money but cannot touch your happiness."

With that he left them and followed the officer out on

deck, where he paused a moment at the rail. Riverboats like this one were lined up as far as the eye could see. Before him on the levee a steamboat clerk flagged those cotton bales that had just been unloaded, while nearby a drayman cursed his mule into motion, heading for the cotton press.

Jared's gaze drifted northward, past the thousands of cotton bales piled on the dock, past the hogsheads of sugar, molasses, and tobacco stacked in neat rows, and the glut of traffic ferrying those goods to the warehouses, past all of it to the slate roof of the French Market. His eyes lingered there, and he smiled. The words of the man at the poker table still rang in his ears: "A man who is lucky at cards is seldom as fortunate . . . in life."

"Not this time, my friend," he said aloud, "not this time."

The young officer standing behind him cleared his throat. "Captain's waitin' on you, sir."

Jared followed him up to the wheelhouse, where a tall man with a neatly trimmed white beard put out his hand.

"Mr. Durant, is it? I'm Captain Willis."

Jared met his gaze and knew at once that he was being unfavorably assessed. On the whole, there was no love lost between riverboat captains and gambling men.

"You have a message for me from Mr. Valmont?"

The captain handed him the envelope without a word. Jared broke the seal and unfolded the note. There was an acknowledgment of Jared's last missive, followed by words of encouragement, and then a final sentence: "She is in New Orleans, I can feel it. Find her, Monsieur Durant, no matter the cost!"

Jared let the wind take the paper and carry it away, and then he watched as it wafted down into the dark green water of the river, where it finally disappeared from sight.

Valmont was so damned certain that he would succeed,

but Jared had begun to believe otherwise. He'd visited the convent and all of the charitable institutions in the city to make inquiries. He'd checked all of the marriage and death certificates at city hall. He'd talked to those families with whom the child and her maid might have taken refuge. He'd even taken out notices in the local papers. Thus far, though, there'd been no trace of Louise Valmont. Soon he'd have to inform Valmont of the facts. While the child and her maid may have landed in New Orleans all those years ago, they'd likely left the city since then, and tracing them further would be all but impossible.

"I was instructed to give you this as well," Captain Willis said, interrupting Jared's thoughts.

He handed Jared a bank draft for a handsome sum, but Jared only shook his head.

"Send it back to him. More money won't help."

The captain's brow crooked in surprise. "Sir?"

"I'll send word if I need funds," Jared replied. "Please tell Mr. Valmont for me that I'll do all that I can."

With this, Jared quit the levee. There was nothing more he could do in Valmont's behalf until he could meet again with Antoine Bredou, the Creole friend Valmont had mentioned. Perhaps he might provide a fresh approach to all of this.

Jared had plans for this afternoon, in any case. Despite a gray autumn afternoon sky that threatened rain, he walked several blocks toward a jeweler's shop on Canal Street, intent upon spending the whole of his morning's winnings on a present for Dellie. He'd not seen her in two days, but for all of that time he'd been debating with himself about her. At length he'd decided. If she wanted to be courted, then he'd oblige. He'd play her game if game it was, for Jared Durant had determined to possess the Witch of Gallatin Street, wager or no.

CHAPTER
7

Jared noticed her on the opposite banquette as he crossed Bienville Street, and despite the dark, enveloping cloak she'd wrapped herself in, he knew it was Dellie.

"*Bonjour,* mademoiselle," he said as he came up behind her.

When the slight figure stiffened at his voice, he thought that he might have been mistaken. "Still in New Orleans, Monsieur Durant?" she replied, hiding yet beneath the hood of her cape.

She did not slacken her pace, and so he walked along at her side. "I've not yet finished my business here."

Dellie stopped then and turned her face up to him. "I understood that one in your profession could find business wherever he chose to travel," she said to him, her expression strangely blank.

Jared took a step toward her, and she stepped back in reply, putting her back up against the brick of the building that fronted the street. "Ah, but I have varied interests, mamzelle," he told her, "and have not yet enjoyed all that New Orleans has to offer."

He touched her arm, and she caught her breath in reply. It was the response he'd hoped for. It told him that despite her efforts to prove otherwise, Dellie was not indifferent to him. All at once the brisk wind pushed back the hood of her cloak, and Jared met her eyes, wide and dark as the overcast sky.

In a moment she was hiding again beneath her cloak, but he'd seen the truth in those blue eyes, and it left him invigorated. Yes, he did love a challenge.

Dellie continued on her way, and he followed at her heels. "There's a definite chill in the air this morning," he said to her. "But you needn't worry, Dellie. It can't last long in this climate."

It was not pretentious. Jared told himself that Dellie was not the sort who'd be impressed by gaudy baubles. It was elegant nonetheless: a delicate bracelet made up of ivy leaves of wrought gold and set with pearls. He had very nearly decided upon it but took one last look at the jeweler's case, just to be sure. It was then that he saw the locket. It was oval-shaped, with two initials upon its face in flowery script: *LV.*

"Where did this come from?" he asked the gentleman behind the counter as he pointed at it.

"A young lady," the man replied, clearing his throat, "in straitened circumstances. It became necessary for her to sell her jewelry, and I obliged her. You understand how it is, monsieur? If you like the piece, the engraving can be changed—"

"Her name," Jared inquired anxiously, "tell me her name!"

"That I cannot do, monsieur. Such a lady would not want it known. . . ."

Jared cursed himself for not having had the foresight to ask Valmont if there might have been other pieces of jewelry in his daughter's possession. "Tell me where I can find her, then," Jared insisted. "I will pay."

The man's eyes lit up suddenly. "There is an address, I think," he said and hurried to his desk to take out a ledger. "Yes, yes. Here it is."

In a few minutes Jared was hurrying down Royal Street with Dellie's bracelet in one pocket, the locket in the other, and a scrap of paper with an address written on it in his hand, and despite the ominous thunder in the distance, he was certain of success in all of his ventures.

The house was a fine one: redbrick, three stories high, with tall shuttered windows and iron balconies. Jared compared the number on the paper to the one over the door, then removed his hat and raked a hand through his hair before knocking.

The young woman who opened the door at last was clad all in black, her fair hair knotted at the nape of her neck, her pale blue eyes vacant and glazed with tears.

"Monsieur?"

Jared pulled out the locket and held it up for her to see. "This is yours?"

"It was. But how—?"

She regarded him with suspicion then and took a step backward as if she might shut him out.

"Please, ma'am. I assure you I meant no harm. If I might come in, I can easily explain what all of this is about."

She seemed to recover herself and obliged, showing him into a shadowy parlor, where all of the furniture was in hollands. She uncovered a chair for him and perched herself on a corner of the settee. All at once a flash of lightning split the sky, bathing the room for a brief second in eerie blue light.

"Please excuse the state of things," she said in a wavering voice. "I am . . . closing up this house. Now, how may I help you, sir?"

"Let me tell you what brings me here and ease your mind," he replied. "My name is Jared Durant, and I am in the employ of a certain gentleman who is looking for his lost daughter. I'd all but given up hope of finding her, but when I came across your locket with these engraved initials, well, I thought I ought to check things out in the event that—"

The woman shook her head. "My father is dead, Monsieur Durant."

"Mr. Valmont was thought to be dead, however—"

"I don't think you understand," she said. "We buried my father two weeks ago."

The young woman pulled a handkerchief from her sleeve and dabbed at her eyes as her voice drifted off.

The storm began in earnest now, and rain began to beat against the windowpanes. Jared listened in stunned silence. He hadn't even considered the possibility that he might be mistaken, that he'd only been grasping at straws. "I'm sorry, Miss—"

"Villiers, Lorraine Villiers."

"I do apologize for intruding upon your grief, Miss Villiers. When I saw the locket . . . and you are of the right age and coloring. I was convinced I'd found the lady I'd been sent after."

"It is understandable. I only wish there could be such a happy ending for me."

Lorraine Villiers looked vaguely out the window at the rain and went on. "My father threw himself into the river and drowned, Monsieur Durant, but not before he'd wagered and lost everything we had. It is considered a perfectly acceptable pastime for a gentleman: brandy and a hand of cards at Price McGrath's. But Papa, he had no luck with the cards, you see."

Her words hung on the air and struck at Jared's own long-buried memories. He was surprised at the ease with which the old wounds were reopened.

"I have come to terms with all of this now and have decided to find a place for myself elsewhere, away from New Orleans. I will get by, but I shall never have back the life that was once mine, shall I?"

Jared looked into her red-rimmed eyes and tried to find within himself some words of comfort for her, but he was struck dumb. He handed her the locket and went out into the rain.

His mouth was dry as dust. He needed a drink . . . badly. But he did not hurry back to the hotel; he let the rain beat upon his back, soaking through his clothes as he walked on through the deserted streets. The chill was a comforting reality. It helped to keep his mind from straying down long-unused paths and dredging up old hurts that were best forgotten. The rain trickled in droplets over the brim of his slouch hat, and he stared into the shop windows as he passed by, trying to stave off the memories.

Jared reached into his waistcoat pocket and drew out the medal—Kirby's medal, hung on a tattered ribbon—that he kept as a reminder of his failure. Lorraine Villiers was lucky in a way, for she was no more than a victim, who could blame the whole of her misfortune upon her father. Jared did not have that luxury. After his own father had died in disgrace, he had insisted upon taking over as the man of the family. There was no denying now that he himself was just as guilty of destroying the Durants as his father was. It was he who had joined the volunteers fighting in Mexico to satisfy his urge for glory, though he knew full well that young Kirby would insist upon following him out. It was he who had ignored his mother's pleas that the boy was too young to join the army and should be sent home at once. At seventeen Kirby Durant was cer-

tainly as much a man as any in the ranks—old enough
to fight for his country, and in the end, old enough to give
up his life.

It was after the particularly bloody battle at Buena
Vista that Jared had cradled his dying brother in his arms,
knowing even as he watched him slip away that the news
of his death would kill their mother. Jared alone was to
blame for the loss of both their lives.

Jared thought it only a trick of the light when he saw
a familiar face inside the shop of an expensive *couturière*.
This could not be Dellie, wearing an evening dress of midnight blue satin, shot with silver, the dressmaker fussing
over the hem. But yes, it was the familiar tignon that she
always wore, and it was her profile silhouetted on the win-
dowpane.

Jared's breath fogged the glass, and he turned away, a
sickening feeling overtaking him. There was only one way
a woman like Dellie could acquire enough money to have
a gown made by Madame Hélène . . . only one way. And
then Jared realized just how much he'd wanted to believe
Dellie the innocent she'd pretended to be. How gullible
he'd been! The Witch of Gallatin Street had weaved her
spell over him as if he'd been no more than a callow youth.

Why, he asked himself then, had Dellie pretended to
be something she was not? He'd have accepted her just
the same. Perhaps she thought this was the sort of game
he enjoyed. Women of her sort were used to accommodating men's peculiar needs. Or perhaps she had only been
laughing at him all along.

"Damn her! Damn her to hell!"

Jared salved his wounded pride with the knowledge that
they would meet again. But the game was over now, and
very soon he'd have what he wanted from her, one way
or the other. Cursing his foolishness, Jared strode toward

his hotel, vowing to blind himself with drink before the evening was out.

Balancing her parcel in one hand, Dellie pushed open her door and swept inside, anxious to be out of the rain. She removed her damp cloak and tossed it over a chair to dry, noticing at once that the lamp on her table was lit.

"Mama? Are you there, Mama?"

From out of the shadows came Solange LeBreton. Dellie could see now that she'd been waiting there in a chair in the corner. "Where have you been, Dellie?" she asked, her soft voice wavering. "I've been waiting so long. It seemed like hours."

Solange was usually such a happy, vivacious sort, but now here she was twisting a handkerchief between her two hands, her rheumy eyes dark and wide against the pallor of her skin. Dellie could not help but notice, too, that the hem of her pretty yellow gown was torn and muddied.

"Solange!" she exclaimed and rushed to take up the girl's hands in hers. "What's happened? What's wrong?"

"The most awful thing. I had to get away."

Dellie could not imagine what might have wrought such a change in her friend. "How did you get here?" she asked. "I didn't see your carriage outside."

"I walked."

"In the rain? By yourself? Why, it's nearly dark, Solange. Are you mad to try such a foolish thing? No one bothered you along the way, did they?"

The girl shook her head vigorously, then dissolved into tears. "You must read the cards for me, Dellie, right now, right this minute. I have to know."

Ushering her friend to the table, Dellie settled her into a chair, then poured her a glass of wine before taking a place across from her. "Here, drink this, and then tell me what's happened."

Solange only sipped at the wine before setting down the glass. "Papa called me into his study this afternoon," she began, "and he told me that I'm to be married. The announcement will be made at my party tomorrow evening."

"But to whom? One of your beaux?" Dellie asked, though she knew it could not be, else Solange would not be so upset.

"He is a business acquaintance of my father's," Solange replied mournfully, "a gentleman I've never even met. Oh, how could Papa do such a thing to me?"

Solange LeBreton had been pampered and indulged for all of her young life, and though Creole convention accepted that a father had every right to decide his children's future for them, quite obviously Solange had believed that she'd continue to be allowed to have her head.

"You must calm yourself," Dellie said, finding it hard to summon up much sympathy for this girl, whose life thus far had been so comfortable and carefree.

But Solange wasn't wholly selfish, Dellie had to admit. She had come to Gallatin Street and made a friend of Dellie despite their different lives, and she had seemed concerned with Dellie's future, even if it was no more than a game to her.

"Things will work out," Dellie soothed and reached out to smooth back a damp ringlet that had fallen across her friend's dark brow. "Maybe it won't be so bad as you think, once you take the time to get to know the man. He may turn out to be very clever and handsome, after all."

"But there won't be time for that, don't you see? He comes from the Indies. He owns a plantation there and must return at once. He's only in New Orleans for a short stay. I'm to be married in less than two weeks' time and then shipped off to his island."

Dellie was wondering how she would react if she were put in Solange's place, but with the mention of the Indies, her objectivity vanished. Marriage to almost anyone might be a fair trade-off if it took her home again. "Oh, but the islands are so beautiful," she said with a sigh. "Much nicer than New Orleans."

But Solange was not listening. "I envy you, Dellie. No one tells you what to do, no one decides your life for you."

"Sometimes Fate has a hand in those decisions," Dellie replied to this.

"Read the cards for me, then," Solange said, picking up the silver tarot case and laying it on the table before her. "Tell me what my future holds."

Dellie regarded her friend for a long while, knowing she ought to refuse. Solange trusted her, too completely, she realized now. She had no doubt that Dellie's cards would provide the answer to this dilemma, but Dellie wasn't so sure she wanted such a responsibility. The pleading in Solange's dark eyes proved too much for her to bear in the end. She could not refuse her.

When the cards lay on the table, Dellie examined them carefully. There were several that caught her eye at once: the High Priestess, the Six of Swords, the King of Coins, the Sun.

"Here is your gentleman," Dellie said, pointing to the king. "He is dark, with dark eyes—a practical and successful man, and I do see travel for you."

"But will I be happy?"

"I see happiness as well," Dellie told her but did not mention the rest of what she saw—not the cloud hanging over all, nor the fact that Dellie herself had a part to play in Solange's future. Dellie decided to keep silent so she would not frighten her friend, but perhaps the truth was that she did not wholly understand the signs herself.

*   *   *

"Monsieur Durant? The concierge told me that I might find you here. My name is Aristede Grimaud. May I sit down?"

Jared studied the stranger for a moment, then waved a hand at the chair opposite. "Suit yourself. Would you care for a drink?"

"Non, merci," Grimaud replied.

"I think I'll have another," Jared decided and drained the whiskey bottle into his glass as he regarded the man across the table.

The dining room of the St. Louis Hotel was a bit blurry around the edges, but Jared could see Monsieur Aristede Grimaud quite clearly. He was very much the affluent Creole: impeccable manners, impeccable tailoring, right down to the fold of his cranberry silk cravat and the gold handle of his walking stick.

"I wish to speak to you, monsieur," Grimaud began, "about an advertisement that you placed in the *Times* with regard to the whereabouts of Mademoiselle Louise Valmont."

It was the last name that Jared wanted to hear at that moment, following his encounter this afternoon with Mademoiselle Villiers. He emptied his glass one more time but feared he'd drunk himself quite sober. "Do you know where I might find her?" Jared asked the man but turned a wary eye upon him.

"I'm afraid that I do," came the reply. "I am in New Orleans on business, Monsieur Durant, but my home is in the Indies, on the isle of St. Gervais. When I came across your advertisement in the newspaper, the name caught my eye at once. The Valmonts were a powerful family on our island for many years."

Jared studied the man as his black eyes shifted beneath heavy lids. Instinct told him to be on his guard.

"I am sorry to tell you," Grimaud went on, "that the

young woman in question died years ago. There was a slave revolt on St. Gervais. Many people were killed, among them Louise Valmont and her father. They were the last of the Valmont line."

Jared pretended to concentrate on his glass, lifting it up and swirling the dregs of his whiskey. "So it might have seemed, Mr. . . . Grimaud, is it? However, I can assure you that such is not the case. It was Lucien Valmont himself who hired me to locate his daughter."

Aristede Grimaud's face went white. *"Ce n'est pas possible!* Valmont lives?"

Jared nodded slowly, taking particular interest in the man opposite him now. Grimaud had revealed more that he ought to have, and if realizing, he suddenly recovered himself.

"It is a miracle. I cannot believe that he has never returned to our island in all of this time. You must tell me where I might find him. Is he here in New Orleans?"

But it was far too late for Grimaud to continue to play the polite stranger. Jared had seen for himself that this man had more than a passing interest in the Valmont family, and he intended to discover exactly what the connection was. He knew that he must tread carefully with Aristede Grimaud.

"Mr. Valmont is not in the city," Jared replied after careful consideration. "Now, if you will excuse me, sir, I have an appointment to keep. Thank you for taking the time to come and talk with me, though."

Jared left Grimaud with mouth agape, hardly an attractive pose for such an elegant gentleman. He went around the corner and out of the dining room, sidling up beside a potted plant in the lobby to await the opportunity to trail the Creole and discover exactly what his game was.

*　　*　　*

With his hat pulled low across his face, Jared kept to
the shadows as he followed Grimaud through the rain-
slick streets of the Vieux Carré. The man's destination was
a ramshackle cottage on St. Ann Street, and he quickly
disappeared through a high fence that nearly hid the
dwelling just beyond it. From the alleyway beside the
building opposite, Jared waited and watched as the twilight faded into a black, moonless night.

He could not help but wonder what a man like Aristede
Grimaud was doing in such a neighborhood. More than
once as he waited, he'd sought to discover who resided
in the dilapidated house by making inquiries of passersby,
but they would only meet him with wide-eyed stares and
then shake their heads and hurry past.

The evening wore on and still Grimaud did not emerge.
Jared turned up the collar of his frock coat against the
damp night air, edging nearer to the brick wall as he
pulled out a cheroot and struck a match to it. While he
waited, his thoughts turned from his disastrous encounter
earlier today with the woman named Lorraine Villiers to
his discovery of the truth about Dellie, the Witch of Gallatin Street. His expression hardened, and he exhaled a long
stream of cigar smoke. Suddenly the sky lit up with stars
as a fist connected with his jaw. The impact knocked him
back against the building, and before he could recover, another well-placed blow in his midsection doubled him
over.

Jared's jaw throbbed, and the world was spinning cra-
zily. He swore at himself for having drunk too much, for
now his reflexes were dangerously dulled. Shaking off the
vertigo as best he could, he pulled a ragged breath and
coiled an arm to retaliate, but his assailant had the advan-
tage yet and struck one last blow, which left Jared lying
facedown in the muddy alleyway.

"Best for you if you mind your business, monsieur," came the warning. "You don't belong in this place."

Jared gathered his strength and rolled over in time to make out the dark blur of a tall figure before he disappeared into the shadows once more.

A wizened old black man who must have heard the commotion came around the corner then and helped Jared to his feet. "You hurt, mister?" he asked.

Jared shook his head, retrieving his hat and brushing himself off as best he was able. "I'll be fine," he said.

He thought about the warning he'd been given to mind his business. Had he been assaulted because he'd been following Grimaud . . . or only because someone here suspected him of invading his privacy?

"Could you tell me who lives in that house?" Jared asked, pointing across the way.

Surprisingly, the old man took up the challenge. "You ain't from 'round these parts, mister, else you wouldn't be askin' such a fool question. That there be the home of Marie LaVeau, that voodoo queen."

Before returning to his hotel room that night, Jared paid a visit to the telegraph office and sent a wire to Lucien Valmont in St. Louis. The message was brief, only one word, in fact, in the form of a question—GRIMAUD?

CHAPTER

8

Jared stepped out onto the terrace, hoping to put as much distance between himself and the commotion in the ballroom as was possible. The orchestra had just struck up a noisy mazurka, and this, coupled with the mingled voices of a hundred conversations in several different tongues, was harsh on the ear. He promised himself that this particular celebration "in honor of the eighteenth birthday of Mademoiselle Solange LeBreton" was absolutely the last Creole function that he would attend in an effort to locate Lucien Valmont's daughter.

Valmont's friend, Antoine Bredou, had asked Jared to be very discreet in his inquiries, but after his embarrassment over Mademoiselle Villiers, Jared needed no encouragement to take the circumspect approach. He'd all but decided that there was no hope of success. Tomorrow he'd head back to St. Louis, settle with Valmont, and be done with it.

Only one thing still bothered him in all of this, and that was the business of Aristede Grimaud, who, in Jared's opinion, had been far too interested in finding Valmont.

Perhaps it was fortunate that Jared had not been able to locate Louise Valmont yet, for he was beginning to believe that there was much more to this case than he'd been told.

Jared's personal feelings would have had him confront Grimaud face to face, if only to learn if he was behind the attack made on him in the alley, but that would doubtless prove a foolish exercise. Maybe later in the evening he would make a search of Grimaud's hotel room to see what he could make of the man. Yes, that would be the wiser move, Jared thought, and he might just do that—if he were not otherwise occupied. However, he had every intention of being otherwise occupied.

In the pocket of his evening coat rested a velvet box containing the bracelet that he bought for Dellie. When he finished his business here, Jared intended to go to Gallatin Street to deliver the gift and see what she might offer in exchange.

No sooner had Dellie's name come to mind than Jared glanced through the French doors and caught sight of her. She wore the same gown he'd seen her being fitted for in Madame Hélène's shop. It was the color of the midnight sky, shot with silver threads that glittered like shafts of moonlight, and her hair was caught up in a turban of the same fabric.

At her throat was a collar of sapphire teardrops, the very color of her eyes, and matching stones dangled from each ear. Jared could scarcely believe that this elegant lady was indeed Dellie. Contrasted with the garden-variety beauties in the ballroom, she was a wild and exotic bloom, and he could see that he was not the only man whose attention she had captured. As she whirled in the graceful rhythm of the dance, Jared was mesmerized, forgetting for a moment how she had deceived him, but only for a moment.

*   *   *

There was no denying that Solange LeBreton had a flair for the dramatic. In a small sitting room that adjoined the ballroom, she had made a special place for Dellie to tell fortunes. There was a table in the center of the room, and over it was thrown a scarf, patterned in reds and golds. A single candlestick on the table provided the only light in the room, and a sheer drapery hanging across the open doorway added to the shadowy effect.

Dellie sat at the table, riffling the cards absently as she watched the dancers beyond the drape, and wondered if this had been such a wise idea after all. She suddenly felt foolish. This whole scheme had the air of a carnival sideshow, but Solange, who'd come in to wish her well, insisted that such was not the case.

"Every man has an interest in his own future," she said, rather too profoundly. "You have a gift, Dellie, just as your Mama Tess says. The first time I came to see you, you said I would travel, *et voilà,* within the month Papa decided that we would spent the summer in Paris. Your cards warned me of an illness only two days before my maid came down with the fever, and did you not tell me that my fiancé would be dark and handsome . . . and wonderful? My friends will come to you tonight, Dellie, even those who think it only a game. You wait and see."

Solange was right. One by one half a dozen young ladies came into the room to sit at the table and have their fortunes read. There were gentlemen as well, gentlemen playing at this game to please their young ladies, and older, more skeptical gentlemen, who still went away smiling.

It was the most fascinating evening Dellie could ever remember having spent. She decided as she thought on it, though, that this gift Solange spoke of lay not only in interpreting the cards but the people as well, and Dellie had an abiding interest in people. She listened to what they told her of their lives, shared in the confidences she was ofttimes privy to, and helped where she could with a kind word or a suggestion.

There were, of course, those times when the message of the cards was amazingly clear, and Dellie never ceased to be astounded by this. On such occasions very little interpretation was necessary. But there were times as well when the signs were subtle, and much thought had to be given to their meaning. Often in her readings Dellie wished that she could have sought her mother's counsel. Surely Madame Valmont, who had gained such renown for her perception in the drawing rooms of Paris, would have been able to explain the nuances of the tarot to her daughter. Sadly, this could never be.

Mama Tess did not understand Dellie's questions. To her, the world was black and white. The cards did not lie, and you trusted them without question to lead you. How much easier things would have been if Dellie had not begun to see the world in shades of gray.

When the last of Solange's guests had left the sitting room, Dellie went out for a glass of wine to soothe her parched throat. The hour was late, and she knew that before very long, she would be back in her rooms behind Madame Celestine's with only her memories. She could live on the memories, she decided . . . for a while at least.

She had this night danced and made small talk with several handsome gentlemen, though despite Solange's intentions, she'd been careful not to encourage them. She knew that it could only lead to disappointment. She had been introduced to Solange's fiancé and was pleased to find that they seemed well suited after all. Throughout the evening she'd met and been accepted by some of New Orleans's most prominent citizens—all this and yet still managing not to trip on her skirts nor spill her wine. It had been a successful evening, all things considered.

When Dellie remembered that she had left her cards behind in the sitting room, she went to retrieve them. She pulled back the drape, and there, deep in the shadows of the darkened room, sat a gentleman with his back to her. He had her cards in hand and was shuffling them in expert fashion.

"Monsieur," she said as she came around the table, "if you please—"

Dellie held out her hand to him, but he lay the deck on the table, cut it several times, and turned over the top card. It was the Knight of Swords.

At once Dellie's knees turned to water, and she dropped into her chair. Only then did the candlelight illuminate the gentleman's face enough for her to recognize him. It was Jared Durant!

He looked positively arrogant, relaxing in the chair in his evening attire, acting as though he had every right to be here, in this fine house, at Solange's party. The flickering candle's flame was casting golden highlights on his sandy-colored hair, its soft light dancing across the sharp planes of his face, as if to remind her how handsome he was.

"You!" she said when she'd regained her voice at last. "What are you doing here?"

"I might ask the same of you," he replied. "This is a far cry from your usual haunts, mamzelle."

The remark stung her. "I am a guest of Mademoiselle LeBreton," she insisted and wondered at the cruelty in his voice.

Jared's laugh was harsh. "Oh? And do the LeBretons make a regular habit of inviting Gallatin Street harlots to their soirees?"

Dellie felt the blood drain from her face, and the room began to spin. How could he say such a thing? She thought she'd convinced him that it wasn't so. As she snatched up her cards, she turned a disillusioned expression on the

Knight of Swords still lying atop the deck and then eyed Jared with a murderous glare. This was the man into whose hands Fate had delivered her?!

"Tread lightly, Monsieur Durant," she spat, "for I'm certain that you have less right to be here than I. Or have the LeBretons taken to inviting swindlers and cardsharps to their soirees?"

"*Touché,* mamzelle. You've more wit than I might have imagined. What other qualities have you been hiding behind that gentle expression of yours?"

Dellie had heard quite enough and so turned on her heel and left him there. She said a quick good night to Solange, hoping to escape this place in the event that Jared Durant intended to reappear and make a scene, for she wanted no part of it.

Before she could make good her escape, however, Durant descended upon her, taking her firmly by the arm and squiring her through the crowded ballroom toward the door.

"Where are you taking me?" she demanded under her breath.

"Back to Gallatin Street, where you belong," he replied.

Dellie dragged on his arm, but nothing short of an ugly scene would have put him from his purpose.

"What gives you the right to interfere in my life?"

He turned a cold eye on her. "I don't like being lied to, and I damned sure don't like games played at my expense."

They were out of the house now, and Jared led her down the flagged walk and into a cab that seemed to be waiting for him. He gave directions to the driver, and when they were inside and Jared had shut the door, Dellie turned to him. "What are you going on about?" she shouted. "What has happened to you?"

He would not look at her. "Tell me, Dellie, do you play

the poor urchin for every man who comes along, or dare I hope you think me special? How you must laugh at those men foolish enough to be taken in by your little act! But then, I'll wager it's a sly method for driving up the price, eh?"

Each word struck her like a blow. "I do not lie, monsieur," Dellie told him, her voice cold and hard, "and I do not care much for these implications you make."

Jared turned to her at last, and she thought that his expression had softened somewhat, though it was difficult to tell for certain within the darkened carriage. "You didn't have to lie to me, Dellie. I'd have understood. At times I'm not proud of the way I earn my living, either. I thought that we were friends."

He did not speak again, and Dellie sat there, wondering what had happened to the charming man she'd dined with only a week before. What had made him doubt her? And even if it were so, why should he care enough to display such anger?

When the cab came to a halt in the alleyway beside Madame Celestine's, Dellie did not wait to be handed down. She sprang from the carriage, burst through the courtyard gate, and hurried up the stairs, hoping to take refuge in her room.

Jared cursed, dismissing the driver, and following at Dellie's heels, he reached her before she could open her door. Catching her by the arm, he fairly shoved her into the room, where she fell against the table in a rustle of crinolines.

"Be honest with yourself, Dellie," he told her. "Your mother isn't Madame's cook, is she? She's one of Celestine Balfour's whores, and like it or not, that's what she's made of you!"

"No!" Dellie shot back angrily, and then in another moment her ire was tempered with amusement. She could not help it. It was clear to her now that Jared thought Mama Tess was her mother. True, he'd never actually seen her. He couldn't know, but it was a ridiculous picture nonetheless.

All of this must have been reflected on her face, for as a result Jared began to shout again.

"You can't have been invited to the LeBreton's party, so tell me which one of those pompous Creole gentlemen paid for you? Whoever he was, I hope he paid a pretty penny; but he'll be alone tonight, I'm afraid."

Jared's expression was unforgiving now, his eyes piercing her like shards of yellow glass. Dellie could feel his hatred, and despite her anger, tears blurred her vision.

"Whether you believe me or not, the truth is I went there alone."

Jared looked at her: Her eyes were two sapphire pools, brimming over now. Oh, she was a consummate actress, he told himself, but he vowed he'd not be taken in again. "Then tell me, Dellie. Where did the Witch of Gallatin Street come by such a fine gown? And those jewels?!"

He shoved a hand into his pocket and drew out the velvet box, removing the bracelet he'd bought for her.

Grabbing her roughly by the wrist, Jared turned over her hand and dropped the bracelet into her open palm. "What is this compared with your other prizes?" he sneered. "Enough to buy a kiss?"

He dragged her to her feet then and caught her up next to his hard body. Dellie shut her eyes against him. This was not Jared Durant; it could not be. This was Celestine's gambler, come back to inflict still more pain. His hand caught her chin and turned her face up to him for a brutal kiss that drew the very breath from her and left her dazed and hurting.

And then he released her all at once, shocked at what his anger had made him become. The look in Dellie's eyes was fatal. She hurled the bracelet at the far wall and slapped him hard across the face. The sharp crack of contact split the silence.

"Get out!" she screeched at him. Tears were trailing down her cheeks. If she'd had her knife within reach, Jared thought, she'd surely have plunged it into his heart. "Get out of here, do you hear me?! I never want to see you again!"

What was it about this woman that drove his emotions to a fevered pitch? He looked at her, standing there, clenching and unclenching her small fists, as her breast heaved with pent-up sobs. Those brilliant blue eyes were wide now and opaque against a pale face, streaked with tears, causing her to look rather like a wounded animal. If this were an act, then doubtless it was the finest he'd ever witnessed. Could he have been mistaken about Dellie? It was far too late to find out.

"Get out!" she screamed with the last of her strength.

Jared did as she demanded, stumbling out of the door to lean upon the wrought-iron railing of her balcony. Nothing had changed. Above, a profusion of stars still flecked the night sky in a mirror-image of the lighted ships out on the black Mississippi just beyond the levee. The sounds of the drunken gaiety of Gallatin Street drifted upward as surely as it did every night. The world had not changed; Jared Durant had.

He descended the stairs carefully, as if each step were a painful one, and in fact he did feel as though he'd just been kicked in the gut. He sat himself down on the bottom step and put his head in his hands to think.

What, in God's name, had come over him? He'd treated Dellie abominably, raving at her like a jealous husband, and he had no right, no right at all. Whatever she was, however she chose to live her life, it should have been no business of his—but somehow he could not bear the thought of another man touching her.

For half of an hour he must have sat there in the darkness, unable to move. He had to understand the hold she had over him. And then, finally, a crazed laugh burst from his lips. Damned fine gambler he'd turned out to be! In this game with the Witch of Gallatin Street, he surely held the losing hand, but he couldn't bear to fold just yet.

CHAPTER
9

There was a lamp still lit in her room, for Jared could see the patterns that the light made on the floor of the balcony as it escaped through the louvered window shutters. He knocked upon her door, not knowing what to expect. Shoving his hands into his pockets, he dropped his head, and though he could not know it, he made a contrite picture, indeed.

The heavy door creaked open, and then Dellie was standing there before him, bathed in the warm yellow glow of a candle burning somewhere in the room behind her. She did not speak, but only pulled her white silk wrapper closer around her, and as Jared met her eyes, he could not help but be affected by the haunted look she wore.

What struck him most, though, was her hair. For the first time since he'd met her, Dellie was not wearing a tignon. Her hair flowed unbound now in a golden wave over her shoulders. In all of this time Jared had assumed that she was dark-haired, for her brows and lashes were dark. He'd not expected her to be so fair and fragile-looking, and it took him completely by surprise; she looked like an angel, standing there in the half-light.

"I couldn't leave you that way, Dellie," he said before she could come to her senses and shut him out once more. "I had no right to say those things to you. Can you ever forgive me?"

Dellie stared at the floor. *Shut him out!* the voice in her head cried. *Before he can hurt you again.* But her heart would not listen, and so she stepped backward, opening the door wider to allow him to enter. Jared wasted no time in doing so.

There was a chamberstick set in the center of her table and a number of the tarot cards were laid out there as if she'd been reading them. Jared concentrated upon the arrangement of the cards and the odd pictures upon them, each having its own symbolic meaning. What had they told her tonight? he wondered.

Dellie watched Jared as he studied the tarot spread. Could he not see the cards that linked them together? But he knew, surely he knew, else he would not have come back.

The silence lasted for a long time, and it seemed to Dellie that this man, who seemed always to know the right thing to say, now had to struggle to find the strength to face her.

"Why, Jared? Why such anger?" she wanted to know.

"I knew that we were kindred spirits from the first moment I laid eyes on you," he explained, turning back to her, and then the words spilled out. "I care for you, Dellie, more than I've cared for anyone in a very long time, and the thought of you with another man—well, that's something I just can't bear."

His voice vibrated with emotion, and Dellie was touched by this admission, which had been so hard for him to make. Jared reached out for her then, and she went to him at once, resting her head against his broad chest as he folded his arms about her.

"Can you forget all the hateful things I said?" he asked. "Can you forget everything but this?"

Cupping her face in his hands, Jared breathed a warm kiss onto her lips, and Dellie's heart fluttered in her breast like a bird taking flight. There was no longer any doubt in her mind; Jared Durant's hold on her was absolute. She could no sooner send him away than she could stop the sun from rising with the morn, and it did not seem to matter so much to her now that he stood between her and her dream of going home to St. Gervais.

Dellie's perfume laced the air between them, and the exotic blend of carnation and jessamine reminded Jared of the luxuriant garden that bloomed outside beneath her balcony. He edged closer to her, still seeking forgiveness in her eyes, but found himself sorely distracted. Her heady fragrance and the feel of her soft body pressed against him was exquisite torture. His hands sought her shoulders, then drifted along the supple line of her arms, where the silken robe was warm from her skin. A wave of desire rose in him, but he quelled it, knowing that this was a path best trod cautiously.

Gathering the courage to touch him, Dellie reached up and ran the back of her hand along the sharp line of his jaw and then moved to loosen the knot of his white silk tie. The elegant evening attire suited him, she decided. How could any woman resist such a man?

The memories of Mama Tess's lessons had begun to hum in her brain. *"Trust in the cards, ma petite. They will show you the way."* Had not the cards told her that the Knight of Swords would come to change her life? And now here he was—flesh and blood before her. 'Twas Fate, no less.

Boldly Dellie pressed her body against the muscled

hardness of his. Jared groaned in response and buried his face in her hair. "Forgive me!" he pleaded, his voice harsh against her ear.

While Dellie's conscience might have needed convincing, her body did not. Blood pounded at her temples, and its rhythm matched her rising anticipation. Her flesh was hot where Jared's hands had been. "Yes," she whispered.

With that, Dellie slipped her hands beneath his jacket and helped him shrug it off onto the floor. But when she'd unfastened the last of the buttons on his white satin waistcoat, Jared captured her hands in his. "Dellie?!" he said, in a voice half strangled. This was both question and warning.

"It was meant to be," she replied.

Those few words, spoken in Dellie's deep, accented tones, were like music to his ears. Jared needed no further prompting, for he was a man whose resolve had been sorely tested tonight. His lean frame was rigid with barely contained desire, and as he crushed Dellie to him, his mouth turned across hers in an urgent kiss.

In one swift move Jared untied the sash at Dellie's waist, and her wrapper draped open. His hands were soon lost beneath the silken fabric, exploring with great relish, and his deft touch sparked a blaze in Dellie that was both compelling and frightening.

Jared's caresses quickly became more insistent—nearly painful, yet not quite so. A small cry escaped Dellie's lips, but he silenced it with a kiss and swept her into his arms, carrying her into the alcove where she slept. He set her down in the center of her bed, brought the candle from the table and placed it on her bureau, then pulled the drape to shut them in.

As he stripped off his shirt and trousers, Dellie sat in the center of the bed and hugged her knees, focusing on the rapid cadence of her own breathing. She could not

help but watch him undress, nor resist admiring the glistening, muscled planes of his chest and the well-shaped
limbs that lent to him the lithe moves of a cat. Now,
though, this great tawny cat had his sharp golden eyes
fixed on her. She was his prey tonight.

Dellie was ashamed to admit, even to herself, that as
a child she'd hidden herself and watched some of Madame's girls and their clients through the rotted floor-
boards in the attic, in the places where the plaster was
cracked. Madame Celestine's old house had many secret
places, places where one could hide and watch. In the end
Dellie had always turned away. Tonight, though, there
would be no turning away.

Jared came to join her, and the bed creaked under his
weight. Reaching out a hand, he tugged at one sleeve of
her satin wrapper, then watched in silent fascination as
the fabric slipped off her shoulders, baring her body to his
eager gaze. She shook free of the garment, and his eyes
lingered over the swell of her breasts, then wandered from
the narrowing rib cage to the slim waist and the tangle
of her limbs in the bedclothes.

When he looked up again, Dellie had opened her arms,
inviting him into her embrace. But as he caught her up
against him, he felt at once the apprehension in her slender
frame and swore to himself. Damn! Her temperament was
as changeable as the winds. But he'd not be put off again;
his flesh burned now where it touched hers, and his head
was reeling as he fought for control.

With his last ounce of reason he pulled in a deep breath
to restore his calm and decided that, even if this innocence
of hers was only a game, he would still go along. After
all, was he not an expert at gaming? Confident in his abili-
ties, he made up his mind to approach her with a gentle
hand, to pleasure her with aching slowness, and soon, very
soon, her need would be as undeniable as his own.

"Don't be afraid of me, Dellie," he said softly and pressed a kiss against the perfumed nape of her neck.

As Jared's mouth slid along the curve of her shoulder, it left a wake of tingling warmth that spread through Dellie like wildfire. She did not understand the urgency building in her, but when he drew back, she could have cried out, so great was the longing to feel his touch once more.

His voice was deep and soothing. "We're a pair, you and I. We belong together."

When next Jared reached for her, it was only to brush the tendrils of hair from her forehead, yet Dellie could see the fierce amber fire that blazed in his eyes, and she quivered with anticipation—waiting for the moment when the great cat would pounce.

Gingerly his hands spanned her slim waist, then rose to cup her breasts so that he could bury his face in their warmth. A light breath caught at the back of Dellie's throat as his tongue grazed a hardening nipple. She did not resist as he eased her back onto the bed, her soft gold hair fanning out across the pillow beneath her head.

Her eyes had darkened to the color of the midnight sky, her lids heavy with passion. Jared teased her with languorous kisses, fighting all the while against his own rising need, wanting first to awaken the sensuality he knew was within her.

His caresses grew more insistent as his bold hands traveled the satin planes of her perfect body, gilded in candlelight: the soft fullness of her breasts, the fine outline of ribs, the angular hipbones and the creamy soft skin between them. As his fingers crept still lower to seek out the yielding softness between her legs, Dellie gasped in surprise, but Jared again covered her mouth with his own and continued his assault until he felt her relax beneath his hand.

He had his victory soon enough. When at last he drew

back for breath, a feverish moan broke from Dellie's parted lips, and her arms coiled sinuously about his neck. "Love me, Jared, please," she whispered against his ear.

Triumphant, he moved to cover her, parting her slender thighs with the pressure of his own. Dellie's fingers had been entwined in the hair that hung on his neck, but she loosed them now and sent them trailing over his broad shoulders and across the taut muscled line of his arms, which held him poised over her. Her eager hands fanned out over the crisp matting of light brown hair that covered his chest, and then crossed to his back and slipped low, urging him closer.

The uneven rhythm of their breathing echoed in the stillness in the room. Dellie's heart beat madly, and a wild excitement such as she had never known before surged within her as Jared lowered his mouth hungrily over hers. His hardness was pressed against her, and when he could stand it no more, he drove deep inside.

At the moment when their bodies met, a small cry escaped from Dellie's lips. Jared felt the resistance; it was enough to assure him that she had not been playing games with him after all. He was the first. She was his and only his.

Jared held back, taking care with her now, murmuring gentle assurances, raining kisses over her delicate brow until, trembling with the frightening force of her desire, Dellie arched her body against his. Responding with a low growl, he thrust deeper and deeper still, giving over to the primal rhythms of his body, which finally cast them both to heights of ecstasy that, until this moment, neither would have dreamed possible.

For a long while they lay, with limbs entangled, satiated but exhausted from their efforts. Dellie settled at last in the curve of Jared's arm and fell asleep, but he only lay there, studying her features in the moonlight. As he reflected on her innocence, Jared found himself recalling, to his shame, all that he had accused her of. What sort of man had he become who could not see the truth when it stared him square in the face?

From across the courtyard came the sound of shattering glass, followed in rapid succession by a drunken bellow and a high-pitched female voice, issuing a stream of foul curses that carried quite clearly on the night air. This nasty argument was no doubt the result of an unhappy match upstairs at Madame Celestine's, Jared decided. He raised a brow in surprise at the next violent crash, but then a smile twisted on his lips and he only settled himself closer beside Dellie as the battle raged on and more innocent crockery fell victim in the melee.

Not long after this, Jared heard the creak of the back-stairs door nearby. Heavy footsteps crossed the floor as candlelight illuminated the room beyond the drape, and then a woman's voice called out. "Dellie? You asleep, child? Anne-Marie and that man of hers are at it again. Likely she's gonna need you to patch her up when it's all done."

Jared tensed, trying to free himself from the tangle of bedclothes. The woman must have heard his movement, for she called out again. "No need for you to come along. I got me the gun Madame gave to Jonas. Put on your wrapper now, child, and I'll go fetch Anne-Marie."

Suddenly the drapery that separated the bed from the rest of the room was jerked aside, and reacting at once, Jared bolted upright, wresting Dellie from her sleep. He found himself staring directly into the outraged face of a stout black woman, dressed in her nightclothes. She held a chamberstick in one hand and now was pointing a revolver at him with the other.

"*Mon Dieu! Mon Dieu! Qu'est-ce que c'est?!* What goes on here?!"

"Mama Tess!" Dellie cried. "No!"

Jared dared not move lest this woman decide to shoot him where he lay. Dellie took a calmer stance. Donning her wrapper, she went to put a reassuring hand upon her guardian's shoulder.

"Non, maman. C'est le temps. C'est lui, le Cavalier de l'Epee," she said, and then went to the table and picked up one of the cards that lay there.

"You see, he is the one," she repeated and held the card up for Mama Tess to examine.

Jared could see it as well. It was the same card he'd turned earlier this evening.

" 'Trust the cards,' you told me," Dellie went on. " 'They will tell you when the time is right.' "

She laid the card back down upon the table and removed the pistol from the hand of a still-stunned Mama Tess. Taking the lighted taper, she set it on the table as well and helped the old woman into a chair.

Tess was clearly shaken at the sight of the card, and now Jared tried to ascertain what all of this meant. He grabbed for his trousers and put on his shirt, and when he was decent, he went to Dellie's side.

"Is she all right?" he asked. "What were you telling her about the cards?"

"Mama Tess has cared for me all of my life," Dellie explained. "I will always be a child in her eyes. She cannot accept this."

"Have you any brandy? She could use a glass, I think."

"I shall fetch a bottle. There's one downstairs in Madame's kitchen."

Dellie put the revolver on a high chest, out of sight, then disappeared down the backstairs. Jared went to sit across from Tess. "Are you feeling better?" he asked her.

When she was certain that Dellie was gone, the black

woman came suddenly to life and cast a malevolent eye upon Jared.

"What you done here tonight is despicable, mister. That child been haunted near all her life by that card. The tarot tells her such a man will come for her, and she believes. 'The Knight of Swords gonna change my life, Mama,' she tells me. Well, you done that, mister, sure enough."

Jared regarded her earnestly. "I know you care for Dellie, but I care for her, too."

Tess's look was unforgiving. "Don't give me none of your silver tongue, monsieur. I seen you downstairs at Madame's poker tables. You ain't nothin' but a no-account gambler man who says what suits his purpose, not half good enough for my sweet Dellie."

As Dellie searched the kitchen cupboards for the brandy, her spirits were high. Mama Tess would accept Jared, she told herself, after she came to know him. For the first time in months Dellie felt truly alive, and it was all because of Jared Durant. He was exactly what the cards had said he would be: strong and clever and handsome, and more than that, he cared for her. He had told her that he did. That was all that mattered. The Knight of Swords had indeed come to change her life. Having found the brandy bottle at last, Dellie started back up the steps—just in time to hear the last of Mama Tess's tirade.

Tears stung Dellie's eyes as she swept into the room and slammed the bottle down onto the table. And then she turned on Mama Tess, who'd always claimed to love her but not, it seemed now, enough to let her grow up.

"How dare you say such things, Mama? I am not a child. Do you imagine that I have no feelings at all? Am I to be kept by you in this room like a caged bird, without ever a hope of freedom? If you cared for your Dellie at all, you would be happy for me. Now I am a woman."

Tess gathered herself up, no longer needing to pretend at being feeble, and confronted her charge. "A woman, *peut-être,* but no lady . . . and a shame to your sweet mama's memory, that's the truth of things."

With that, Tess left them, closing the door firmly behind her. Dellie stared after her for several long minutes. Her face had paled, and a single tear slipped out and trailed down her cheek. She brushed it away at once and dropped down into the empty chair.

Jared could see that she was trembling. Tess's words had cut her more deeply than any of the awful things he'd said to her tonight. He had to resist the urge to reach over and wrap his arms about her, but he knew it would be better for her to shake off this melancholy at once.

"So that's your Mama Tess," he said lightheartedly. "She's certainly a force to be reckoned with, I'll give her that. Do you know that I'd thought, until I saw her just now, that she was your mother?"

Dellie nodded, and Jared saw that his remark had had the effect he'd desired. One corner of her mouth turned up in a lopsided smile.

"She's raised you as her own for all these years," he said more seriously as he went to the long table where Dellie kept her medicines and brought back two glasses. "It's no wonder she can't let you go."

When he sat down to pour brandy for each of them, Dellie cleared away the cards that still lay upon the table and returned them to their silver box. She hesitated for a moment as she handled the Knight of Swords and then put it away as well.

Jared wondered if what Tess had told him was the truth. Had Dellie only allowed him to make love to her because of that card? It could not be so, he assured himself. She had wanted this as much as he.

Across the table Dellie shut her eyes and tried to will

away the tears. Mama Tess couldn't possibly understand what she felt for Jared Durant. Her words had been so hateful.

"She didn't mean what she said," Jared told her, as if he could read her mind, and pressed the glass of brandy into her hand. "She was angry, that's all."

Jared watched as Dellie sipped at the amber liquid, staring up at him through the dark fringe of her lashes. What Tess had said about him, however, had definitely struck a chord. He'd been so pleased to discover that Dellie was not one of Madame Celestine's girls, but he hadn't stopped once to consider that he himself had robbed her of the very innocence he'd prized so dearly.

As the guilt rose in him, Jared tried to wash it away with the brandy. He hadn't taken the time to consider the future when he'd come back to apologize to Dellie tonight. He only knew that he needed her as he'd never needed a woman before. She made him feel whole and healed, but still he had to ask himself: Was he the kind of man she needed?

In any case, this was the time to make a stand, he knew that, in order to prove he was not the man that Mama Tess had accused him of being. "I'll be leaving New Orleans in a day or so," he told Dellie, and she grew very still at his words. "I want you to come with me."

Dellie felt relief flood through her. Her first thought had been that he was saying goodbye. "Where will you go?" she asked.

"I've business in St. Louis, and after that—well, I don't know yet—maybe we'll see San Francisco. Or anywhere else you'd like."

Her lips curved into a generous smile. At once she thought of St. Gervais. Would he take her there? she wondered.

"I warn you, though," he continued, "your Mama Tess

may not have been far from the mark in her assessment of my character. We haven't talked at all about our pasts, Dellie. I've not the makings of an ideal partner. I think you ought to know that much at least."

"I don't believe it. The Knight of Swords is a forceful man, brave and talented."

Jared stared hard into his empty glass. So she did believe in the tarot. "Do not put so much faith in your cards, Dellie," he warned.

But Dellie had drawn strength from her belief in him as the dashing knight and was excited by the possibility that Jared might help her get home. She was animated now. "What advice is this from a man whose fortunes are won and lost at the turn of a card? You are a gambler, no?"

"Yes, but—"

"Then you, too, must put your faith in the cards, *mon cher.*"

Jared found himself irritated by her logic. He reached across the table and took firm hold of her hands, willing her to look deep into his eyes.

"Dellie," he said to her, "don't you understand? I've no faith left in me at all."

Her lovely face was lit by a serene smile. "No matter. I have enough for us both."

He'd stayed too long, Jared told himself as he crossed Gallatin Street, or perhaps not long enough. When he was with her, his thoughts were disjointed and unfocused, allowing his emotions free reign. But now he'd begun to question the wisdom of his asking her to come away with him.

She had captivated him from the first with the paradox in her nature: innocent yet wise, fragile yet with such a strength of purpose that Jared did not doubt she could heal even his hardened heart. She trusted him implicitly, and therein lay the danger, for, despite the depth of his feelings for her, Jared feared that, in the end, he would destroy her. Hadn't he destroyed everything he'd ever loved?

Lost in thought, he gave only the merest glance to the tall black man he passed, lingering in the shadows of the alleyway: a brawny fellow with a patch over one eye. If he'd not been so preoccupied, he would certainly have been struck by the peculiar fact that he'd seen this same fellow more than once in the past few days out of the corner of his eye, always lagging a dozen or so paces behind him, or lurking behind corners almost out of sight. As it was, though, Jared passed him over as just another wretched denizen of Gallatin Street and strode on, thinking instead of Dellie and trying to stave off remembrances of the brother whose blood still stained his hands and of the mother who'd accused him of being no better than a murderer before she'd succumbed to her grief.

Dellie was a balm for his scarred soul. She had given him everything and asked nothing in return, and now he was contemplating their future together and swearing to himself that he'd make her happy. This, he thought wryly, from a man who'd always lived just one day at a time, who'd not thought of a future for himself in many, many years. Perhaps he did have some faith left after all.

CHAPTER
10

Dellie stared hard at the cards laid out on the table. She hadn't been able to sleep at all after Jared left her, and so, with the dawn, she'd turned to the tarot, hoping to find some peace in introspection.

The High Priestess was the card that she'd come to identify with herself, and beside it now lay the Moon, Death, and the Tower. Dellie had seen this ill-fated combination only once before, but she'd never forgotten. These were the cards she'd thrown on the night of the fire on St. Gervais.

Their meaning was abundantly clear: deception, change, ruin. . . . Dellie hesitated before turning over the final card, willing with all of her might that it should be the familiar man on horseback, her protector, the Knight of Swords. But when the last card was turned, it was the Devil's face leering up at her. All five cards of the *Arcanes Majeurs,* indicating that the matter was out of her hands.

Before another minute could pass, Dellie swept the five cards back into the deck and put it away into its silver case, closing the lid upon which were chased her initials.

She backed away from the table. Instinct would have had her run to Mama Tess at once, but what had happened last night had driven a wedge between them. Dellie knew exactly what Mama Tess would make of those cards—and of Jared's invitation.

She was more anxious than ever. She paced the length of her room, seeking solace in thoughts of Jared Durant. He had said that he wanted to take her with him, hadn't he? Anywhere she wanted. The kiss he'd left her with last night had been enough to drive away any doubts. Still, it was a difficult decision for Dellie to make. If she left New Orleans with Jared Durant, she'd have to leave Mama Tess as well, but she would be going home.

The absence of the card of her protector in the ominous spread seemed prophetic. Was the deception that the tarot alluded to of Jared's making? Now even the cards would have her doubt his intentions. But Dellie would not believe it. It did not matter what Mama Tess had taught her about Fate, nor what Celestine had taught her about gamblers. She had put her faith in Jared Durant, and she would sooner burn the trusted cards in the hearth than believe her lover false.

Dellie gave off stalking the room like a caged cat and busied herself instead by brewing a tea made with lemon balm to ease her jagged nerves. From the larder she sliced bread and cheese, and when she had eaten and drunk down her potion, she felt better almost at once. By the time she opened her shutters to face the day, she was ready to attribute most of her distress to the delusions of an over-taxed, overtired brain and determined to ignore the portent of the five cards.

It was a gray morning, quiet and still, as if the whole of the city sensed the impending storm, for storm there would be. The sailors had read the signs. The river, normally glutted with traffic, flowed freely today as ships sought safe mooring. Stevedores on the levee moved at twice their normal pace to transfer the cargoes that lined the docks into the safety of nearby warehouses. New Orleans had learned, over the years, the wisdom of caution in the face of the hurricane.

The day seemed ripe for disaster, yet Dellie tended to her chores, choosing to pretend that this morning was no different from any other. Her only deviation from the daily routine was to gather up some of her things and pack them into a carpetbag, for, almost without realizing, she had decided. When Jared Durant left for St. Louis, she would go with him, and when he had finished his business there, she would ask him to take her to St. Gervais.

With her mind made up, Dellie thought next on how she would explain things to Mama Tess. It was this confrontation she dreaded most of all. If last night's tirade was an example, Tess would not accept the news graciously. Somehow, though, she had to make her understand how much things had changed since Jared Durant had stepped into her life.

First, though, Dellie had to settle her debts. She went to her bureau and drew out an envelope which she'd hidden beneath her clothes, then she gathered up the velvet box that contained Madame Celestine's sapphires, slipped it into her apron pocket along with the envelope, and went out to the balcony and down into the courtyard, thereby avoiding crossing Mama Tess's path in the kitchen. She had not the stamina for sparring yet this morning.

When she entered the main house, she found Madame's parlor empty, and so she knocked upon the door of her boudoir.

"Entrez!" Madame called out.

Dellie did so, standing in the doorway to watch as Celestine, who was dressed for the day but still seated before her vanity table, pulled a silver-handled brush through her dark curls. Dellie marveled at the grace in her every move. It was no wonder so many Creole gentlemen had fallen under her spell.

"Good morning, madame. I've come to return your sapphires," she said.

Drawing the jewel case out of her apron pocket, Dellie went to put it in Madame Celestine's hand. "Thank you for lending them to me."

But Celestine would not take it. "I meant for you to have them, Dellie, to keep."

"Oh, madame, I could not. They are yours; it wouldn't be right."

"I shall never wear them again, and who is there to wear them after I am gone?"

"You have always told me that a woman's jewelry is her insurance for the future. I cannot take that from you."

Dellie held out the case once more, and reluctantly Celestine accepted it. Next, Dellie pulled out the envelope and gave it as well to Celestine.

"What's this, *ma chère?*" Madame asked.

" 'Tis the money to pay for my party dress."

"There is no need to—"

But Dellie was firm. "You have been too kind already to Tess and me, madame. I insist that you have it. The Valmonts always repay their debts."

Celestine looked as if she might argue but only sat quietly for a moment before reaching to brush a tear from her eye. "You are a good girl, Dellie. Now you must sit and tell me all about your party last night."

She pointed out an overstuffed chair in a near corner of the room. Settling into it, Dellie began at once to relate to her the events of the night before—excepting, of course, her fateful encounter with Jared Durant.

The older woman listened with great interest, and Dellie was surprised to learn that Madame Celestine was familiar with a good many of the guests who'd attended the party.

"You look different today," Madame noticed. "You met a gentleman last night, perhaps, who struck your fancy?"

"No," Dellie replied quickly. "Well, that is to say—"

Dellie was not a very good liar, and when she met Madame's inquiring gaze, her story simply tumbled out. "I have indeed met someone, madame, someone very special. But you will not approve—after all of your warnings."

Celestine seemed to find it amusing that Dellie should be concerned at all with gaining the approval of one with such a reputation as hers. "I am in no position to judge," she told her. And then with trepidation in her voice, she asked: "Is it the gambler, then?"

Dellie nodded, relieved that Madame Celestine had guessed the truth. "He is not like the other men who come here, madame, not like any man I've chanced to meet. He cares for me, I know that he does, and yet Mama Tess despises him."

Celestine grew pale and stared for a long while at her reflection in the mirror. "Oh, my poor child. I was sure you'd turned that man away, that there'd be no need to tell you—"

"Tell me what, madame?"

"Emma came to me a few days ago," Celestine began. "She said she'd heard a pair of men make a wager at the bar. One of them was your gambler. Dellie, he bet another man five hundred dollars that he could bed you within the week."

Dellie sprang out of the chair. "It's not true. Jared would never do such a thing. She's lying!"

"No, Dellie, she's not. Come and sit here close to me, and we'll talk."

But Dellie could not stay to hear another word. Traitorous thoughts were welling within her, and she clamped a hand over her mouth to stifle a sob as she quit the room.

In the dining room of the St. Louis Hotel, Jared Durant had just finished his lunch and was lingering over a second cup of coffee, hoping it would restore his vigor. He'd returned to the hotel early this morning only to find that, in his absence, someone had ransacked his room. His belongings had been searched, but he'd found nothing missing, and he'd spent over an hour putting things back in order before he finally got to bed.

He was kneading his brow, hoping to stave off a headache, when Silas Crane approached his table.

"Good morning," Jared said to him. "Have you come to sample the hotel cuisine, Silas?"

Crane took a seat and put a match to his cheroot. "Just come to pay my debt, Durant. I suppose I'll have to eat crow this morning. I'll be damned if you didn't do it, just like you said you would."

For a brief moment Jared was baffled, and then he remembered the bet. With a sinking feeling he realized that Crane's informant must have seen him at Dellie's last night. Thinking now on how much she'd come to trust him, he was sorely ashamed. What sort of man was he to ever have involved himself in such a wager? But he would not fail her now.

"Much as I'd like to take your money, my friend," he said, "I'm sad to say you're mistaken."

Crane's eyes widened in surprise. "What? Why I was sure—"

"I guess I'm not as persuasive a fellow as I thought. I couldn't make an impression on the lady at all. So you were right, you see. I'll make out a draft for the five hundred and have it to you by the end of the day."

Crane got up and started to walk away, shaking his

head in amazement. He'd gone only a few steps when he turned back. "But we bargained on a week, and you have two days yet," he reminded him.

Jared only shrugged. "I know a losing hand when I see one."

After Crane left him, Jared finished his coffee and then stared into the bottom of his cup, wondering how long he could go on pretending that Dellie would be better off with him.

"Monsieur Durant?"

He looked up at the woman and very nearly did not recognize her. It was Madame Celestine, but she was dressed in a sober black gown, with a veiled bonnet obscuring her features.

How much she had heard of the conversation that had just transpired he could not say, but there was fear in him as he rose and offered her a chair.

"Madame? What can I do for you?"

"I've come to speak to you about Dellie Valmont."

Jared had no doubt that she knew of the wager; he could see it in her eyes. His heart dropped—and then her words struck him. "Dellie . . . Valmont?" he repeated slowly.

Could it be? He had never considered such a possibility. Dellie had not mentioned her past, and he had not questioned, for there were things in his own past he'd just as soon forget. Now all at once his eyes were opened: a fair-haired woman nearly twenty years in age, a devoted black woman who'd raised her from childhood.

He told himself that he'd have seen the truth sooner if his emotions hadn't gotten in the way. But still he could scarcely believe it. The attraction he felt for Dellie damned near blotted out reason and perspective.

"Yes, Dellie Valmont," Madame Celestine replied. At first she appeared uncertain about the confused look he wore, but soon thereafter anger possessed her. "Don't pretend you don't know who I'm talking about, monsieur, for I know quite well that you do."

Jared was growing more than a little irritated now himself. "If Dellie is Louise Valmont, if you've all known who she is, then why did none of you respond to the ads I placed in the newspaper?"

"Which ads are those, monsieur?" she queried.

"The ads seeking information about her that I placed in the *Times* and the *Star.*"

Madame Celestine shook her head. "You do not understand the ways of our city yet, monsieur. The *Times* and the *Star,* they are for *les Americains.* Those of us who live in the Vieux Carré read only the *Picayune.*"

"Dellie *is* Louise Valmont," Jared repeated blankly.

It was not this realization, however, that left him preoccupied and suddenly full of dread. It was the other, illfitting pieces of the puzzle: the odd behavior of Aristede Grimaud, the ransacking of Jared's hotel room, and the attack that had been made on him in the alley, and more than any of these—the memory of the black man he'd crossed in the alley the night before, a hulk of a fellow wearing an eyepatch.

Jared realized now that he'd seen that same man several times in the past few days. Had he been shadowing him? Was he responsible for what had been happening these past days? Perhaps someone else was hoping to learn the whereabouts of Louise Valmont, and if that was the case, then Jared had led him straight to Dellie.

CHAPTER
11

Dellie woke with a start. Her heart was drumming and her mouth had gone dry, but it was not from the exhilarating effects of the storm brewing. This morning she'd run out on Madame Celestine because she couldn't bear to listen to any more speculation about Jared Durant and had taken refuge under the arbor, protected by the heavy foliage of the garden. This had been her favorite hiding place as a child, a place where she could go to be alone and sort out her thoughts. She must have dozed for a time, but now she sat hugging her knees as she tried to reconcile what Madame had told her with the sweet words Jared had whispered in her ear last night. Was she a fool for ignoring the lessons of her childhood? Were all gamblers the same?

Closing her eyes, Dellie tried to deny it, tried to deny what the cards had warned her of this morning. She resolved to put it out of her mind, and gathering herself up, she drew a ragged breath and decided that even if it was true, there was no good in sitting and feeling sorry for herself.

A keen wind had begun to howl, rattling the shutters

on their hinges. Dellie crossed the courtyard, ducked beneath a wildly swaying canopy of fringed leaves, and let herself into the kitchen. "Mama?" she called out. "Mama, are you here? We must bolt all the shutters, the storm's nearly upon us."

The kitchen was full of the delicious aromas of the meal being prepared, of biscuits baking in the hearth oven, and the spicy gumbo bubbling in the copper pot upon the stove. But Mama Tess was not to be found.

Dellie started up the inside stairs that led to her own room, thinking maybe Tess was there. She hesitated midflight when she heard the sound of voices from above in her room.

"Why have you come here?" Dellie heard Tess ask in her Creole French. The words were fraught with anxiety. "Why can't you just leave us be?"

A gentleman's voice responded. "It's been a long time . . . a very long time, hasn't it? Now, don't give us trouble. You know what I've come for. Where is she, Tess?"

Dellie did not recognize the voice, but responding to the fear in Mama Tess's tone, she pressed her back against the wall of the stairwell, not daring to move. This man was looking for her. Who was he?

"She's gone away," she heard Tess say next. "She's got her a man now. They went off early this mornin'. Her man come to take her away."

"You're lying," the stranger accused. "But I've no more time to waste. I only wanted to come and pay my respects to an old friend. Thomas here will have the truth from you . . . one way or another. Thomas, you see that she tells you all that we need to know."

"Yes, sir, jes' as you say."

"*Adieu,* Tess."

The door slammed shut as the stranger left by way of

the balcony stairs, and there followed the echo of heavy footsteps crossing the floor above.

"She's gone, I tell you," Tess said, her voice rising to end on a hysterical note, "and she'll not be back."

Thomas must have struck her then. Dellie heard a heavy pounding repeated and then a sickening crack. At this, Tess cried out.

Dellie was paralyzed with fear for a brief second, but all at once a surge of panic seized her, and she rushed up the remaining stairs and burst into the room, where an evil-looking black man was pummeling Mama Tess.

"Best for you if you tell me, ol' woman. Where is that precious child of yours?"

Dellie looked upon Tess's face, mottled with purple bruises, her mouth cut and bleeding. Enraged, she drew her knife, and giving vent to her fury with a wild screech, she rushed headlong toward the black man. "Leave her alone, you bastard!"

"Dellie, no!" Tess cried out, and Thomas turned around just in time to snatch Dellie's wrist as the wicked point of her knife creased his shoulder, tearing his sleeve and drawing a thin line of blood.

"So here you are, little one," he said, and an evil grin split his face.

Before Dellie could think to react, his big fist swung around and connected with her temple, throwing her off-balance. With his other hand he snapped her wrist like a twig of kindling. The knife clattered to the floor. He reached for it, but Tess pounced on him, dragging on his arm to keep him away from Dellie.

Numb with pain, Dellie struggled against the throbbing in her head, trying to rise. She knew that Mama Tess could not fight off this man on her own. All at once she remembered the pistol that she'd taken from Tess the night before. With Tess still holding Thomas back, Dellie went to the tall chest and reached up for it.

Ignoring the dull ache in her wrist, she braced one hand with the other, pointed the pistol upward, and fired to draw Thomas's attention. And then she took aim at the huge black man. Her head was swimming, and lights flashed before her eyes. Dellie feared she would not have the strength to fire again.

Jared could not be certain that the sound he'd heard had been a gunshot. The wind was whistling in his ears, flapping the ends of his gutta-percha cape, and kicking up anything else not nailed down. He clamped a hand onto the crown of his hat, keeping the brim low to deflect the wind, and hurried on. Perhaps it was only a shutter he'd heard, banging against a building and yet—

He took the balcony steps two at a time and pulled open the door without bothering to knock. Tess lay sprawled on the floor near his feet, only barely conscious and wailing in French. One eye was swollen shut, and her broad face was misshapen with bruises and streaked with blood.

At the far end of the room stood Dellie, frighteningly pale and reeling on her feet as she endeavored to use both hands to steady the pistol she had pointed at the intruder, a black giant with an eyepatch. Jared cursed. It was the same man who'd been following him.

"Come along quiet, now. You don't want for me to mess that pretty face of yours no more, do you, missy?"

Jared winced to see Dellie's bloodied brow and, in response, felt a rage rising in him which he feared he could not control.

"Don't touch her again!" he shouted, drawing the man's attention.

But the black giant continued to advance on Dellie, seemingly bent on finishing the job he'd begun. Jared moved quickly to put himself between them. "Why are you here? Who sent you? What do you want with her?"

The man did not reply, but boldly took one step forward and then another. To stop him, Jared coiled a fist and, concentrating all his energy, thrust it into his opponent's midsection, intending to fell him like a huge tree. Unfazed by the impact, the big man stood unmoved, and following a mere moment's hesitation, struck a blow that caused Jared's head to snap backward. The room was spinning, yet Jared managed to strike several times more before the giant's massive fist found its mark and sent him sprawling against the bedstead.

Swiping a hand across his mouth to staunch the blood that flowed from the cut on his lip, Jared shook off the dizziness and clutched at the bureau for support. Before he could get to his feet, though, there was a loud report. The black man swayed and dropped to the floor, a circle of crimson staining his shirtfront.

Dellie had had to concentrate all of her energy to raise the pistol again and fire. But when she looked at the blood and realized what she'd done, her strength evaporated, and she sank to the floor.

Jared righted himself and came to kneel beside her. She lay unconscious now, barely drawing breath. He tried but could not rouse her. A dark smear of blood streaked her temple just beside her left eye, where an ugly, purplish weal was forming. She looked so pale and still that he feared the worst. This was his fault, all of it. It was he who'd led the man to Dellie, he who'd pushed his way into her life and spoiled her innocence.

For the first time in many years Jared Durant sought to bargain with God. If she lived, he vowed to make no claims on her. If she lived, he would see her safely into her father's hands and disappear from her life. It was the kindest thing that he could do, he told himself. After a

long while he reached out and ran his fingers lightly along
her pale cheek. At his touch she stirred.

Jonas appeared in the door just then, and behind him
was a breathless Madame Celestine. "Monsieur Durant!"
she cried out as she stepped into the room. "You left me
so suddenly; I knew that something must be amiss. What
has happened here?"

"I'm not quite sure myself," Jared said as he lifted Dellie into his arms. "See to Tess, will you? She's been hurt
badly."

Celestine went to her at once, and some of the girls tried
to come up then to see what all the commotion was about.
Mon Dieu! Celestine cried when she saw the old black
woman. "Jonas, come help me carry Tess downstairs to
her bed. Emma, run and fetch the doctor at once! The rest
of you go back to your rooms. *Allez!*"

"I wouldn't move her until the doctor's had a chance
to look at her," Jared advised. "Just get some blankets to
make her comfortable."

Jared settled Dellie onto her bed, drew out his handkerchief, and after dipping it into the water pitcher beside her
bed, he wiped the blood from her face. The bruise on her
temple was swollen and discolored, but the cut was not
very deep, and he was soon able to stem the bleeding.

As he tended her, her eyelids fluttered. "Jared? What
happened?" she asked weakly, and then her eyes widened,
as if the memory had come back all at once, and she cried
out. "Where's Mama?" With renewed panic she began
thrashing on the bed. "Mama!"

"Hush, Dellie! Hush!" he pleaded and bent to fold his
arms around her.

"Mama Tess . . . Where is she? Is she badly hurt?"

Jared eased her back down on her quilt. "Lie still," he
ordered. "Celestine is tending her, and the doctor's been
sent for."

"I've killed that man," she said.

"I don't know yet," Jard replied. "You may have. But you had no choice. Can you tell me who he was? What he wanted?"

Dellie shook her head. "When I came up, he was hurting Mama Tess. I had to stop him. I charged at him with my knife, but he was too strong. And then I remembered the pistol."

She squeezed her eyes closed as if to shut out the memory, and Jared went to the washstand to wring out the handkerchief, stained with her blood, in the basin. He turned back in time to see that Dellie had somehow gotten to her feet and was standing near the foot of the bed. Her eyes, wide with anxiety, were searching the room for her beloved Mama Tess, and when she spotted her, lying bloodied and helpless on the floor, she cried out sharply. As she attempted to go to her aid, though, she swayed on her feet, and Jared only just managed to catch her up in his arms before she collapsed.

Again he lay her down on her bed and wiped the fresh blood from her brow. Only when he was sure she was resting did he turn his attention to the black man laid out on the floor. Dropping on one knee before him, Jared studied him without compassion. Amazingly, the man was still alive. "What's your name? Who do you work for?" Jared demanded.

"Thomas," he replied, and sputtered a cough that rumbled through his barrel chest. "Ol' Baron Samedi, he gonna come for Thomas now, sure 'nuf."

"What's that you say?" Jared did not understand. He could see that the man was dying; there wasn't much time. "Damn it, man! I asked you who's your master?!"

Thomas let go a crazed laugh that sapped his remaining energies. "Sometime Papa Legba he got his eye on me, and I do his bidding. Sometime it be Damballah hisself," he said, his dark eyes glazed. "But I am a free man now, monsieur."

With that the last breath of life left him. He had spouted only nonsense; Jared had learned nothing.

Celestine meanwhile was ministering to Tess, who had begun ranting hysterically in French. She kept repeating Dellie's name, that much Jared was able to understand, and it caught his attention now. Celestine replied in soothing tones, trying to calm her.

"What is she saying?" Jared wanted to know.

"She's not making much sense, I'm afraid. She says that you must take Dellie away, far away from here, to some safe place. She's suffering from the shock, I think. I've told her that she doesn't have to be afraid, that the man is dead and can't hurt her now."

"And she's not convinced?"

"She says he'll return—" Celestine tried to explain.

"The dead man?"

"Someone else. The Evil One. Satan's spawn. That's the most sense I can make out of it."

"What is his name? What does he want?" Jared asked. "Did she tell you that?"

"He's come for Dellie, she says . . . and she keeps speaking of something called the 'Eye of the Serpent.'"

"What the devil does that mean?"

Celestine shook her head. "I've never heard of such a thing before."

Jared went to kneel beside Tess. He was appalled by the extent of her injuries. Her face was bloodied and swollen, distorting her features.

"His name," Jared said to Celestine, who was cradling the old woman's head in her lap, blood staining her skirts. Jared wanted to be quite certain of his adversary. "Ask her to tell you the man's name."

But it was too late for such questions. Tess lay quiet,

her breathing shallow and rasping. Jared surmised that, aside from the obvious injuries, those within that could not be seen were far worse. She seemed calmer now, but only, he feared, because she'd given up the fight. She'd used all her might to save Dellie, and Jared wanted to ease her mind now. "Dellie's father—" he started to explain.

The old woman shook her head. "He is long dead, monsieur. She has only you now."

There was a long silence before she reached to lay a hand on his arm. "Care for her, monsieur," Mama Tess whispered to him as she closed her eyes for the last time.

Jared knew that she must have been truly afraid for Dellie, else why would she entrust her to him with her last breath? Her dislike for him thus far had been plain enough. He put a hand on the old woman's shoulder. It was his way of letting her know, even if it was too late, that he would do as she asked.

He had to admit a grudging admiration of her spirit. Not many would have borne the burden of raising another woman's child and loved her as her own for all these years—without recompense—but Tess had, and despite a brutal beating, she had not betrayed her charge. In the end her life had mattered little when compared with Dellie's safety.

Small wonder, he told himself, that Tess had disliked him on sight. She had recognized him from the first for the failure that he was. "Not half good enough for my sweet Dellie," she'd said to him, and she'd been right. This was no time for recriminations, though. Failure or not, Dellie's life was now in his hands; Mama Tess had put it there.

He got to his feet then and went to examine Thomas's body. The clothing was shabby and worn, and he had but a few coins in his pockets. The only item on his person that was out of the ordinary was a small bag of red flannel that he'd worn about his neck, suspended on a leather thong. Inside, Jared found a few bits of bone, ashes, and what looked to be a mixture of herbs.

"Gris-gris," Celestine explained as she came up behind him and saw it in his hand. " 'Tis a voodoo talisman to keep him from harm."

Jared's brow went up. "Not too effective in this case," he noted with a caustic air.

"The lives of many in this city are ruled by such practice, monsieur. Surely Dellie has told you that much."

"She has explained that, in order to help some of her more superstitious clients, she has had to pass off her herbal remedies as 'voodoo' cures, but I'm afraid I don't hold much store in magic charms, be it a horseshoe, rabbit's foot, or—what was it you called it?—*gris-gris.*"

Jared noticed a mark on the inside of Thomas's forearm then and studied it carefully. It was a tattoo, or a brand of some kind: the fleur-de-lis with a circlet of laurel leaves around it. He remembered that he'd seen such a design before—on a piece of jewelry worn by the man who'd hired him: Lucien Valmont.

A shudder traveled along his spine as he considered, for the first time, the possibility that the man who was paying him to find Louise Valmont might not be who he claimed.

What if Lucien Valmont had, indeed, died in the slave uprising on the isle of St. Gervais thirteen years ago? What if the man calling himself by that name in St. Louis was not Dellie's father at all, but an impostor who had hired Jared to find her in order to fulfill some other, more sinister purpose? Tess had told him that Valmont was dead, and she had certainly sensed danger, but Tess could not explain her reasons now. Jared had to trust his instinct alone, and instinct told him to tread carefully.

He'd been bumbling about for these past few weeks like a blind man, he realized now. If his suspicions proved true, then there was a whole new set of questions that needed answering. Who was this impostor, and what was his game? What motive could he have for wanting to find Louise Valmont? And what exactly was the Eye of the Serpent?

Old Dr. Fortier arrived soon thereafter and examined Tess's battered body with a furrowed brow, shaking his head all the while. He ordered Jonas to carry her downstairs and then came to have a look at Dellie. Celestine followed, standing beside Jared on the opposite side of the bed.

"What do you think, Doctor?" she asked.

"Other than the broken wrist, the damage is slight. She'll recover fully with rest . . . and time."

"I think not, Doctor," Jared said with quiet resolve.

Both Celestine and the doctor turned to him in surprise.

"You mean to tell me my business, monsieur?"

"In this case, Doctor, I do. I would say that the young lady has suffered a vicious beating. I would say that she is dying . . . that she is already dead."

Dr. Fortier was astounded by this observation, and he looked once again upon his patient. "You are mad, monsieur! Do you not see her, lying there before you? Her color is coming back. Her pulse is normal. She is breathing easily. All the signs are good. I don't understand such talk."

"I think that I do," Celestine said, after a while. "You see, Doctor, Monsieur Durant proposes that in order to save her life, Dellie Valmont must be presumed to be dead."

"Exactly so," Jared replied and looked about the room to make certain they were alone. "The man you see lying there on the floor is not solely responsible for what has happened here, Doctor. He is only a pawn. The real culprit is still out there somewhere . . . waiting. He did not get what he came for, and given the chance, he will surely strike again, so until I can find out who he is and what he wants of her, I must keep Dellie out of his reach."

"This is highly unorthodox. I cannot condone such a falsehood."

"You needn't do anything against your principles, Doctor," Celestine assured him, taking up Jared's cause. "All we ask of you is silence. We will take care of the rest."

"Do not inform the police about any of this," Jared said to Celestine. "I'd venture to say that many such things go unreported in this part of town. Tell your girls that Dellie and Tess are dead—that they were murdered by a one-eyed black man who was seen running from the house. Do not hesitate to tell this story to anyone else who might ask.

"Have Jonas make a pine box for Thomas here," he continued, "and put the body inside and nail it shut. And then, just as soon as you are able, bury it in the cemetery, in a plot beside Tess, with a marker that reads 'Louise Valmont.' Do you understand?"

"I do," she said.

Dr. Fortier finished bandaging Dellie's wrist and gathered up his bag. "I do not like deception," he told them plainly.

Celestine glared at him. "And who will your silence harm? Need I remind you of all of the kindnesses that Dellie has shown those of us who live in this quarter? Have you forgotten so quickly the times she ministered to our sick so that you might have the time to devote to your wealthy Creole patients?"

"She's always been a pleasant child, always asking my advice, wanting to know more about doctoring, and she does have a natural gift for healing others," he admitted. "All right, for Dellie, then. I shall keep silent."

"Thank you," Celestine replied and saw him to the

door. A chilly blast of wind swept in as she opened it. "Take care," she said. "The storm will soon be upon us."

When he was gone, Celestine returned to Jared's side. Jared could see that her color was not good, and her breathing was decidedly uneven. All of this excitement had been taxing for her, yet she continued to maintain her control of the situation. "You, too, must leave at once, monsieur," she told him. "I've a cabin on the Bayou St. John, at the end of the old bayou road. It's not far, and no one knows of it but Jonas and me. You could take Dellie there until it is safe."

Jared eyed her in cautious surprise. "You trust me with Dellie? Even knowing about the wager I made with Silas Crane? That is why you came to see me this afternoon, madame. Isn't it?"

Celestine nodded. "I came, and I heard you send that man away. Whatever your motives were at the start, Monsieur Durant, I believe you care for Dellie now. Tess put her faith in you. I shall as well."

"Thank you, madame," he said. "I will take Dellie to your cabin until I can sort all of this out."

"What else can I do to help?"

"You must go to your room now and rest. Dellie has told me of your fragile health. After all of this, she would not want you to take sick, too. I shall ask Jonas to point out the way to your cabin, and we'll be on our way as soon as I can pack a few things for Dellie."

Celestine waved a hand toward the carpetbag resting on a nearby chair. "Already done. She was planning to leave with you, if you recall."

Jared was sure he detected a glint of reproach in Celestine's eyes.

"I shall have Jonas saddle one of the horses for you,"

she said next. "Take care, Monsieur Durant. And pray remember Tess's warnings about a great evil . . . and the dead man's talisman. If there is voodoo at work here, you must leave nothing to chance."

CHAPTER
12

The humid night air was redolent of incense and smoke. From her hiding place in the shadows of the wood, Dellie listened to the church bells of the St. Louis cathedral in the distance, tolling the hour. There was only a sliver of a moon for light, but by the dark waters of the Bayou St. John, the world was bathed in the bloodred haze cast by a brilliant bonfire which flared in the clearing and illuminated the strange proceedings.

Steam rose up from the huge iron caldron that was set upon the fire, and black men in loincloths and women in tignons and loose white gowns cast offerings to the *loas* into the pot. And then they began to dance the calinda, just as Dellie had seen them do so many times on Sunday afternoons in Congo Square.

With the drums keeping beat and an old fiddle scraping out the melody, the dancers abandoned themselves to the primal rhythms, bowing and swaying like a grove of saplings in a windstorm. A series of chants rose up, and then bottles of whiskey and tafia were handed around, with each participant taking a generous swallow before passing the bottle on to the next in line.

Dellie stepped out of the sheltering grove to take a closer look. She was lulled by the languid rhythm of the drums, her perception dimmed by breathing of the pungent incense pervading the air. Time spun out, and she drew closer despite herself.

No one in the clearing seemed aware of her presence. Calling upon the saints and their voodoo gods to join them, they continued their celebration with rising fervor. But at the height of the frenzy, the dancers drew apart, and a lone woman appeared at their center.

Slowly she began her own dance, her long dark hair flailing out behind her as she whirled, golden bracelets jangling as she waved her arms over her head in sinuous fashion. The skirt of her blue cotton dress flared out in a wide circle, exposing slim ankles beneath. This was Mamzelle Marie herself, and a hush fell over those in the clearing as they watched their queen in silent fascination.

She sidled up beside one reveler, then quickly abandoned him in favor of another, flitting through the crowd like an exotic butterfly. And then all at once, she stopped dead still.

"I see that there is one among us tonight who would dare challenge the power of the *loas,* the power of the great Marie LaVeau," she said.

"No!"

"Never!"

"C'est impossible!"

"Mais oui, mes amis . . . une petite sorcière," she went on, "who promises to cure the people of New Orleans of their ills with her potions, and read for them their futures in the devil's own cards."

Dellie felt a surge of panic. She wanted to run back into the safety of the wood, but her feet were rooted to the spot.

"You need not fear me, *ma petite,*" Marie LaVeau said to her. "I've only brought you a gift, that's all."

She reached into her pocket, withdrew her hand, and tossed something toward the great caldron. There was a hiss of steam. The flames rose up, blazing white-hot, and blinded Dellie for a time.

When her sight was restored, she saw a man beside the voodoo queen, a tall man with sharp features, his eyes as black as pitch. He was leering as he reached out his hands, beckoning to her. Marie LaVeau was laughing; they were all laughing.

"Who are you?" Dellie cried.

"Don't you know me, little one?" he asked her. "I am called by many names. I am Ogoun Balandjo. . . . I am the evil one . . . the devil himself. I am the avenger, and I have come for you."

Before her eyes his looks began to change—melting, as if made of wax, then sliding across the planes of his face, forming into a grotesque expression. Now he was the devil of her tarot cards, come to life and standing there before her. She screamed.

"Hush! You don't have to be afraid, Dellie. It's all right now. It's all over."

After a great effort Dellie opened her eyes and looked up to see Jared, sitting on the edge of the cot where she lay. His face was haggard, shaded with the stubble of a beard, but concern for her was written plainly on his features.

"Where are we?" she asked him as she surveyed their surroundings: a snug little room, sparsely furnished and lit by half a dozen candles that had been placed about.

"Celestine's cabin on the Bayou St. John," Jared replied. "We've been here for more than a week now, but you've been feverish for most of that time."

Dellie was surprised, but before she could question him again, the wind kicked up, screeching through the trees outside. It rattled the shutters and set the door to banging in its frame, as though someone were trying to get in. Her nerves were still on edge from her nightmare, and instinctively she threw her arms about Jared's neck, hiding her face in his chest. The throbbing in her bandaged wrist began anew, reminding her of the attack she and Tess had suffered.

"It's only the storm," he told her, his voice hushed and soothing. "I'd wager we've weathered the worst of it, though."

Dellie drew back as if she'd been burned. With all that had happened, she'd nearly forgotten. "I'd wager"—those words brought it all back. Yes, he'd wager on almost anything. She did not know if she could trust him.

"Where is Mama Tess?" Dellie asked, with apprehension rising in her. "Why is she not here with us, too?"

Jared was very still. "Tess was badly hurt," he explained, bowing his head so that she could not read his expression.

Dellie was trembling. She had suffered a great deal, and her nerves were overwrought. Jared feared she could not bear another upset. "She couldn't be moved," he said. "The doctor has seen her, and Celestine will care for her. It was Tess herself who made me promise to get you out of the city. She sensed great danger, Dellie. Do you know why?"

Dellie only shook her head.

He grasped her shoulders firmly and stared deep into her eyes. "It's important that we discover what all of this is about. Tess says that there was another man in your room besides the black man. Did you recognize him? Did he tell you who he was or what he wanted?"

Dellie considered his words. No matter what she believed about him, she had to admit he was trying to help. "I only heard his voice," she explained. "I was hiding on the kitchen stairs, and he was gone by the time I came up. He knew Mama Tess, though; he called her by name. He asked her where I'd gone. 'You know what I've come for,' he said to her. 'Where is she?' His accent was French, but I'd never heard the voice before."

So Tess had not been merely raving. The man whom she'd called the Evil One had, indeed, been after Dellie. But why?

Jared searched his mind, trying to remember any details that might help piece together this puzzle. At last he spoke.

"First of all, Dellie, you must tell me the truth. Are you Louise Valmont of the Valmonts who lived on the isle of St. Gervais in the West Indies?"

Dellie was startled. "Who told you? Was it Tess? Or Madame Celestine?"

He shook his head. "That's not important right now."

Jared contemplated asking her about her father but thought better of it. He could not make mention of the man who'd hired him until he was certain that he was who he claimed to be. At this point that likelihood was doubtful. Dellie had told him the other intruder had been a man with a French accent. The man calling himself Valmont had had a French accent, but then again, so did probably half the people living in the Vieux Carré. The man calling himself Valmont had been wearing an emblem identical to the tattoo Jared had found on Thomas's body. Could this be significant—or only coincidence?

Jared knew that as soon as he was able, he'd have to go back to New Orleans. He had yet to question Aristede Grimaud, to find out what his interest in the Valmonts was. Perhaps Grimaud could help to shed some light on all of this.

"Have you ever heard of something called the Eye of the Serpent?" he asked Dellie next.

She regarded him suspiciously. "Yes, but what has it to do with anything that's happened?"

"Celestine said that Mama Tess spoke of it, after the attack."

"It's part of an old island legend, that's all."

Jared was intrigued. His instincts told him that this might be another important piece of the puzzle. "Tell me all that you know of it."

He plumped up the pillows at the head of the cot, and Dellie settled back into them with a sigh, feeling her strength returning.

"Mama Tess told me the story when I was only a child. The Eye of the Serpent is a stone, you see, a priceless emerald that is said to be at least as large as a sea turtle's egg. As the story goes, it was mined by the Indians of Mexico and made into an offering to their serpent god. They believed that their god endowed the stone with great powers. It fell into the hands of their Spanish conquerers and eventually became a part of the treasure that the legend says belonged to Lucien Valmont."

"Your father?"

Again Dellie eyed Jared warily. She could not help but wonder at how he'd learned so much about her. "No. No, of course not. My father was one of many in our family to bear the name. The first Lucien was a privateer, who came to the Indies carrying letters of marque from the king of France. He made a career in raiding Spanish galleons, and when, after years of successful plundering, he decided to retire, the king gave him a large tract of land on St. Gervais."

"Yes, but what of the treasure?"

"Lucien, it is said, kept the most spectacular of the spoils for himself. Objects of gold and silver, brooches and necklaces encrusted with jewels, and of course, the great emerald."

"But what became of all of these things?" Jared wanted to know.

"It *is* only a legend," Dellie replied, thinking he was putting far too much store in the colorful tale.

"What does the legend say, then?"

"Lucien the privateer was an odd sort. He had retired a very wealthy man. He didn't need money, and he really had no wish to sell off his treasure, so one day he sealed it all up in a sea chest and buried it somewhere on the island. The legend says that he entrusted the secret to his son but made him vow never to attempt to retrieve the chest, except in the event of a most dire need—and only if the very fate of the Valmonts hung in the balance."

"Sort of an insurance against poverty for his family," Jared commented.

"You could say that. The secret was supposed to have been handed down through the generations from father to son." She paused for a long moment. "Maybe Lucien wasn't such an odd sort after all."

"It's more than likely that in the intervening years some financially strapped Valmont dug up old Lucien's treasure and made off with it," Jared noted.

"The Valmonts always enjoyed great prosperity on the island," Dellie protested. "My father and his father and all those who came before them—they worked very hard to build a successful sugar plantation. I suppose the island people found it amusing to believe we'd been dipping into some ancient cache of pirate's treasure, but it wasn't so. If anyone truly believed in this fanciful tale, St. Gervais would be more full of holes than a wedge of Swiss cheese."

"Someone must believe it," Jared replied. "But I think that, rather than dig up the entire island, he's decided to go to the source, to the one person most likely to know the secret . . . the last remaining Valmont."

Dellie felt the blood draining from her face. Could this be why a stranger had come calling for her? Why the black man had beaten Tess? All this grief on account of an imaginary treasure?

"I don't know any secrets," she insisted, pressing a hand to her forehead. "I swear to you, I don't. I want to forget all about everything that's happened these past few days. Please, Jared."

Jared was sorry for having frightened her, but she didn't seem to understand the seriousness of this business. But then, she didn't know the truth. Maybe if he told her that Tess was dead, she could better realize that whomever they were up against, whatever his objective, he was possessed of a dangerous determination.

Somehow, though, when Jared looked down on Dellie's pale features surrounded by a soft halo of golden curls strewn across the pillow, he could not bear to tell her. There would be plenty of time for the truth later; he could not upset her now.

He noticed the furrows in her brow and bent over her to smooth them with his hand. "Trust me, Dellie," he whispered. "I'll keep you safe. You can forget all that's happened. No one will ever hurt you again, I promise."

Dellie looked up at him, wondering at the tenderness in his voice. She ought to have asked him right then if what Madame Celestine had said was true, but she could not put out of her mind the image of Jared facing off against a stranger and risking his life for hers. Perhaps she'd been wrong to doubt him at all—perhaps they'd all been wrong. In that moment Dellie realized that she was in love with Jared Durant . . . undeniably . . . inextricably.

Jared still bore the marks of the encounter with the black man. His jawline was marred by the knot of a greenish-colored bruise, and a thin line of congealed blood tugged at the corner of his mouth where his lip had split.

Almost on its own, her unbandaged hand moved to caress his bruised face, brushing back the shock of hair that had fallen across his eyes, and then it wound behind his neck, pulling him down to her.

Jared could feel the warmth of her breath on his face, her fingertips playing with the hairs on the nape of his neck. "Please, Jared," she entreated, her deepened voice inviting him. "Help me forget."

Her soft body twisted provocatively beneath him, urging his response, and at once a fierce longing coursed like fire through his veins. But he held back, unable to forget the vow he'd made not to touch her again. The woman lying beneath him with her charms so seductively displayed by the deep neckline of a thin chemise and her full lips parted now in anticipation of his kiss, was not a witch—nor some poor unfortunate child whom he had rescued from Gallatin Street. She was Louise Chandelle Marie-Thérèse Valmont, a young lady born of an aristocratic family, who might well be an heiress and certainly deserved more than a man like Jared Durant could offer her.

The moment of hesitation seemed endless. Dellie pressed closer, sorely testing his resolve as her fingers fluttered along the line of his collarbone and set to work unfastening the buttons on his shirtfront. The rasp of his uneven breathing filled the small room, and then, when he could stand it no longer, he dragged himself out of her arms and quit the room, closing the door with a shuddering slam.

Sunlight filtered in through the closed shutters, and somewhere on high a warbler whistled its bright song. The storm had blown itself out at long last.

Dellie opened her eyes to the new day, and cautiously raising herself upright on the cot, she winced as the blood began to pound in her bruised temple. On makeshift tables about the room were pools of congealed wax where candles had burned late into the night until they'd finally burned themselves out. With her first thoughts she was beset by an undeniable fear. Last night Jared had pushed her away. As she began to examine the dark corners of her soul, she was plagued by a chorus of familiar voices, of old conversations, which had first warned her of the danger: *"Your beauty will draw men to you, ma chère, but not always the right sort of men." "He ain't nothin' but a no-account gambler man who says what suits his purpose." "He made a bet that he could bed you in a week's time."*

Dellie put her hands to her ears, as if that might stop the voices in her head, and pulled herself up from the bed. After she'd doused herself with cold water from the basin in the corner, she put on a clean skirt from her carpetbag, which she found nearby, and opened out the shutters, turning her face up to the warm sun and breathing of damp earth and moss.

For the first time she noticed the isolation of this haven of Celestine's. The wood in this place was thick and verdant, the dirt road leading up to the cabin almost overgrown with brush. It was the perfect hiding place.

There was a movement in the bushes nearby, and Dellie's heart stopped at the sound. A closer look told her it was only a horse tethered to a low branch. It was not Jared's mount, for she had heard it nickering from its spot on the lee side of the cabin. No, someone else was here. Again she felt a tingle of apprehension run through her. She went to the door that separated this room from the next, and when she pulled it open a crack, she could hear low voices.

"It's all been taken care of, then?" she heard Jared inquire.

"Just as you instructed," a woman replied. "We buried her in the graveyard three days ago."

"And has anyone come 'round asking questions?"

"Anne-Marie said there was a man last night—a Frenchman."

"A Frenchman?" Jared echoed. Dellie could hear the trepidation in his tone. "What did he ask? What did she tell him?"

Dellie was curious. The whole of their conversation had an air of secrecy about it, as though they meant that she should not hear. She tried to open the door wider to afford herself a better view, but the hinges began to creak in protest, and so she had to content herself with peering through a thin crack lest she be discovered. She could scarcely make out the two figures seated at a table near the hearth, but by now she had determined that the other voice was a familiar one. It was Madame Celestine.

Dellie felt the relief wash over her and would have gone out to greet her, but what Madame said next paralyzed her. "He asked about Dellie. Anne-Marie told him the whole story. She said that Tess and Dellie had both been murdered by a big black man wearing an eyepatch—that someone saw him as he ran off—"

Dellie could not breathe. Her whole body began to shake, and she had to cross her arms over her chest to quell the tremors. She recalled the first words she'd heard Celestine speak: *"We buried her in the graveyard three days ago."*

Who? Who had they buried? Dellie feared the answer. She feared she already knew and yet would not allow the thought to form in her mind. *"She said that Tess and Dellie had both been murdered . . ."*

"We've done everything—just as you asked," Celestine

said to Jared then. "Now I think that you owe me an explanation at least, Monsieur Durant. Tess did not trust you from the first, did she? And you cannot deny making that unforgivable wager with Silas Crane, even if, in the end, you would not collect. As for me, well, I'm not so naive as to think you're just a riverboat gambler passing the time with a beautiful young girl who's caught his eye. Who are you, and what is your interest in Dellie Valmont?"

Dellie waited anxiously for Jared's explanation, but it was not at all what she hoped to hear.

"Oh, I'm a gambling man, right enough. But as you say, it wasn't the poker tables that brought me to New Orleans. I was a Pinkerton man for a time—"

"A detective?"

Dellie saw him nod. "Mr. Pinkerton and I parted company, but by then I suppose I'd acquired a reputation of sorts. I was hired in St. Louis by a man who'd heard of me. He paid me a great deal of money, to find Louise Valmont—Dellie, as you call her—and bring her to him."

Dellie shut the door and turned away, then pressed her back against it as if she might shut out what was transpiring on the other side. She felt strangely numb. Her legs buckled, causing her to slip down until she was sitting on the floor, hugging her knees.

Jared had been paid to come to New Orleans, paid to find her and take her to St. Louis. I did not occur to her at that moment to ask herself by whom or for what reason. She only knew that she had been used and betrayed by a man she'd cared for, by a man she'd been foolish enough to believe cared for her.

Dellie wanted to run to Celestine at once and tell her that she'd been right all along about Jared Durant, but she was too ashamed. She needed now to find the comfort she'd known all of her life in her Mama Tess's arms. But

Celestine had as much as said that Tess was dead. Dellie was on her own.

With a firm set to her jaw she picked herself up and, dusting off her skirt, began to shove her things into her carpetbag. She'd leave here at once. Get out of New Orleans and go back home. Yes, home to Belle Terre. The words alone were enough to bring feelings of comfort and security to Dellie. She'd saved enough money for her passage—but no, she'd given that money to Celestine, to pay for the dress. What would she do?

She remembered Jared's coat, hanging from a peg on the other side of the door. Gamblers always had money; someone had told her that once. Cautiously she eased the door just wide enough to reach out. Jared and Celestine were still deep in conversation across the room, and so she was able to remove his billfold from the inside pocket of his jacket and quietly close the door.

When she had her prize in hand, she opened it and counted the bills. Jared Durant had more than seventy-five dollars! She took it all, telling herself that he owed her at least that much for all the grief he'd caused. Despite her anger, the guilt crept in, and so she reached into her carpetbag to pull out the silver box that held her tarot cards. Surely that was worth something; he could sell it if he liked.

As she stared at it, a tear slipped from the corner of her eye. She brushed it away, impatient with herself for her weakness, and tossed the box onto the bed, scattering cards across the quilt. Surveying the lot, she reached out, almost against her will, to pick up one of the cards. She looked at it for a long while before she gave in to her spleen and ripped it in two. Wrapping herself in her long cloak, she climbed out of the window and headed for Celestine's tethered horse. Behind on the bed lay the Knight of Swords—torn in two jagged halves.

CHAPTER
13

Celestine leaned across the table, her brow marred by deep lines. "But who was this man?" she asked Durant. "And why did he want you to find Dellie?"

"He claimed to be Lucien Valmont, Dellie's father," Jared explained. "He told me that he'd escaped from St. Gervais when the slaves revolted, and that all these years he'd thought his daughter was dead."

"What changed his mind?"

"One day he came across a diamond brooch. He was certain it had belonged to his daughter and had been in her possession at the time of the revolt."

"Tess did have some small pieces of jewelry with her when she first came to me," Celestine remembered. "How wonderful it would be if her father should still be alive, after all these years." She regarded the man across the table for a long moment. He was staring hard at his folded hands, and his brow was creased in a thoughtful frown. "But something bothers you in all of this, monsieur. I can see that. What is it?"

"I'm not so sure anymore that the man who hired me

137

was Lucien Valmont. To be quite honest with you, madame, I'm not all that good at what I do," he said to her. Pulling himself out of his chair, he began to pace the floor, keeping his back to her all the while. "I was . . . once, but when Allan Pinkerton finally decided to end our association, it was because I'd become a liability. A drunk who's fond of gambling with his own life can't always be relied upon to do the job. It was only by accident that I came across Dellie, and even then I didn't realize who she was until it was too late."

Celestine felt a fondness for Jared Durant despite her better judgment and wondered if he truly deserved the harsh judgment he'd dealt himself. "If this man who hired you is not Lucien Valmont," she asked him, "then who is he, and what does he want with Dellie?"

He turned back to her now. "Do you recall what Tess said, just before she died? She mentioned 'the Evil One' and 'the Eye of the Serpent.' "

Celestine nodded, though still wearing a puzzled look. "It makes no sense at all."

"Not to you or me, but Dellie had heard of such a thing. She told me last night that this Eye of the Serpent is an emerald, a part of a pirate's treasure that once belonged to the Valmonts. Legend says it is buried somewhere on St. Gervais and that certain members of the family know the location."

"All this trouble on account of an old legend? It's hard to credit."

"Yet Tess believed it was so, and now she's dead. Whoever is responsible for that certainly doesn't have Dellie's best interests at heart. This treasure is the only plausible motive I can find at this point."

Celestine watched as Jared took down his coat from the peg where it hung on the closed door. "What will you do now?" she asked him.

"I'm going into the city. There are some people I have to see. I'm hoping they will be able to shed more light on all of this. I'd appreciate it if you would stay here with Dellie. After what's happened, she needs to rest. And you must try to get some rest yourself. All this exertion can't have been easy for you."

"I shall be fine, monsieur," Celestine assured him.

He put a hand on the door and then turned back to her. "I haven't told Dellie about Tess yet. I—I just couldn't find the words. She's already suffered too much."

Celestine smiled at him. "You're in love with her, aren't you?"

Jared met her eyes for a brief moment, then turned away without responding.

"*Bonne chance,* monsieur," she called after him. "And if it matters at all, I think you're very good at what you do."

Dellie tied Celestine's horse behind the shed in the alleyway, and pulling the hood of her cloak up over her head to hide herself, she started for the kitchen, hoping against hope that she would find Mama Tess there in her small room at the back, lying in her bed and recovering from her injuries, just as Jared Durant had told her. She'd throw herself into the old woman's arms, and then this nightmare would be over.

But Tess's room was empty. The tall shutters were closed, and only the merest slivers of light stole in between the cracks to cast bright patterns on the dingy walls. As Dellie stepped inside, her foot struck something on the floor, and she bent to pick it up. It was an overblown flower from the garden outside, its vivid red color faded and tinged with brown.

She drew a tremulous breath. There was on the air the sickening, stale odor of wilted flowers and burned wax . . .

the smell of death. It drove her from the room, and she stumbled out into the afternoon sunlight that flooded the courtyard, still hiding behind her cloak, with her carpet-bag tucked up under her bandaged arm.

Almost at once one of Madame's girls leaned out of one of the upstairs windows and called across the yard. "If you've come about the cook's job, you'll have to come back tomorrow. Madame's not here now. But do come back. We've buried our Tess and little Dellie now, and we don't know how we shall manage without them."

The girl's head disappeared from the window in a flutter of curtains, and Dellie only stood there as she came to accept the truth at last. Her Mama Tess was dead. Jared Durant had lied to her about this, just as he had about everything else. Her hand closed into a tight fist, crushing the flower she'd been holding. Petals rained down onto the flagstones, followed by the twisted remains of a stem.

Dellie made her way up to her own room then and was startled by the sight of herself as she walked past the mirror that stood on her dressing table. She removed the bandage that had been wrapped over her bruised temple, and shook out her hair to cover the spot. Her face was frighteningly pale, her eyes glistening with moisture. She turned away quickly to concentrate on her packing. She had not wept since the night her father died, and she wasn't about to start now. Mama Tess had hated tears; she would not want them on her account. Dellie thrust everything she owned into the large portmanteau and the carpetbag—her clothing, the packets and bottles of her medicines, her favorite books—and when she could carry no more, she turned away from the alcove.

She wanted to be out of this house, out of this city, as quickly as she could manage it. Everywhere she turned here, there was a memory of Tess. She simply could not bear it.

When at last she shut the door on those whispering voices and the half-remembered visions of her childhood, she stood on the balcony and looked out over the river. A cloud of thick smoke wafted down on the wind from the steamboat docks, then dissipated to reveal a majestic brig midstream, her sails set and glistening white in the autumn sun. But today, though she would finally realize her dream of sailing home on board one of these vessels, Dellie could find no cause to celebrate. With a trembling hand, she reached to take down her wind chimes, placed them in her bag, and left Madame Celestine's for the last time.

Not until she'd walked well beyond the French Market did she throw off the hood of her cape. She wore no tignon today, and tossing her head, she closed her red-rimmed eyes and let the breeze catch in her fair hair, fluttering it out behind her. She'd not hide any longer. The 'Evil One' who was responsible for Mama Tess's death likely had fallen for Jared and Celestine's ruse and believed her to be dead. She had no wish to discover who he was. What good would that do? Soon she'd be out of harm's way and safe at home at long last.

Dellie made her way from one transport office to the next along the waterfront, attempting to secure passage aboard an Indies-bound ship. To her dismay, she found that most of the lines did not have such a route on their regular schedules, and of those who did have ships that made a stop on the islands, none had departures scheduled until late the next month.

On the levee a commissioner barked orders to a grumbling gang of stevedores who were rolling cotton bales down the gangplanks and stacking them in neat rows. A drayman shouted a foreign curse at the heads of his braying team, and Dellie stepped back quickly so as to avoid being run over by the heavily laden wagon, which shook the pavement beneath her feet as it rolled by.

The last shipping office on the row, Meade & Co., was quiet by comparison. A clerk stood idly behind the counter, and across the room a porter was tagging baggage as it was given to him by a pair of passengers.

"May I help you, miss?" the clerk asked.

Dellie set her bag down on the floor and, straightening her spine, did her best to sound like a lady, even if she did not look the part. "My name is Louise Valmont. I should like to arrange passage on the first available ship to the Indies, if you please. I wish to travel to the city of Marigot on the island of St. Gervais."

The young man checked his schedules. "We have the *Polynesia* sailing on the twenty-third of this month, which makes a stop on that island."

"But that's two weeks from now," she pointed out, unable to hide her distress. "Isn't there anything sooner? I was told that you might have another ship—"

"Well, yes, miss. There's the *Phoebe Ann.* She sails for California this very afternoon, with a stop in St. Gervais, but I'm afraid that she cannot take on—"

"I'm not particular about the accommodations," Dellie told him as she fought the panic rising in her. She would not stay in this city, not another day. "I'm not carrying much baggage. Please, sir. If you could just look again and see if something might be arranged. It's most important that I leave at once."

The clerk went through his papers another time, shaking his head all the while. "I'd like to help, miss, but I'm afraid there's nothing I can do."

Dellie only stood there in the middle of the floor. Her bandaged wrist had begun to throb unbearably, and her head was aching. Tess's murder and Jared's betrayal had sapped the remainder of her strength. The island was the only haven she knew, and now it seemed she'd not be able to reach there for some time to come.

Suddenly a hand touched her arm. "Dellie, is that you?"

Dellie looked up to see Solange standing there before her.

"*Mon Dieu,* it is you!" the girl cried. "This is a miracle! When you did not appear at my wedding, I came to say goodbye—they told me that both you and your Mama Tess had been killed."

Before Dellie could reply, Solange squired her to a bench and sat down beside her. "Are you all right, *mon amie?*"

When Dellie opened her mouth to speak, she had to choke back a sob. "Tess is dead, it's true," she explained as soon as she'd regained her composure, "but I was only injured."

Solange noticed the bandage as Dellie held up her hand. "Oh, my poor Dellie," she said. "All this must be awful for you. But what brings you here? Did you discover that I was leaving for my new home today and come looking for me?"

Dellie shook her head. "I came, hoping to leave the city myself. I can't bear it in New Orleans a moment longer, and I wanted to go home to St. Gervais."

"Why, that is wonderful. I, too, am headed for St. Gervais. Isn't it the most remarkable coincidence? My husband's plantation is on that same isle. We can travel together."

Dellie was surprised to hear it, but she did not meet her friend's eyes for fear she would again dissolve into tears. Instead, she concentrated upon her hands, which were now folded neatly in her lap. "I should like nothing more, Solange, but the clerk has just told me that there is no room on board for me."

Solange looked as fresh and attractive as ever in her

fashionable traveling dress of lavender grosgrain and a straw bonnet decorated with violets and blond lace, but her delicate features were shadowed by a frown as she considered Dellie's dilemma.

"Surely some arrangement can be made," she remarked and then called to her husband, who had, for all of this time, been giving instructions to the baggage clerk across the room.

As he approached them, Dellie pulled her cloak closer around her so that he might not see her shabby dress. She'd never been ashamed to look like a gypsy on Gallatin Street; it was a part of her disguise. But Solange's well-bred Creole husband believed that she was a lady same as Solange, and she didn't want to spoil that image.

When Solange had explained the problem to him, he nodded slowly. "Wait here, mademoiselle," he said to Dellie. "I shall see what I can do."

He crossed to the counter, and Solange's dark eyes followed him all the way. Dellie could see that her friend was enamored of her new husband, in spite of her initial fears, and believed he could accomplish anything he set out to do. More than once while they waited, Solange patted Dellie's hand and assured her that all would be well.

Dellie took this opportunity to study Solange's new mate. She had only seen him once before, at the birthday ball, and then only from a distance. He was a man of proud bearing with an athletic build. Years in the tropical sun had bronzed his skin, and this was accentuated by the light-colored suit of clothes that he wore. Beneath his wide-brimmed hat his hair was thick and black, swept off a high forehead, now creased in thought as he conversed. All of his physical characteristics were strong and well-defined, but without a doubt his keen black eyes were his most striking feature. He had a commanding presence, and Dellie thought to herself that this was exactly the sort of man with whom Solange could find happiness.

He turned then to flash them a brilliant smile, looking very pleased with himself, as if an inspired thought had just occurred to him. After exchanging only a few words with the clerk, he returned.

"It's all settled," he told Dellie. "You shall sail today along with us on board the *Phoebe Ann*. Mind you, the cabin isn't a spacious one—"

Dellie could scarcely believe it. Her spirits lifted instantly. "*Merci, merci beaucoup, monsieur.* I am sure I shall be more than comfortable."

"However did you manage it?" Solange wondered.

"It was nothing miraculous, *ma chère*. I merely informed the young man that my manservant, who was to have been traveling with us, has decided to stay on with his family in New Orleans. I suggested that you be given his cabin, Mademoiselle—" He hesitated. "I'm afraid I do not recall hearing your name."

"Oh," Solange put in. "This is my good friend, Dellie—that is, Mademoiselle Louise Chandelle Marie-Thérèse Valmont. Dellie, this is my husband, Aristede Grimaud."

To Jared's dismay, he learned nothing in New Orleans that would help him clear up the mystery behind Tess's murder and the attack on Dellie. Antoine Bredou was not able to give him any information about Lucien Valmont. Although they had been acquainted for some six years, Bredou could neither confirm nor deny that the man he'd been doing business with was who he claimed to be. Jared's uneasiness was increasing.

And as for the questions he'd had about Aristede Grimaud's relationship to the Valmont family, they remained unanswered. By the time Jared located the hotel where Grimaud had been registered, the man had already checked out. The desk clerk could tell him little more than that Grimaud had recently married a local girl. As he understood it, the couple was returning to Grimaud's island home to begin their new life together. Jared made inquiries with the passenger lines that serviced the Indies, but it seemed that he was destined to remain one step behind. When finally he'd tracked down the only line with a departure scheduled that day for the Indies, it was only to learn that the ship had already sailed. Grimaud had gone back to St. Gervais.

Jared returned to his own hotel, anxious for a hot bath and a change of clothes. As he crossed the lobby, though, the young clerk behind the desk called out to him and handed him a message: "Most urgent you meet me at once. I am on board the *Savannah,* Toulouse Street & the levee. Valmont."

So the man calling himself Lucien Valmont was in New Orleans. This only heightened Jared's suspicions. He could well be the one responsible for the attack on Dellie. "When was this note delivered?" he asked the boy.

"Early this morning, sir."

Jared's expression revealed nothing as he pulled the watch from his waistcoat pocket and flipped open the lid. Eleven forty-five. Valmont would not expect him now until morning. But the later the hour, he reasoned, the greater the element of surprise would be. With Dellie safely out of reach, hidden away in the cabin and in Celestine's care, he decided to force the truth from the man calling himself Lucien Valmont—one way or another.

Jared strode across the gangplank and onto the main deck of the *Savannah,* where the watchman was resting himself on the capstan. Jared drew a long cheroot from the case in his breast pocket. As he struck a match to it, the orange glow illuminated the hard lines of his face beneath the brim of his hat for a brief second before it went out. "Evening, friend," he began. "Mr. Valmont on board?"

"This time of night, I'd 'spect so. You got business with him?"

"He sent word for me to meet him."

"Up those stairs, then, second cabin on your right. Maybe you ought check with the captain first, though, seein' as how it's late."

"Thanks, I'll do that," Jared told him.

But he had no intention of consulting the captain nor alerting anyone else to his presence. He went up to the promenade deck and leaned against the gingerbread railing, calmly drawing on the cheroot as he studied his surroundings. Most of the crew was likely ashore by now, availing themselves of the diversions to be had in the whiskey cribs and boardinghouses on Gallatin Street. Light filtered out through the draped windows of a few of the passenger cabins, and the gay sound of music and laughter carried across the deck from the saloon astern, but the majority of those still aboard the *Savannah* had settled in for the night.

Jared tossed the stub of his cheroot down into the black water of the river. He trod lightly as he crossed to Valmont's cabin, to keep his bootheels from striking the deck. Standing before the windowed door, he peered through the small space where the curtains hadn't been drawn together completely. There was not much to see; the room was dark within. It would be a stroke of luck, he thought, to find Valmont there alone in his bed.

He put a hand on the knob but, as he'd anticipated, it was locked, and so he reached into his cigar case for the slender metal tool he'd not had occasion to use since leaving Pinkerton's employ.

Only a few minutes later Jared was inside. His heart was pounding as if it might burst, and there was a creak of leather when he pulled his revolver from its holster that seemed to reverberate against the walls of the spacious cabin. He froze in his tracks but was immediately reassured by the sound of even breathing coming from the bunk. When his eyes adjusted to the dimness, he made out Valmont's still form lying there.

By focusing his anger on this man he believed responsible for Dellie's misfortune, he steeled his nerves. With his confidence restored, Jared lit the lamp, sat himself down in a richly upholstered velvet chair, and pulled back the hammer of the revolver he was pointing at Valmont.

"Who's there?" the Frenchman called as he rolled over and slowly dragged himself into an upright position. And then he saw Jared. "What is this, Monsieur Durant?"

"Don't even think of shouting for your men," Jared warned him. "I can put a hole in you and be out that door before anyone realizes what's happened."

Valmont shook his head and swiped a hand across his sleep-glazed eyes. He was clearly perplexed. "We had an agreement. I thought you were working for me. The last time we spoke—"

"A lot has happened since the last time we spoke," Jared shot back. "Now I want you to tell me what you are doing here in New Orleans."

"I got your message," Valmont replied, "and came at once."

By this time, though, Jared wasn't listening. His anger had peaked; he'd decided that he would wait no longer for answers. Leaning forward in the chair, he leveled the revolver again for emphasis. "I don't like being lied to, mister. I want to know who you really are and why you're so anxious for me to find Louise Valmont. And I want the truth this time!"

"I've given you nothing but the truth, monsieur," Valmont protested.

"Let me tell you what I think," Jared began. "I think you're not Lucien Valmont at all. I think Lucien Valmont died thirteen years ago in a slave uprising, and that you're some sort of an opportunist who's taken the name only in order to suit your own needs. I think you hired me to find Valmont's daughter because you believe she's got something that you want. And what could that something be? The Eye of the Serpent, perhaps? Or the Valmonts' buried treasure?"

"Who told you of such things? It's all nonsense. There is no treasure."

"Tess didn't think it was nonsense."

"Tess?" Valmont repeated the name gently. "You've found Tess? She is alive? Then my Louise must be with her. I must know, monsieur. Have you found my child?"

"We've not yet determined that she is your child, nor indeed that you are who you claim to be."

"Bring Tess here to me," Valmont said, anxious now. "She will tell you that I speak the truth, that I am Valmont."

"I'm afraid that's impossible. Tess is dead. But then you already know that. She was murdered by a black man who'd been following me for the past several days. I figure he's one of your men because he was branded with a tattoo of a fleur-de-lis, of the same design I saw on a piece of jewelry you were wearing when last we met."

Valmont threw off the bedclothes and picked up the dressing gown that lay at the foot of his bunk. Jared kept a cautious eye on him as he put it on and reached next for an ivory-handled walking stick that was propped up within reach. Leaning heavily against it, he struggled to his feet and with great effort made his way across the cabin, dragging his lame left leg behind him. "I do not get about so easily lately," he explained. "These changes in the weather can keep me laid up for weeks at a time."

Jared felt the gun in his hand waver as doubts came to him. Valmont could barely walk; how could he be the same Frenchman who'd been wandering the streets of New Orleans in search of Louise Valmont?

When he reached his bureau, Valmont opened the velvet case that rested atop it and rummaged through the contents. At last he came across what he was looking for and held it up for Jared to see. It was the fleur-de-lis stickpin. "This design is a part of my family crest," Valmont explained. "All of the slaves that once belonged to my family were marked with it, but I have no hold on any of them now."

He tossed the piece back into the case and turned to face Jared without fear. "Now, Monsieur Durant, please, you must tell me what you've learned of my daughter."

Jared holstered his revolver, trying to re-form his thoughts into something that half made sense.

"Please, monsieur," Valmont prompted.

"She is safe," Jared assured him.

"Then you must take me to her—at once!"

All there was to do now was to reunite Dellie with her father, but as Jared recalled the way she'd touched him in the cabin, the way he'd nearly responded despite the promise he'd made himself, he knew he could not face her again.

"You can find her in a cabin on the Bayou St. John," he said, dragging himself from the chair to head for the door. "Follow the road that leads from the city, and when you come to a junction, take the left fork. It's the only place you'll see."

Valmont opened his mouth to protest, but Jared cut him off before he could speak. "Do not ask me to come along. Our business is concluded, monsieur."

"But you'll want to be paid, once I've found her."

"You can keep your money," Jared told him and quit the room, knowing the peace of mind he sought could only be found at the bottom of a whiskey bottle.

CHAPTER
14

As the open landau bounced along the dirt road that cut through the seemingly endless expanse of cane fields, it seemed to Dellie as if she were watching scenes from her past. In the twilight she could just make out the shadowy outline of a sugar mill, with its tall sailcloth vanes silhouetted against the night sky, exactly like the one that had once stood on Valmont land. She also spied the field hands who had finished their day's work and were now trudging home along the side of the road, single file. Further ahead in the distance lay a sprawling plantation house with a deep veranda supported by white pillared posts.

It was all so very familiar that Dellie could easily have imagined that she'd found the home she thought she'd lost so long ago, but Aristede Grimaud was sitting across from her on the carriage seat to remind her that, in fact, this was *his* empire.

And he was quick to point up the differences. "Things have changed greatly in the time you've been away, Mademoiselle Valmont. Landowners can no longer exploit black slaves in order to reap their profit. Those Negro workers you see are employed by me and paid a daily wage for their work."

Dellie could not help but feel that this was a pointed reference to her family, who for so many years had been the major landowners on the island, but when she turned her eyes upon the man across from her to gauge his intent, she was met with only a polite smile.

"But I must be boring you ladies with all this talk of business. I hope you can forgive me. I confess that I was trying to impress my bride. But now I promise I shan't say another word about it."

"You have every right to be proud of what you've accomplished," Solange said, entwining her arm in his.

"Look there now and you will see your new home," Aristede told her. "The original structure was of a more modest size, but we have made many additions and improvements over the years. I hope you find it to your liking."

Aristede had been kind enough to invite Dellie to stay with them until she could reacquaint herself with St. Gervais and sort out her plans. Solange was delighted, but the invitation made Dellie realize that she hadn't given much thought to the future. She only knew that first thing in the morning she intended to ride out to Belle Terre.

The driver had turned the horses into the drive now and pulled up just before the steps. "Mother will be so pleased to have company," Aristede said. "She's been ill so often lately that we've all but given up on socializing."

Dellie could see that Solange was apprehensive about this meeting. Aristede had spoken with great pride of his mother, Dominique. He'd referred to her as a woman of exceptional beauty and grace, and Solange had confided to Dellie soon after that she feared that Madame Grimaud would find her somehow lacking. Dellie told her she was only being foolish; her mother-in-law would see her for the kind and lovely young woman that she was.

Aristede helped them down from the carriage and escorted them up the steps and across the veranda, where a maid promptly opened the double doors. "Where is Madame, Henriette?" he asked the thin black girl, who wore a neat white apron over her gray cotton dress and a tignon over her dark curls.

Henriette whispered a reply which Dellie did not hear, for she was fully entranced by her surroundings. It was an elegant house, just what she would have expected of Aristede Grimaud. The foyer was spacious and airy. Just ahead was a broad staircase leading to the upper rooms, and she could see on the wide landing a carved mahogany table upon which was set a porcelain vase filled with fresh flowers.

"Oh, Dellie, it's much nicer than I thought it would be," Solange whispered.

"It's magnificent," Dellie said.

To the right through an archway was the parlor. It was tastefully furnished, but what caught Dellie's eye was the portrait of a young woman hung over the fireplace mantel. She was a striking beauty with finely etched features, her dark hair piled atop her head and strung through with ribbons in the Grecian style, and she wore a diaphanous white gown in a simple style of the past generation.

Dellie found herself unable to turn away from those dark eyes. "The woman in the portrait. Who is she?" she asked when Aristede rejoined them.

"It is my mother, Dominique. My father was an artist from Paris, you see. He came here to the island to paint this portrait. They fell in love and were married soon after."

"Such a romantic tale!" Solange remarked.

"Without a happy ending, however. Two years after I

was born, he was traveling home to France, and his ship was lost at sea."

"How sad for you . . . and your mother," Dellie replied.

"Will we meet her now, Aristede?" Solange wondered.

"I'm sorry to say that my mother has already retired for the evening. Another one of her headaches. She will join us for breakfast tomorrow, if she's feeling up to it," Aristede told her. "For now, I'm certain that you ladies would like to see your rooms. Henriette will show you the way."

St. Gervais was exactly as Dellie remembered it. From the window of her room, she could look out over the whole crescented curve of the island, lush with tropical greenery, and the sparkling turquoise waters that surrounded it. She was sure that nothing on earth could compare with the beauty of St. Gervais.

Dellie did not wait to be called for breakfast the next morning. Immediately upon rising, she requested the use of a horse from the stables, intent on riding to the far side of the isle so that she might set foot once more upon Valmont land.

Dellie discovered soon enough that the village of Marigot had lost none of its cosmopolitan charm. Already there were people in the coffee shops and clustered here and there along the banquettes to share the morning's gossip. The ladies, who were dressed in the latest fashions from Paris, chattered on about the empress Eugénie and the goings-on at the French court as if unaware that it was all an ocean away.

The waterfront markets were bustling with humanity, the stalls filled to bursting with the bounty of the island. Fish, crab, and shellfish were displayed by the tubful. Baskets of bananas, yams, mangoes, breadfruit, and coconuts lined the walkways, and flower sellers offered bouquets of fragrant blossoms such as frangipani and white ginger.

Dellie managed to avoid all of these temptations, but she did make a stop at the bakery, where she purchased some honeyed biscuits. She had one with coffee for her breakfast, and after tying the rest up in her handkerchief, she went on her way.

Away from the village the roadway was worn deep into the dusty, red earth with cane fields rising up on either side. When she'd gone farther still, Dellie found herself riding beneath a thick canopy of leaves that nearly shut out the morning's light. She listened in wonder to the flutelike song of a whistling bird hidden somewhere in the branches above and the shrill squawking of parrots, whose coloring of green, orange, and blue rendered them all but invisible amidst the vivid jungle foliage. Memories rushed over her, and a smile came to her slowly. Yes, she was home at last.

Sadness twisted her heart, too, as she reminded herself that she'd returned without Tess. For all those years in New Orleans, Mama Tess had cared for her without a thought to her own needs, and Dellie had hoped to repay her by bringing her back to the island one day and finding a little house where they could both live quietly. But now that dream could never be.

Giving vent to her frustration, Dellie snapped the reins and gave the big bay stallion her heel, and in response he jerked into a gallop. She leaned forward in the saddle, wanting to think on nothing but the wind whistling in her ears and the salty breeze that caressed her face and tangled her unbound hair, but suddenly she found herself blinded by brilliant sunlight as the dense jungle of tall trees gave way to a clearing.

She pulled up and blinked to adjust her eyes in time to see that several wattle and daub huts had been constructed on the seaward side of the road, where half a dozen bare-foot black urchins in tattered clothes sat in the dust, play-ing a game with sticks. Dellie waved a greeting and continued at a less frantic pace, noticing now the familiar landmarks: the limestone bluffs that rose up from the sea, the blue mountains in the distance, the stream that coursed through the wide valley, its bed strewn here and there with rust-colored volcanic boulders.

Once the whole of this valley had been planted with sug-arcane to feed the mill that had stood nearby. Once a hun-dred or more field hands had tended the crop, sweating day after day in the hot sun to assure a profitable harvest. Once Dellie had walked this very road, able to lose herself in the tall fields of cane—for this was Belle Terre, Valmont land.

A feeling of trepidation crept over her as she drew near the spot where her home had stood. She'd seen the flames that night so many years ago when she'd stood on the deck of the ship in the harbor, and yet as she directed her mount up the road, she expected to see the big white house still standing there, its wide, shady veranda providing a wel-coming shelter from the heat of the late-morning sun.

There was no sign of the house, however, no sign at all that any building had ever stood in this place. The trees here were not so tall as elsewhere, but the choking vines had spread over all. The jungle had wholly reclaimed the land. Dellie dismounted, tying off the reins on the low branch of a flowering bush. She advanced cautiously, pull-ing her skirts close about her to keep them from catching on the straggling undergrowth as she searched for some sign of habitation. For almost two hundred years the Val-monts had made their home on this spot—how could every trace have been wiped out in only one night?

Perhaps, she told herself, she had miscalculated. Per-haps this was not the spot after all. It had been more than a dozen years since she'd set foot on this ground. It was possible that she was mistaken about the exact location. Deep within herself, though, Dellie knew that she was not mistaken. She tore at the vines with her hands, hoping to uncover something familiar, but with no success. The exercise had caused her bandaged wrist to throb, and she rubbed it impatiently. She walked around in circles, finally stamping her foot in frustration. But instead of striking the spongy ground of the jungle floor, the heel of her boot had struck upon something hard.

She bent down and saw a moss-covered flagstone, and her heart leaped with joy. This was a portion of the front walk. By tracing the steps in her memory, Dellie soon discovered a stand of charred and rotting timbers, and when she stumbled across a pile of stones that had once been the parlor fireplace, she threw herself upon it.

She could not determine the reason why, but this part of the jungle seemed as hushed and solemn as a church. Only the murmur of the sea breeze rustling the leaves overhead broke the stillness—and, too, the sound of her own mournful sobs. In this place she felt herself no more than a little girl again, and so she gave in, allowing emotion to overwhelm her. She wept for her father, as she had never been able to do when Mama Tess was alive, and she wept for Tess herself, who had given so much and asked so little in return. And the bitterest tears she wept were for the loss of something which she did not wholly understand even now . . . for the emptiness within herself that she'd hoped would be filled when she was home once more.

She could never go home, she realized now as she looked about her. Her home was in ashes, and she was no longer the same little girl she'd been when she left. The comfort of her island could not fill the void that had been created by the deceitful riverboat gambler who'd stolen her heart.

Dellie returned to Grimaud's house that afternoon in a plaintive mood. She left her horse with the stableboy and was grateful when she met no one in the foyer or the hall as she made her way upstairs to her room. She needed time alone now to think on what she was going to do with her life. The trip to Belle Terre had made her finally face up to the fact that the past was dead. Mama Tess had tried to tell her that often enough, but Dellie had never listened. She'd preferred to believe that if she came home, somehow she could have her old life back. Now she'd seen for herself that it just wasn't possible.

What choices were there for her then? She could not stay with Solange and Aristede indefinitely. She needed employment. The tarot had been a source of income for her in the past, but she'd thrown the cards away, and she knew that never again could she put such faith in them. What would she do?

Threading through her thoughts came a voice as if in reply, a voice with a deep Virginia drawl. *"We're a pair, you and I. We belong together."* . . . *"I'll be leaving New Orleans . . . I want you to come with me."* . . . *"Trust me, Dellie. I'll keep you safe. . . . No one will ever hurt you again, I promise."*

Lies, that's all they'd been. How could she have expected anything more from a man so well used to lying? Still, Dellie could not prevent the words from creeping into her thoughts at odd moments like these and tormenting her. Oh, when would she be rid of them?

There came a knocking at the door. "Dellie? Are you there?"

Pulling herself out of the window seat, Dellie went to unlatch the door, and Solange swept in. She looked prettier than ever in pale green muslin, a lace cap resting on her dark curls.

"Where have you been all morning? You must see my room, Dellie. You won't believe it. I shall feel like such an elegant lady here. There's a silk chaise set before the hearth and a writing desk for my correspondence. Aristede says all the carpets and furnishings came straight from Paris. This house is even more spacious than my home in New Orleans."

"Perhaps later I'll come and see," Dellie said, putting her off. "I've been riding all morning, and I'd like to rest a bit now."

"But you'll miss lunch, and besides, I haven't told you the most exciting news of all. Aristede has decided that we must have a party so that he might introduce me to the neighbors."

"How nice for you. You'll be able to meet all the other young wives and make some new friends here."

Dellie couldn't help sounding a bit resentful. Solange's life had so easily fallen into place, while Dellie's had only fallen apart.

"You sound as if you're not coming," Solange commented.

"I don't belong at such a party, Solange," Dellie told her, "and I can't stay here with you forever. I'll likely be gone by the time—"

"The party is planned for next Saturday; you'll stay with us till at least then, won't you? Oh, you must come. You're my friend, and I insist."

Dellie sighed deeply, and Solange took this as an assent. "Good. Now we must think of a costume for you. This is to be a fancy dress ball, you know. Aristede has decided he shall play Napoleon, so of course I must go as his Josephine. I'm to wear one of Madame Dominique's gowns, the very one she wore to have her portrait painted."

As she spoke, Solange made her way to Dellie's wardrobe and threw open the doors. Her pert little nose wrinkled to see the meager selection there. "There is the dress you wore for my party," she said, tapping her foot on the floor as she thought on it, "but it won't do at all."

"Won't do for what?" Dellie wondered.

"For the costume I have in mind," Solange explained. "You must have something entirely different. White, I think. I shall send Marie in later to take your measurements. She's my new maid, and Aristede says that she can stitch as fine as any French seamstress. We'll have her make you a new gown. And then there are the shoes to consider, the shoes must be special."

"Whatever are you going on about?" Dellie asked her friend.

"Your costume. For the costume ball. Dellie, haven't you been listening?"

Dellie kneaded her brow. All this excitement was giving her a headache. "What costume is that? I'm afraid I can't recall exactly what it is that *we* have decided upon."

"Why, Cinderella, of course."

CHAPTER
15

On the night of the masquerade ball the Grimaud house was transformed. Vases of fresh-cut flowers were set upon all the tables, and garlands of greenery twined over the stairway rails and draped on fireplace mantels. All of the furnishings were removed from the parlor, a corner set apart for musicians, and comfortable chairs placed along the walls for the guests. The French doors at the back of the house were all opened out, and there were colored lanterns hanging in the garden.

In spite of her apprehensions about the evening, Dellie felt like a princess in her costume and stood before the cheval glass in her room for a long while, admiring the handiwork of Solange's maid. Cinderella's gown was of fine white satin, edged with gold embroidery. Its deep-cut bodice laced up the front, and the skirt was worn over panniers in the style of a century past.

The talented maid had even come in to help Dellie dress, after she'd finished with her mistress, and had done up her hair in a mass of soft curls arranged atop her head, with a white rose perched daintily over one ear. A white silk mask trimmed in gold lace completed the ensemble. And there were special slippers, just as Solange had promised—not glass, as the fairy tale intended, but satin, covered in crystal beads that caught the light and glittered when she walked about the room.

By the time Dellie went downstairs that evening, most of the two dozen guests who were expected had already arrived and were milling about the parlor. Standing in the archway, she admired the elaborate costumes. Among those assembled were a pair of Harlequins; a portly Father Time complete with hourglass, hooded cape, and long white whiskers, which had been pasted on his chin; Julius Caesar in a crimson tunic, his brow crowned with laurel leaves; a fancifully bejeweled gypsy; and a youthful Cleopatra, queen of the Nile, who carried a fruit basket wherein basked a rubber snake.

Dellie scanned the crowd for Solange and Aristede and found them at last, immersed in conversation at the far end of the room. They made a handsome couple indeed and were quite convincing as Bonaparte and his Josephine. All the guests seemed to recognize their host, even though he was masked, but their attentions were captured by his charming new wife, and Dellie could see that Solange had already won their approval.

"Dellie!" Solange exclaimed and took up her hands as she drew near. *"C'est merveilleux!"*

"Ah, mademoiselle," Aristede Grimaud chimed in, "how lovely you look tonight."

"Merci, monsieur. It seems your wife is all the fairy godmother I shall ever need."

"One way or another," Solange retorted, "I intend to see that you meet your prince and enjoy a happy ending, just as I have." With this, Solange slipped an arm through her husband's.

Regardless of her friend's good intentions, though, Dellie doubted that there was much chance she'd find a prince in her future.

But it was not some prospective prince who caught Dellie's eye soon after that, it was the woman sitting beside the hearth, almost directly beneath her own portrait. In the week that she'd been here, Dellie had met the ailing Dominique Grimaud only once, for the woman seldom left her rooms. Even disguised beneath a black lace veil, Dellie recognized her and was surprised to see that Dominique's health had improved sufficiently to allow her to attend the party welcoming her daughter-in-law.

Even with her illness, Dominique had barely changed at all in the years since the painting of her portrait. She was truly a woman of exotic blood. Her skin was cinnamon-colored, her dramatic features contained within a perfect oval of a face. Gazing into her black eyes with their seductive slant, Dellie could see where Aristede had come by his own hypnotic good looks.

This evening Dominique Grimaud was dressed as a Spanish lady in an elegant evening gown of wine-colored taffeta, trimmed in black lace. Beneath her black lace mantilla, her smooth, dark hair had been drawn back into a plaited chignon, threaded with only a few strands of silver to remind one of her age.

From her appearance it was hard to believe that she was an invalid. When the company moved into the dining room, she carried herself proudly and was an eager participant in the dinner conversation. But later on, after the dessert of meringues floating in brandied cream had been served and consumed, Dellie noticed that a change had come over her. Whereas earlier she had been vibrant, possessed of the vigor of a woman half her age, now all at once it seemed as though she'd used up her reservoir of strength. Her color faded away, leaving her complexion yellow and pasty, and her hand was trembling quite noticeably as she lifted her spoon.

Aristede did not miss the change in her, either, and as he came to escort her into the parlor where the other guests were mingling and the musicians had already begun to play, he asked her: "Have you taken your medicine this evening, Mama?"

"I—I don't recall," she replied. "I was so anxious about the party, fussing over my dress and my hair, and—oh, my head aches so."

"Shall I fetch Dr. LeClerc, madame?" Solange inquired.

"Yes, child, please do," Dominique replied.

Solange ran off to the parlor, and Dellie, who had remained in the dining room to have a word with her friend, came forward now. She was accustomed to making herself useful and so went to stand behind Dominique's chair and spoke to her in soothing tones.

"Here now, let me help you," she said and began to massage the woman's temples much as she had done on those occasions when Mama Tess had been plagued with a headache.

She could feel a strong pulse beating beneath her fingers, but eventually the tension in Madame Grimaud's slender frame eased under her ministrations. The woman's color had not improved, though, and there were beads of perspiration forming on her brow.

"Thank you, dear," Dominique said in a breathless voice. "That is so much better."

Dr. LeClerc, the stout little man with a wisp of hair over each ear who was costumed as Father Time, bustled into the room then with Solange close behind.

"You are in pain, madame?" he asked, taking up one of her hands.

"Another of her headaches," Aristede explained. "She's forgotten to take her medicine."

The doctor clucked his tongue. "Too much excitement," he said, and when he noticed Dellie, who had continued to knead Dominique's temples all this while, he asked: "Are you a nurse, mademoiselle?"

"I have had some experience," Dellie admitted.

"You have capable hands," he told her, and then as he left the room, he turned to Aristede. "I think your mother needs to rest now."

Aristede obliged, sending one of the girls who was clearing the table after Sophie, Madame Grimaud's personal maid. The woman appeared in only a few minutes. She was of an advanced age, with stooped shoulders, her brown skin cracked like worn leather, and a shock of wiry gray hair escaping from beneath her colorful tignon. From the moment she entered the room, Dellie was uneasy, for the woman fixed her beady, black eyes on her with a baleful glare, as though Dellie herself were responsible for her mistress's distress.

"Madame has not had her medicine this evening. See that she gets it," Aristede instructed, "and then put her to bed."

"*Oui,* monsieur," the old woman replied. "Do not worry yourself about it. Sophie will care for her. Haven't I always?"

"Rest now, madame," Solange put in. "Aristede and I will come up and see you later on."

Dellie stepped back to watch as Madame Grimaud leaned on the old woman's arm and allowed herself to be led from the room.

" 'Tis a chronic condition," Aristede explained for Dellie's benefit. "She manages well enough so long as she remembers to take her medication."

Dellie joined the others in the parlor and would have

been content to settle herself in a chair in the corner, but as she passed a group of elderly gentlemen, she heard a bit of conversation that caught her attention.

"How in heaven's name can I be expected to treat these poor people," Dr. LeClerc was saying in a loud voice, "when they continue to practice their pagan beliefs? All I hear is 'voodoo' in every quarter, and it's gotten worse, I tell you. Even those who ought to know better are subscribing to it. I go to treat a simple skin rash, and the damned fool thinks he's been hexed."

"I understand your frustration, Doctor," Dellie heard herself say to him. "Our own Dr. Fortier in New Orleans had much the same trouble."

This comment was met with a soft chuckle from the other gentleman whom Dr. LeClerc had been addressing.

"Did he, now?" LeClerc replied. Dellie could see that he was trying to ascertain her identity but without success. "Well, then, young lady, you must tell me how he dealt with the problem."

"He got on well enough by accommodating the people's beliefs whenever he could manage it."

The doctor pulled on his chin, a puzzled look overtaking him. "So you propose I get myself a snakeskin rattle and set up practice as a witch doctor?"

These words conjured an amusing picture, and Dellie felt that the gentlemen were enjoying themselves immensely at her expense. "Hardly," she replied, irritated that no one seemed to be taking her seriously, "but it might help to understand your patient's way of thinking and treat him accordingly. The man suffering from a rash, for example: If you prescribe a certain jar of salve, tell him it is powerful *gris-gris,* and if he paints himself with it every day, in three days' time the 'fix' will be undone. If you treat a child for lung congestion with a garlic poultice, tell his parents that the smell will ward off evil *loas*. It's not so much the method of the cure as the presentation."

LeClerc's brows arched in surprise, and he studied her more carefully now. "You seem to know quite a bit about this yourself, mademoiselle, for one so young."

"I do have somewhat of a facility with herbal cures," Dellie told him, "and so Dr. Fortier allowed me to help where I was able."

"She sounds like a competent hand," one of the other gentlemen put in. "Perhaps you ought to hire her on as your assistant, LeClerc."

Everyone clearly thought this a humorous notion, and LeClerc responded with tongue in cheek. "Not at all a bad idea. If you should ever require employment, mademoiselle, I shall be happy to hire you on the spot. I'm getting too old to handle all of this nonsense myself."

Dellie was not amused by their humor, but it was her own fault, she supposed, for offering an opinion when she had not been asked.

As the evening wore on, Dellie was asked to dance by several young gentlemen. However, not one among them struck her as princelike. She tried nonetheless to keep a smile on her face, if only to please Solange, who was so anxious for Dellie's happiness.

At midnight Dellie thought it might be appropriate for her, costumed as she was, to take flight. But this was the time for unmasking, and only now did she realize that she had been garnering a good deal of attention from the guests. Aristede had not missed their curiosity, it seemed, for he came to take her hand, and turning to the crowd, he raised a hand.

"Mesdames et messieurs, I should like to present to you my wife's good friend and our houseguest, Mademoiselle Louise Chandelle Marie-Thérèse Valmont."

With this he reached to remove Dellie's mask. A hush

fell over the assemblage, but it was promptly followed up by the buzzing of whispered conversations.

"The Valmont child?" she heard someone say.

"But I thought that she—"

"She cannot be the same one."

"Where do you suppose she's been for all these years?"

Dellie felt her cheeks flush with color. She was unaccustomed to such scrutiny and did not like it at all. She came perilously near to bolting from the room, but felt Aristede's grip on her hand tighten as if to reassure her. "I'm certain you are all curious, and so I shall explain the circumstances to you, and then perhaps, for Mademoiselle Valmont's sake, we can let the matter rest. It seems that mademoiselle's maid helped her to escape the horrors of that night of the uprising. This faithful servant took her away to New Orleans, where she has been living for all of this time. I was no less surprised than all of you to discover that my new bride's friend was one of our own, and I know that you will all welcome her home with open arms."

Everyone was very kind after that, and Dellie was thankful to Solange's husband for the way he'd handled the situation. She was politely engaged by several people who shared with her their fond remembrances of her father and even of his father. There were few on this island who did not know the name of Valmont.

Still somewhat uncomfortable, Dellie attached herself to a covey of young ladies. These were her people, she reminded herself. This was the life she'd always said she wanted. Surely within this diverse group there would be a place for her. She listened to their conversation, hoping to find common ground. She did not find it.

"What sort of costume is that meant to be, do you suppose?" she heard one of the ladies say, nodding her head toward a woman across the room.

"I couldn't begin to guess, my dear, but she is rather too old to be showing so much of her bosom."

"Have you seen DeVille's daughter? Poor thing will never catch a husband if she keeps dressing herself like a dowdy governess."

Dellie took in the endless, petty discourse, her only comment a disappointed sigh.

She first noticed him standing in the doorway as though he'd just come in from the garden. He was tall and dressed in a knee-length coat, breeches, and jackboots. He had not deigned to remove his mask: a black kerchief tied over the top of his head, with two holes cut for his eyes. Atop this he wore a jaunty tricorn hat, and Dellie could not help but think of her ancestor, the pirate Lucien Valmont, when she saw him staring at her, bold as brass, with his arms folded across his broad chest and a menacing combination of cutlass and revolver tucked into his wide sash.

She could not recall being introduced to him at all. In fact, she was certain that he'd not been at the table for dinner. Who was he, then, this late arrival?

"Wouldn't you agree with that, Mademoiselle Valmont?" someone asked her.

"Hmm?" Dellie replied absently and responded without ever having heard the question. "Oh, yes, as you say."

She had turned away for only a moment, but when she looked back he was gone. Had he been no more than a product of her imagination?

All at once the pirate was standing there before her, one arm extended as if he were inviting her to dance, yet he did not speak a word. She heard a collective intake of breath from the ladies beside her. This was the most exciting thing that had happened all night. Intrigued, Dellie accepted the unspoken invitation and allowed him to rescue her from her boredom and squire her to the center of the floor. Whispers followed them out.

"Why, did you see that? Who is he?"

"I don't know, but he has the most devilish look about him."

As the silent pirate led her through the smooth steps of the waltz, Dellie wished that there were no mask to hide his face, wished that there were more light to see by than just the soft glow of candles overhead in the chandelier. This was curious, indeed.

"Do you intend to dance with me and yet speak not a word all the while, monsieur?"

He did not reply. He was so close she could feel his chest rise and fall with his breathing, but she was no nearer to understanding this mystery. Dellie was held fast in his arms, and he whirled her across the floor in a deft move that left her breathless.

"You dance well, monsieur, but then, I suppose many ladies have told you so."

Try as she might, she could not draw him out. She studied him more thoughtfully now. The candlelight fed the gleam in his deep-set eyes and cast golden highlights on his longish brown hair, which was caught up in a queque and tied with a ribbon. "I sense that you do not belong here, *monsieur le pirate*. You're not the same as them," she told him, tossing her head at the assembled guests.

At this he looked deep into her eyes as if in reply. She had no trouble reading his meaning. "Neither am I, you say? Well, you're right. Once I thought that I belonged among them, but I was wrong. I see that now."

The pressure of his hand on her increased, but this time she could not guess what he was trying to tell her. She only knew that she felt a kinship with this stranger.

"Why have you come here this evening?" she asked. "And who are you? I wonder. 'Tis a shame you will not speak; I do so need a levelheaded friend on this island, monsieur. Someone quite apart from these useless folk with their parties and petty jealousies. There are so many important questions running through my brain, so many decisions I must make now—"

Dellie knew at once that she'd gone too far. How could she have voiced her innermost thoughts aloud and confided in this stranger? It was his odd silence which had drawn her out, she told herself.

Her agitation caused her to miss a step in the dance, and she trod on the hem of her gown, which made her stumble. The pirate caught her in his arms, pulling her close against him.

He pulled in a ragged breath. "Dellie!"

Was that longing she heard in his voice? And how did he know her name?

Recovering the steps, he continued to lead her on in the dance as if nothing had happened. But something *had* happened. The sound of Dellie's pounding heart filled her ears; all her senses were heightened, in fact. She knew now who he was, though she could scarcely believe it. She stiffened in his arms. He tightened his grip in reply.

"Have you come all this way after your money, Monsieur Durant?" she said in a voice as cold as ice.

"So you know who I am, then?" He sounded almost disappointed.

Jared let his eyes wander over her. He'd almost forgotten how beautiful she was. Tonight she looked as though she'd stepped out of the pages of a fairy-tale book in her elegant white gown, her bright golden hair swept up, and those tendrils which had escaped framing her face in soft curls. Her dark blue eyes were wide and opaque against translucent skin, yet there was no mistaking the change in her. She looked older, warier.

"Of course I know who you are," she said then. "You are the gambler, the man who makes his living on the misfortune of others, as I have learned well enough."

Jared knew she had run from him in New Orleans, yet he did not expect such venom, did not expect to see such hatred in her eyes. What had caused the change in her? "You must listen to me, Dellie," he said.

"There is nothing you could say to me that I wish to hear."

Still following the movements of the dance, Jared suddenly swept her across the floor and through the French doors and out into the garden, knowing that she could not protest without causing a scene. When they were alone at last, he released her, and Dellie responded by picking up her skirts and fleeing as far away from him as she could—to the very edge of the flagstone terrace, where she turned her back on him and clung to the stone balustrade.

He followed her with a purposeful stride, and doffing his hat, he removed his mask and cast it to the pavement, revealing himself to her. "I'm a gambler, it's true," he explained, keeping his voice even, "but I have also on occasion been employed as a detective, and it was in that capacity that I was hired by Lucien Valmont . . . to find his daughter."

Dellie turned on him. The look on her face was cold and unforgiving. "Liar!" she spat.

"For God's sake, what's happened to you?" Now his words were fraught with concern. "Why won't you listen to reason?"

Dellie thought that she'd rid herself of any lingering affection for him, but when she allowed her eyes to rest on his familiar features, she felt herself drawn in by the warmth in those golden eyes. Her composure was crumbling, and she knew that she was not strong enough to face him alone for much longer.

"All that I've told you is true, whether you believe it or not," he went on. "Your father escaped the fires that night, just as you did."

Dellie covered her ears with her hands to shut out his lies. She would not let him take her in again. Jared Durant would not be here tonight on this island, she told herself, unless there was some sort of profit in it for him.

"Oh?" she retorted, able to speak only in halting breaths, "and to repay this man who hired you, you made a wager with your saloon friends that you could bed his daughter before the week was out?"

The words struck Jared like a blow. So she did know of the wager. Little wonder she hated him. He could not blame her, yet still he had to try to make her understand. "I cannot excuse what I did," he responded, expelling a long sigh of regret. "It was stupid and childish—but I swear to you, I did not know when I made that wager that you were Valmont's daughter. I imagined that all the women at Celestine's were—"

At that very moment Aristede Grimaud came out onto the terrace. He must have sensed Dellie's distress, for he eyed Jared warily and went at once to her side. "Mademoiselle?"

Dellie turned her attention back to Jared. "My father," she said, edging nearer to Aristede, "died more than a dozen years ago during the slave revolt. Ask anyone here tonight, and they'll tell you. Ask Monsieur Grimaud."

"I did try to tell you, monsieur, when we met in New Orleans that Lucien Valmont was dead," Grimaud explained coolly.

He offered his arm, and Dellie linked hers through it, obviously grateful for his aid. Jared felt a hatred of the Frenchman welling in him. He wished now that he'd made Lucien Valmont tell him all he knew about this man Grimaud, instead of allowing himself to be put off.

"I would suggest," Grimaud continued, "that the man who hired you was an impostor."

Though Jared had himself considered that same possibility more than once, he wouldn't give Grimaud the satisfaction now. "I don't believe that."

Shutting her eyes, Dellie reminded herself of all the lies Jared Durant had told her thus far and felt her strength returning. "Think about this, monsieur. If my father were alive, then why has he never come back to claim his land? And where is he now?"

With each word, Jared could feel her slipping further away from him. He could not expect to gain her trust, but he had to make her listen. Tess was dead, and Valmont was missing. He did not know yet who was responsible, but there was no doubt that Dellie, too, was in danger.

"I sent your father to Celestine's cabin," he explained. "When he learned that you had run off, that you were headed for St. Gervais, he came after you. I followed him here only to discover that he had disappeared. His ship arrived in Marigot three days ago. He went ashore, and no one has seen him since. It's only a matter of time before I learn what's become of him. Until then you must trust me, Dellie."

"I've trusted you once too often already," she said, sounding weary. "Find this man who claims to be my father, bring him to me, and maybe then I'll believe."

"Can't you see that you're in danger?" he persisted.

"And how much of this danger was fabricated by you?" she shot back, "in order to draw me out, to get me to—"

Dellie could not continue. She did not wish for Aristede Grimaud to hear of her shame.

"Have you forgotten about Tess so soon?" Jared retorted. "She saw danger, too."

Dellie tried to speak but only a small cry escaped her lips before she pressed a hand over them. Grimaud moved behind her to put his hands on her shoulders. "That's quite enough, monsieur," he said. "You've had your say. Now I think you ought to leave. Rest assured, as Mademoiselle Valmont is my guest, I shall make it my business to see to her safety."

There was nothing that Jared could do. He looked once more to Dellie, hoping to catch a glimmer of remembrance in those vivid blue eyes, but she cast them downward in response, concentrating instead upon the pattern of the flagstones beneath her feet. And so he turned and walked away.

CHAPTER
16

Dellie decided to put Jared Durant entirely out of her mind. The very next morning she rode to Belle Terre and wandered over the ruins of her home once more, discovering things that she'd missed the first time: an overgrown plot that had once been the kitchen garden and where some of Mama Tess's herbs still bloomed; the family cemetery behind the house, with its gate rusted shut, the markers barely visible for the dense foliage; and the overseer's stone cottage near the sea, which had been miraculously spared.

She explored the abandoned cottage at great length, noting its state of utter disrepair but still allowing the germ of an idea to plant itself in her thoughts. She could not stay with the Grimauds forever. This cottage was, after all, on Valmont land. Why could she not claim it for herself?

All the while she'd been walking amid the ruins, Dellie had felt saddened by the fact that the work of generations of Valmonts had come to naught. There was no great house, no sugar mill, no bustling plantation. It was as if there had never been a Valmont on this island at all.

Only after a great deal of contemplation did Dellie realize that she herself might change things. *She* was a Valmont. The land belonged to her now, and she made a promise to restore her family's name, no matter how long it took.

Only two days after their meeting at Grimaud's party, Dellie arrived at the office of Dr. LeClerc to take up his offer of employment. He was astounded at first and then concluded that she must be playing a joke.

Dellie thought she appeared serious enough, with her hair tied up in a kerchief and an apron over her worn calico dress, but the doctor still could not allow that a young lady of her like would be equal to the thankless drudgery of nursing. She proved him wrong almost from the first, following him tirelessly even through the meanest sectors of the town and not hesitating to give help where she was needed, no matter how menial or unpleasant the task.

Helping Dr. LeClerc in his work gave Dellie a close look at the daily lives of the former slaves who resided on St. Gervais and convinced her that emancipation had not bettered their lot by much. Although Aristede Grimaud had seemed proud of the fact that his field hands were paid to work for him, Dellie soon learned that their wages were piteously low, and while a slave owner was obliged to feed his workers and provide them shelter, there were no such demands made on an employer.

The result of this was that the employer's profits were increased while the freedman quickly used up all of his meager earnings in providing for his family. The system as it was was little better than slavery, with little chance for improvement or advancement.

As Dellie saw it, only those who elected to live away

from civilization could truly call themselves free. When emancipation came, they had spurned employment in the cane fields or on the wharves in Marigot and had instead turned to the land and the sea to eke out whatever sort of life they could manage on their own.

In spite of the doctor's warnings about the dangers, Dellie insisted upon making treks on her own to more remote locales where resided the poorest of the island's black population. These were the people most in need of medical attention, she told him plainly; there was only the matter of gaining their trust.

Dr. LeClerc did not seem at all surprised by her willfulness, as if such a trait was to be expected in a Valmont. However, he pronounced her need for aiding the unfortunate quite unheard of in ladies of her class and wondered aloud about the sort of unusual influence she'd lived under while in New Orleans. Dellie was beginning to see that she could not go on living between two worlds. The time was coming when she'd have to make a choice about the sort of life she wanted for herself.

The one thing that drew all of the former slaves together, yet still kept them distrustful of Dr. LeClerc, and of Dellie as well, was their belief in voodoo. Made up of remnants of their native African religions with odd bits and pieces of Christianity thrown in, voodoo offered these all-but-powerless people a way, with charms and powders and hexes, lighted candles and incantations, to control the world around them.

Dellie knew well enough from her years in New Orleans how futile it was to attempt to convince them otherwise, and so she set out to win them over with some magic of her own—offering them, where she was able, her teas and ointments, poultices and powders, and a host of harmless concoctions suitable for nonmedical complaints.

She came across so many freed blacks branded with the

Valmont mark that she could not help but feel some amount of responsibility for their condition. Perhaps it was this that made her so persistent. In the first week her visits seemed to accomplish nothing, but she returned again and again to the ramshackle villages, determined to make her presence felt and to convince the wary that she could be trusted.

Often while out on these excursions, Dellie would sense an unseen presence, as if someone were watching her. And then once she turned quickly enough to see that it was Jared Durant who'd been following her at a distance all the while, just out of sight. After that, although they never spoke, he did not try to hide the fact that he watched over her, and while she would not confront him, she could not help but wonder. Was he still searching for the man who'd claimed to be her father? Or was he after something else?

Dellie continued her work with the poorest of the island people. She was so anxious to find a purpose to her life on St. Gervais that she did not even stop to consider that her actions might earn the displeasure of some on the island. . . .

She was awakened her first morning in the stone cottage by bright splashes of sunlight that stole in between the louvered shutters and splayed across her bed. Somewhere on high a bird was trilling a melodic reveille while the sea breeze rustled the leaves beneath it. Brushing the sleep from her eyes, she raised herself up and threw aside the bedclothes. She'd not felt this content in years. Here, in this house, on the land where she'd been born, she hoped she would be able to forget all that had happened to her in New Orleans.

Solange had come yesterday to help Dellie settle in. As she looked over the accommodations, however, she wrinkled her nose and begged Dellie to come back with her.

Dellie insisted that she was pleased with her new home. She had made her choice.

There were only three rooms in the cottage. The bedroom was small, with only enough room for a narrow bed and a battered chest for her clothes. The parlor was empty but for a rocking chair donated by Dr. LeClerc, which Dellie had put in one corner. The kitchen, though, with its stone hearth and pair of windows that faced the sea, was a cheery place.

Once the filth and cobwebs had been swept away, it all seemed much more pleasant, but there was still much to be done before Dellie could truly feel at home. She wanted to scrub the tiles on the kitchen floor and arrange all of her medicines in the pantry and have a look to see if anything remained of what had once been the kitchen garden out back.

Anxious to begin, Dellie dressed promptly, tied up her hair, and with a pail over her arm, went to fetch some water. As she stepped out onto the walk, a flash of color beneath her feet caught her eye. She moved aside quickly, sweeping her skirts back so that she could see the walk.

There on the flagstone just outside the kitchen door was the image of a coiled serpent drawn in blood. Nearby in the grass, its feathers matted with its own dried blood, lay a slaughtered white hen, insects buzzing about the carcass.

Dellie clamped a hand over her mouth, and a shudder ran through her as she remembered the dream she'd had that night in the cabin on the Bayou St. John: "There is one here among us who would dare challenge the power of the *loas*. . . ."

But this was nothing supernatural, she told herself; it was only a prank. Someone was trying to frighten her. She went to fetch the water and, returning, stepped around the bloody picture as she went into the kitchen for a scrub brush.

All the while she could not rid her mind of the leering face of the devil she'd seen in her dream, nor of the taunting words of the voodoo queen, Marie LaVeau. Somewhere on this island was just such a woman, Dellie told herself, one who resented her attempt to usurp her power, and she had sent a clear message.

Dellie knew well enough that the only real power of a mambo, as the voodoo priestess was called, was the power of suggestion, that her success lay in her ability to frighten her followers into submission. Well, she told herself, Dellie Valmont was not wholly without weapons in this battle, if that's what it was to be, and with a determined set to her jaw, she vowed she'd not be scared off by childish tricks.

She was on her hands and knees, working to remove the bloody picture outside her door with a scrub brush, when out of the corner of her eye she saw Jared Durant ride up the path.

"Still here, are you, monsieur?" she said, without looking up. Despite her cool tone, Dellie could not stop wondering what his game was this time.

"What's this?" he asked as he dismounted and came up behind her.

"The local voodoo doctor stopped by last night to pay her respects, and as I'd already gone to bed, she left her little greeting here on my doorstep."

"Written in blood?"

A look of uneasiness had settled on Jared's face, but Dellie only nodded and continued to scrub the flagstone vigorously. "It was a rather crude picture of a snake. I imagine the intent was that I should recoil in horror, pack up my satchel of herbs and roots, and flee back to Marigot."

"Perhaps that's an idea you should consider," he told her. "I will admit that you have been a great help to the poor blacks in the village, but as for the others, those who do not want to assimilate—maybe it would be wiser if you left them to take care of their own."

Dellie finished her scrubbing, tossed the brush into the pail beside her, and wiped her hands on her apron. "I'm only offering them my help," she told him as she got to her feet and opened the kitchen door. "Those who live away from Marigot need it most of all."

Jared followed her in. "Perhaps they do, but ask yourself for whose benefit you're doing all of this, Dellie, theirs . . . or yours?"

Stung by his suggestion, Dellie turned on him in hurt surprise. "What do you mean? I want nothing from them."

"I think that you do. I've watched you as you look on their slave tattoos, especially those who bear the Valmont mark, and I think that somehow you feel responsible for their plight."

"And if I do, is that so wrong?"

"You had no part in any of their suffering," Jared replied gently.

"I reaped the benefits of their labors, same as any of the others—"

"You were only a child then. You're not the same as those others now. I think you know that, even if you won't admit it. You say that you believe your father was killed on the night of the revolt by his own slaves, yet you bear those slaves no malice at all, and in fact, you do all that you can to help them."

Jared came to lay his hand upon her shoulder, but she jerked away as if she'd been burned.

"Would you have me hate everyone whose skin is black?" she retorted hotly. "Every little child I see playing on the roadside? Every mother working in the field?

Mama Tess was black and Madame Celestine. If not for them, where would I be?"

"You'll get no argument from me on that score," Jared assured her. "I only sought to point out how the years you spent on Gallatin Street have changed you. You give so much to others, but you've got to think of yourself, too. You have a life of your own to lead."

Dellie expected him to reach out for her again, but instead he turned away, pretending an interest in the collection of jars on a shelf across the room. "No matter what you believe of me, Dellie, I am your friend. That's why I'm telling you this. You're a beautiful young woman, and you ought to be thinking about a husband . . . and children," he said, swallowing hard, "instead of hiding out here all alone. There are plenty of eligible gentlemen on this island who'd consider themselves damned lucky to have a woman like you for a wife."

With his words hanging in the air, Dellie closed her eyes to hide the pain as the wound she'd been nursing in her heart was wrest open once more. She ought to hate him, after all that he'd done. She ought to be glad of his indifference. But when he described himself as her friend, no more than that, the word had such a hollow sound that she could scarcely bear to hear it.

"Why are you here? What do you want from me? Why do you torment me so?" Her voice was breathless and uneven, and the questions had tumbled out before she could think.

Jared turned to her, and their eyes met briefly before Dellie was able to mask her hurt.

"I've not yet finished the job I was sent to do," he replied quietly and started for the door. "I never meant to hurt you. I'll keep my distance from now on, if you like, but have a care in your dealings with these voodoo people, Dellie. They don't take kindly to outsiders."

"You may be right," she said, wishing against all her better judgment that she could stop him from walking out that door. "These people may not want my help. It's been more than a week now, and they've yet to come to me, even with all my encouragement."

"Be proud of what you've accomplished already," he told her.

When he was gone, Dellie sat for a long while in her rocking chair, trying to understand the complexity of the emotions he had aroused in her. It would have been so much easier to hate Jared Durant, and yet she saw now that she could not, no matter what he'd done—but then, neither could she trust him.

She was still sitting there half an hour later when Dr. LeClerc rapped on her door.

"Are you there, mademoiselle?" he called out when she did not answer at once.

Pulling herself out of the chair, Dellie shook off her reverie. As soon as she opened the door to him, LeClerc presented her with a large parcel. "I had my housekeeper, Madame Rousseau, put together some things for your larder," he explained.

"How thoughtful of you, Doctor," Dellie replied, taking up the package. "Come in, and I'll make us some tea."

LeClerc followed her into the kitchen and watched as she began to unwrap the items and put them one by one into the pantry. "I still don't approve of your living out here all alone, you know."

"I really am quite capable of taking care of myself," Dellie assured him.

"I don't doubt it," he admitted. "You have been a tremendous help to me in my work, more so than I would ever have imagined. But you're so young. You need the company of friends of your own age—young gentlemen who'll pay you compliments and try to win your heart."

"Perhaps I'm not meant for such things," Dellie answered sharply. She could see that she had shocked him and tried to suppress her irritation. Twice today she'd heard this same argument, but she could not fault Dr. LeClerc for his concern. "My heart is a bruised and battered thing, Doctor, and not much of a prize for any man, I'm afraid. Now, please go and sit in the parlor, where you'll be comfortable. I shall bring your tea directly."

As he did so, there came a knock upon the kitchen door. Dellie peered out through the louvered shutters and could make out the figure of a tall black woman just outside. She was shabbily dressed, with a worn shawl thrown over her mended calico, and she was barefoot, but still she bore herself proudly. A thought came to Dellie as she studied the woman. Could this be the voodoo priestess, come back to see what her handiwork had wrought?

Ignoring the hammering of her heart, Dellie went to open the door. "Can I help you?" she asked, trying her best to hide all emotion.

"Mamzelle? You are Mamzelle Valmont?"

"I am," Dellie replied.

The woman did not look convinced, and Dellie's suspicions about her motives increased. What sort of game was this?

"How can it be? The Valmonts all are dead," the woman insisted, "killed in the fires many years ago."

"Believe me when I tell you this," Dellie retorted in a voice full of icy calm. "I am the child of the Valmonts, raised up from the ashes of the great fire just as the gum and chestnut trees that now stand upon the ruins of my home. The Valmonts belong to this land, and no one can ever drive us from it. And you may tell that to anyone who wishes to know."

She moved to shut the door, but before she could, the young woman stepped onto the threshold. "I mean no harm, mamzelle," she explained, sounding more anxious now. "I had to know the truth. People in Marigot say you are a powerful root doctor, and so I've come to ask your help."

Dellie was surprised to hear this. When she had recovered, she stepped aside to allow the young woman in. "What is your name?"

"Amelie," came the reply. "My own people tell me I must not come here." She hesitated before continuing. "But I would face the devil himself if it would help my son."

Amelie unwrapped her shawl to reveal an infant, who looked to be about six months old, resting in the cradle of her arm. "He does not eat. He does not sleep. He does not even cry."

Dellie reached to take the child from his mother and laid a gentle hand upon his brow. "He is feverish," she noted.

"I do not want charity," the woman said. "I will pay you, mamzelle. I have some money, only please make him well."

"How long has he been ill?"

"Three days now. The fever comes and goes."

"And has he not been treated at all?"

Amelie shook her dark head. "I was told that it was a fix, put on me by a jealous woman—so I'll never see a child of mine grown to manhood. I've bathed him in special waters, lit candles, and made offerings, all just as I was told to. I've already lost two babies, mamzelle. I won't lose another."

Dellie was angry all at once. She could not believe that anyone would advise such nonsense as treatment for an illness. She poured some of the tea that had been steeping and offered the woman a seat at the kitchen table. "Wait here," she said. "I'll see what I can do."

With the child in her arms Dellie went through the drape into the parlor, hoping that Dr. LeClerc had overheard what had transpired in the kitchen. One look told her that he had. He reached out immediately for the child and took him into the bedroom, instructing Dellie to fetch the medical bag from his saddle. She did as he bade her and met him in the bedroom. LeClerc had already placed the child on her bed and unwrapped it from its blankets.

"I can ease the fever with my boneset tea," she told him, "but you are far better qualified to determine the cause of this sickness than I."

"The child must be made to take in more fluids," LeClerc explained, his voice barely a whisper. "Tell the mother that it is essential."

He went on to examine the boy carefully, explaining the various symptoms to Dellie, voicing his observations about the possible causes of such an illness, and finally giving her a set of instructions that the mother should follow in order to hasten the child's recovery.

"Will you not speak to her yourself?" Dellie asked.

"It took every ounce of the woman's courage to defy the beliefs of her people and come here. She has put her trust in you, not me."

Dr. LeClerc reached into his bag and rummaged through the contents, finally drawing out a small bottle. "This powder must be mixed with water and given to the boy, a spoonful twice a day. Now go out and tell the mother what must be done."

Dellie did as he told her and promised Amelie that she would look in on the child in a day or so. When she had shown the woman out, she returned to the parlor, where Dr. LeClerc was waiting.

"We make a fine team, you and I," he said. "Perhaps I was wrong to try and dissuade you. You have a rapport with these people, and if they come to trust you, by working together we might just do some good after all."

"I'd like nothing more," Dellie told him.

She knew well enough what the decision meant. Sooner or later she would be forced to confront the voodoo priestess who'd left the mark of the serpent in blood on her doorstep, and yet she was not afraid.

CHAPTER
17

Perched on an outcropping of rock at the edge of a meadow overlooking the ocean, Dellie Valmont surveyed her domain. The grant from the king of France had ceded to the privateer Lucien Valmont all the land, from coast to coast, between the Blue Mountains and the rivière Ste. Marie. It was the most extensive tract of land on St. Gervais, and now it belonged to Dellie. What use she would make of it, she could not begin to guess, but for now she was content to simply revel in the beauty of the landscape. This was her home, her Belle Terre, and she hoped that her love of the land would be enough to fill up and heal her heart.

"Dellie? Dellie?"

The waves pounding the rocks below nearly drowned out the voice, but when the call reached her ear at last, Dellie turned to see Solange crossing the meadow. Thorny weeds were tugging at the hem of her white lawn dress, and the brisk wind had swept off her bonnet, leaving it to hang down her back suspended by its ribbons.

Dellie waved a greeting to her friend and rose to meet

her. "Solange, what brings you here? I thought you'd decided that my new lodgings were too rustic to visit."

"Don't tease, Dellie," Solange said, frowning in annoyance as she surveyed the tears that the brambles had made in her skirt. "I've come all his way, even handled the carriage on my own. You must read the cards for me."

"I'm sorry, *chère amie,* I cannot," Dellie replied with a shrug of her slight shoulders. "I've thrown them away."

"You've what? Oh, how could you? Whatever shall I do now?"

Solange stamped her foot impatiently. Dellie took up her friend's gloved hand and squeezed it. "Sit down here and tell me what's happened to upset you so. Have you had a fight with Aristede?"

"No. No, it's not that at all," Solange explained as they both sat down upon the rocks. "He's been so wonderful. I know I can be silly and childish at times, but Aristede understands and is patient with me. I could not ask for a better husband."

"Well, then, what is it?"

"It's his mother, Madame Dominique. I'm afraid of her, Dellie. She doesn't speak to me at all, and sometimes she gives me the sharpest looks, almost as if she hates me."

Dellie put on a smile and smoothed Solange's tousled curls with a gentle hand, doing her best to soothe the excitable girl. "Dominique is ill and in pain. Even if she does have an unpleasant look on her face at times, I'm certain it's not meant for you."

"There's something else," Solange said. Slipping the strings of her purse from her arm, she untangled them, opened the bag, and rummaged inside. "I found it beneath my pillow yesterday morning. At first I thought it only a child's plaything, but then as I looked on it—"

When finally she came upon the object she'd been searching for, she held it out to Dellie. It was a doll, fash-

ioned crudely out of lengths of plaited straw. Dressed in
a scrap of brightly colored silk, it was crowned with a lock
of hair exactly the color and texture of Solange's, and a
length of black cord was knotted several times around its
neck.

Dellie took the doll from Solange's outstretched hand
and examined it. The symbolism was clear enough.

"It's one of those voodoo charms, isn't it?" Solange's
voice was fraught with anxiety. "You know about such
things, Dellie. Do you suppose Dominique put it there to
frighten me off?"

"Of course I don't believe such a thing," Dellie
snapped. At times it was hard for her to be patient with
Solange, who was forever acting like a spoiled child. "You
haven't been speaking this way to Aristede, have you?"
she queried. "He may be the very soul of understanding,
Solange, but I don't think it wise to villify his ailing
mother—and with no proof at all."

"I know I oughtn't to blame Madame Dominique, but
she dislikes me, I can feel it, and she resents my presence
in the house." Solange pouted prettily, then dropped her
head and stared hard at her hands, folded neatly in her
lap. "I haven't said a word to Aristede, though."

"Good," Dellie told her. "More than likely one of the
house servants is responsible for this. If you dealt a sharp
word to your maid, perhaps, or complained about a meal
to the cook—"

"Yes, I suppose you're right."

With that, Dellie stuffed the doll into her apron pocket.
"Now you must forget about this, Solange. It was a spite-
ful bit of mischief, but no more than that."

For the first time Dellie noticed how pale Solange
looked today. There were shadows marring her lovely features, too, and she was trembling, even with the warm

tropical sun beating down on them. "I wish you hadn't thrown away your cards," she said wistfully.

"I know, *chère amie,*" Dellie replied to this, "sometimes so do I."

The following evening Dr. LeClerc invited her to a dinner party in his home. She ought to have guessed at his game when he entreated her more than once to be sure and wear her "prettiest frock," but she did not suspect anything until she stepped into the parlor, wearing a white muslin decorated with ribbons and pink rosebuds, which Solange had given her, and found herself being stared upon by at least a dozen expectant faces.

The old doctor introduced her to them, one by one. She was Louise, last of the renowned Valmont family, dear Lucien's daughter, who has been living abroad for many years. And the dinner guests? They were some of the wealthiest families in Marigot—each of whom, by some fortunate coincidence, had a son of marriageable age.

This soirée was an ill-conceived notion from the first. The dour matrons all eyed her warily, determined to guard their precious offspring, and Dellie knew it was only a matter of time before they discovered that Mademoiselle Valmont, since her return to St. Gervais, had been living alone, outside the bounds of polite society, and associating with persons who would doubtless be considered unacceptable.

Dellie was not in the least disturbed by this, but she could not help but be disappointed in Dr. LeClerc. She'd thought after all he'd said to her the day before when he'd visited the stone cottage that he understood what sort of life she had decided upon for herself. Watching him, though, as he squired her around the room like a proud papa, presenting her to his guests, she could not fault his intentions, and so she endured the party for his sake.

It was late in the evening, after the gentlemen had finished their brandy and cigars, that the young messenger from the Grimaud estate arrived, asking for the doctor. "There's been an accident. Someone up at the big house has been hurt," the boy said. "You must come at once."

The news brought Dellie to her feet. "Solange? Is it Solange?" she inquired anxiously.

"Can't say, mamzelle," he replied. "I was only told to bring the doctor."

Dr. LeClerc apologized to his guests, excused himself, and went to fetch his medical bag. Dellie managed to exit unnoticed shortly thereafter and met him in the hall.

"Take me with you," she entreated. "Solange Grimaud is my friend. If I can help in any way, it would help to repay the kindness she has shown me."

"I can manage, my dear. Stay and enjoy the remainder of the evening."

"I must know that she is safe," Dellie insisted.

"Calm yourself, my dear. It could just as well be one of the servants, or this accident may turn out to be nothing serious at all."

Dellie did not believe it, not for a moment. "If you cannot take me with you, I shall find my own way," she told him.

Seeing that she would not be dissuaded, LeClerc relented at last. "Come along, then. I'll have Madame Rousseau explain to the guests. . . ."

The drive seemed endless. As the open carriage jogged along the road, Dellie stared out on the shadowy landscape and said a prayer in the hope that this "accident" was nothing serious after all—and that they would arrive to find her friend unharmed.

As they drew up in front of the house, Dellie saw a tall figure on the front steps. It was Aristede, and he was coming down to meet them in the drive.

"It's my mother," he told Dr. LeClerc as he helped the old man down. "She had another one of her headaches, and so her maid put her to bed early. She awoke a short while ago to discover that there was a fire in her room. A fallen chamberstick set the bed-curtains afire, and she must have panicked. She tried to put it out with her hands."

It was not Solange, after all. Dellie could not help but breathe a sigh of relief at the news, and then guilt washed over her. She was forgetting poor Madame Dominique, who surely did not deserve more suffering.

As LeClerc hurried inside, Aristede finally noticed Dellie there on the carriage seat. "Mademoiselle? I didn't expect—"

He seemed to hesitate and then reached out a hand to help her alight.

"I was dining with Dr. LeClerc when your message came," she explained, feeling rather foolish all at once, "and I thought that—that there might be something I could do."

Grimaud studied her and then flashed that disarming smile he wore so well. "How kind you are," he said at last, taking her by the arm to lead her up the steps.

"Where is your wife this evening?" Dellie wondered, for she could not imagine that Solange would want to be anywhere but at the center of all the excitement.

"She was not feeling well after supper, and so I sent her to bed. She is such a fragile flower; I must take special care with her."

Dellie smiled. How lucky Solange was to have such a thoughtful husband! If only she could put aside her childish fears, she could be so happy.

"Is your mother hurt badly, do you think?" she asked him then.

"There are blisters on her palms which the doctor will

have to tend, but I believe she's suffered more of a fright from the mishap."

"I can well imagine her alarm—to wake up with the flames all around her. It must have been awful."

"She's had a nervous condition for some time now. I fear that this will only aggravate her situation. . . ." Aristede's voice drifted off as his brow furrowed in concern.

"Dr. LeClerc will see that she's made as comfortable as possible," Dellie assured him.

He pulled in a deep breath that seemed to restore his vigor. "Well, then, Dellie, let's you and I go into the parlor and wait while he tends her," he said.

Once inside, Aristede poured them both a glass of sherry and came to sit beside Dellie, who was perched on the sofa. "We've missed your pleasant company, my dear," he told her.

"You flatter me, monsieur. But you forget that I know something of the running of plantations. More than likely your business affairs have kept you too busy to even notice my absence. All is well, I hope."

"Very well, indeed. I made an important . . . acquisition, you might call it, and Fate has given me the opportunity to finally settle an old debt that's been haunting me for years."

"That is good news for you, then."

"I understand that you've been working with the doctor and making quite a reputation for yourself among the islanders."

Dellie could not gauge by his comment whether he approved of this or not. "I've been helping where I can," she replied without elaborating.

Leaning closer, Grimaud broached a new subject. "I hope that you've had no further trouble from that meddlesome fellow who accosted you at our party. What was his name—Durant? Take care, my dear. He's not the kind of man to be trusted."

"I know that well enough, although I do wonder why he's come all this way," Dellie said, giving voice to her thoughts.

"He wants something from you; that's clear to see. And believe me, Dellie, a man of his sort wouldn't hesitate to use any trick to get it."

"But I have nothing of value," Dellie insisted.

"Nothing?" Aristede echoed, and one dark brow crooked upward in disbelief. "I wouldn't say that, my dear."

Dellie blushed, lowering her head. During the long silence which ensued, she pondered the question carefully. What could Durant be after? And then quite by chance, she recalled the conversation that she and Jared had had in Celestine's cabin. He'd questioned her thoroughly, anxious for any information she might have. Oh, what a fool she was not to have realized before!

"The Eye of the Serpent," she said softly, and each word pierced her heart. "He's come after the pirate's treasure."

"It's only a legend," Aristede replied, regarding her closely. "Isn't it?"

"I'd always thought so," Dellie told him, "but now with all that's happened, I'm not so sure."

The disappointment must have been visible on her face. Aristede reached for the decanter and refilled her glass. "Have you thought about your future, Dellie?" he prompted gently. "Do you plan to remain here on St. Gervais?"

Dellie nodded, sipping at the sherry. "There may be nothing left of my family fortunes, but there is still the land."

"But what good is that?" he wondered. "There are precious few individuals on this island who could afford the upkeep on such an acreage, and even fewer who have an eye toward purchase."

"That suits me well enough," Dellie replied, "for I do not plan to sell."

Aristede's dark eyes widened. "If not sell, my dear, what then?"

"I intend to make my home there. I have already moved into the stone house on the grounds near the sea. It was once the overseer's cottage, I believe. It is not large nor fashionable, I'll grant you that, but it is comfortable enough to suit my needs."

"Yes," he said, and a serious expression came over him. "Solange has mentioned this to me, but I feel it no less than my duty as a friend to try and dissuade you from such a plan."

"A Valmont on Valmont land. 'Tis where I belong."

"A fragile young lady, accustomed to city life, proposes to live alone, miles from the village. However shall you manage?"

Dellie was not daunted by the dismal picture he'd painted with his words. "There is a well on the property and ample wood for the hearth. I daresay I can draw water and lay a fire as well as any other."

"You do have spirit, Dellie Valmont, I'll give you that much, but what sort of income will you have to live on?"

"Dr. LeClerc has offered me a small salary. I shall manage."

Dellie could see by his vexed expression that Aristede Grimaud was unaccustomed to being argued with. "I shall buy up a parcel of your land," he offered next. "This will give you money enough to buy a comfortable house in the village at least."

"I will not sell," Dellie insisted.

Aristede shook his head in resignation. "It is not safe, nor wise—a woman alone."

"Nevertheless, it is what I want. I do understand, my friend, that you wish only what is best for me, and I thank you for that. But I am not accustomed to a sheltered life. If you knew how I have lived my life till now, you would not fear half so much for me."

"And if you knew the sort of evil you may one day face on St. Gervais," he retorted, "you would not be half so bold."

CHAPTER
18

Dr. LeClerc came downstairs looking serious indeed. He and Aristede closeted themselves in the study for a short while, and then they both emerged to join Dellie in the parlor. She could see there'd been angry words between them.

"How is Madame Grimaud?" she inquired.

"Well enough for now," LeClerc replied, but the dour expression remained fixed on his face.

Aristede's response proved more enlightening. "The doctor has remarked to me that my mother's maid, Sophie, is . . . well, getting on in years and might not be the best choice to tend her needs in her present state. I have suggested that one of the other housemaids takes over in her stead; however, it is the doctor's opinion that a more qualified person be on hand, for tonight at least. He has suggested that you might be willing. I told him that I could not think of asking such a favor." He cast an irritated look at LeClerc. "However, the doctor is adamant."

"Of course, I shall be happy to do all that I can," Dellie told him at once. "That was my intention from the first."

Dr. LeClerc's instructions were quite specific. Dominique was resting now and was not, under any circumstance, to receive more of her medication until he returned tomorrow. Her bandages were to be changed when she woke in the morning and a fresh coat of salve applied to her blistered palms.

Before he left, LeClerc took Dellie aside and pressed a key into her hand. "I have locked the cabinet where Madame's medicines are kept," he told her. "See to it that it remains that way, and take special care not to leave her unattended. In her present state, another dose could kill her."

Dellie could not miss the message behind LeClerc's words. Here was the reason, she surmised, that Dominique had been taken out of Sophie's care. The old woman was obviously so attached to her mistress that she could not bear to see her in pain, and LeClerc suspected that if Dominique awoke in the night, Sophie might unwittingly offer her more of her medication which, as he'd pointed out, could prove fatal.

And so Dellie found herself spending the night under Aristede's roof. Dominique had been moved from the scene of the fire to an adjoining room. Dellie arrived to find her resting peacefully enough, asleep in the center of the large bed, beneath a draping of mosquito *barre*, her hands swathed in bandages.

She set her chamberstick on a small table, making a place for herself on the deeply upholstered wing chair that stood beside the bed. Untying a length of ribbon from the decoration on her gown, Dellie threaded the key that Dr. LeClerc had entrusted to her on it and hung it around her neck.

By the flickering light of the candle, she took in the surroundings. It was not hard to guess, by the sparse furnishings done in deep shades of red, that this had been a gentleman's chamber, likely Aristede's father's, though there was no trace of personality left within its walls now. Over the hearth there was a mantel of heavy, carved wood and set upon it a clock and a Chinese vase. A writing desk and bureau stood empty on an adjacent wall, and across the room, tall shutters opened out onto the gallery, allowing the ocean breezes to sweep in and flutter the mosquito *barre* and the candle's flame.

Aristede had lent her a novel from his library to pass the hours, but after a time her eyes grew tired, and she tucked it into the chair beside her. With Dominique still fast asleep, Dellie got to her feet and paced the room, first turning her attentions out onto the gallery to admire the night sky and then crossing the room to the door leading to Dominique's dressing room. She opened it cautiously and was met at once by the acrid odor of smoke still hanging on the air. The bedchamber where the fire had been was beyond this dressing room, and with curiosity spurring her on, Dellie went back for her chamberstick. Just a quick look, she told herself; there'd be no harm in that.

With the candle to light her way, she passed a mirrored vanity table, a black lacquered cabinet, and a tall chest of drawers in the small anteroom before she opened the opposite door and stood on the threshold of Dominique's bedchamber.

The fire had done more damage than Dellie imagined. Though the servants had already stripped away the bed-curtains, the mattress, the carpets, and some of the furnishings, the scorch marks were yet visible on the floral wallpaper and on the wood floor. Staring upon these reminders of the blaze, Dellie shuddered, thinking how close Aristede's mother had come to losing her life.

As the stale odor of smoke filled her lungs, she found herself suddenly overwhelmed by old memories: of fires in the cane fields, of clinging to Mama Tess's hand and

running through the jungle, of boarding a ship and looking
out over an island in flames.

Dellie turned away at once, closing the door as she
stepped back into the dressing room. There she drew a
breath of clean air and looked up to see her own pale face
reflected in the vanity glass.

Anxious to put aside the old nightmares, Dellie turned
her concentration on the first thing that caught her eye—
the cabinet beside the vanity table. It was a beautiful piece,
decorated with floral patterns and fantastic dragonlike
creatures. Seeing the lock set into its frame between the
two doors, she decided that this must be the cabinet Dr.
LeClerc had mentioned, where Dominique's medicines
were kept. She took the key from around her neck and
fitted it in the lock and opened the doors.

On the first shelf was an assortment of vials, bottles,
tins, and, most significantly, two bottles of morphine powders. So this was the "medicine" that Dominique relied
upon so regularly to soothe her headaches. It was no wonder LeClerc had been wary. How much had she come to
depend upon the drug? Dellie wondered.

She did not mean to pry, but when she noticed a cord
hanging from one of the drawers within the cabinet, she
pulled open the drawer to put it in its place, and her eyes
widened. Inside was a collection of fetishes, voodoo amulets, which were made with packets of dried herbs, small
bones, feathers, and even a piece of snakeskin. Could these
things belong to Aristede's mother? Dellie had not imagined that Dominique Grimaud would be the sort to believe
in magical cures, but then when she recalled the many
Creole ladies who visited Marie LaVeau, Dr. John, and
other practitioners of voodoo in New Orleans, it did not
seem like such a farfetched notion, especially if Dominique was desperately searching for a cure for her painful
headaches.

Dellie shut the cabinet doors and relocked them.

"What are you after, mamzelle? What's locked in there ain't none of your concern."

Dellie looked up, her heart drumming frantically, only to see the reflection of Madame Grimaud's maid behind her in the mirror. The woman was eyeing her with suspicion.

"Oh, Sophie, it's you," Dellie said after breathing a long sigh of relief. "You very nearly scared the life out of me. I was only making certain things were locked up, as the doctor ordered."

"Meddling old man," Sophie muttered.

"What brings you here so late?" Dellie wondered. "I thought Aristede—Monsieur Grimaud—had relieved you of your duties for this evening."

"Madame's fretful. Maybe you been too busy to notice," she chided.

Dellie put the key around her neck once more, went to Dominique's bedside, and lifted the drape of netting. The woman, who'd been peaceful enough only moments ago, was now thrashing beneath the bedclothes, moaning and muttering under her breath.

Looking across the room, Dellie noticed Sophie still lingering in the doorway. "Go on now," she told her. "I'll see that Madame is made comfortable."

The old woman leveled a gimlet eye on her and stood her ground. Dellie only sighed in response and turned her attention back to her patient.

"Be still, madame," she entreated, grasping Dominique's shoulders firmly. "It's all right. You're all right now. But you must rest—"

All at once the thrashing stilled. Dominique's dark eyes opened wide, and she regarded Dellie in surprise. "Who are you?" she demanded, sounding quite normal.

"It's Mademoiselle Valmont," Dellie told her. "I'm a

friend of your son's. We met at dinner a few days ago. Do you recall? You've been hurt, and the doctor asked me to stay with you tonight."

"You're not. You can't be." A note of hysteria crept into her voice now. "They're dead, all dead. They had to die, every one . . . to pay for their sins."

Dominique's black eyes were wild; her head jerked from side to side as if her torment were increasing. Then all at once she reached out to lay a bandaged hand on Dellie's arm, and thrust her face even closer. Her pallid skin looked waxy in the aura of candlelight. "Where is it?" she hissed. "I must have it!"

Dellie pulled back, frightened by the woman Dominique had become. Was she mad?

"You know where it is. They all know. I need it, do you hear?"

Dellie tried to make sense out of Dominique's ravings. She decided that the woman must be asking for her medicine. "The doctor has said you mustn't have any more of your medicine tonight," she told Madame Grimaud in a firm voice. "I know you must be hurting, but try and rest."

And with that she began to knead Dominique's brow. "Try and rest."

She repeated the words again and again until at long last she felt Dominique's tension easing. In a few more minutes the dark eyes had slipped shut, and the woman drifted off to sleep.

Dellie slumped into the chair beside the bed and stared on Dominique's still form as the woman's anxious words resounded in her head. "They had to die, every one . . . to pay for their sins." That was what she'd said, but what did it mean? Crossing her arms over her chest to quell the chill that coursed through her, Dellie tried to convince herself that these were no more than the ravings of a woman grown too dependent upon her morphine.

*   *   *

Jared grudgingly opened his eyes as the bell in the church tower struck the noon hour. He felt as if he hadn't slept at all. For nearly three weeks now, each day from daylight till dusk, he'd scoured the island for some trace of Lucien Valmont. He'd found none. The islanders he questioned had all regarded him as if he were crazy. Valmont was dead. Everyone knew that—everyone, it seemed, except Jared Durant.

He dragged himself out of bed, splashed cold water from the washstand over his haggard face, and reached for the shirt and trousers he'd left draped across the chair. It was time to face the facts. He might never find Lucien Valmont, if indeed that's who he was. He might never know the mystery in all of this. As for Dellie, she did not need his protection, she'd proved that time and time again. His actions had made her despise him, and he could not undo what he'd done. Why then did he keep on?

When he was dressed, Jared went down to the dining room of the inn, which was at this hour bustling with activity. He managed to find a table for himself in a quiet corner, gave his order to the waiter, and went on musing.

His money would run out soon, and then the choice would be made for him. Perhaps it would be best to leave now, tonight, before he was tempted to see her again. If he stayed on, he might only make things worse. He could go back to St. Louis and forget he'd ever heard of Lucien Valmont and St. Gervais. The only regret he had in all of this was hurting Dellie.

"Bonjour, monsieur. May I join you?"

Before Jared had a chance to reply, Aristede Grimaud sat down across the table. There was a long moment of silence while Jared studied him. He had disliked Grimaud from the first, and the Frenchman's look of smug assurance only strengthened that feeling now. Aristede Grimaud was too cultured, too well groomed, too rich. . . .

Grimaud tented his fingers and leaned back in his chair. A ray of sunlight glinted off his gold signet ring. "I shall be brief, monsieur, as I do not wish to intrude upon your meal. How much will it cost me to send you back to New Orleans?"

Jared regarded him more closely, thinking he must have heard wrong. One look told him that he had not. "Do I understand, Grimaud, that you wish to be rid of me?"

"Mademoiselle Valmont is a good friend of my wife's and I, monsieur, and we do not wish to see her hurt. Your insistence upon dredging up the past—indeed, your very presence here—distresses her greatly."

Jared knew that what Grimaud said was true, yet he was enraged by the man's high-handed attitude. His expression showed no trace of the emotion roiling within him, just beneath the surface. The only indication of tension, in fact, was the clenching and unclenching of his fists as he considered his next move. If Grimaud thought that this little interview would dissuade him, then he was wrong. It made him all the more tenacious. He'd hold on, just a little while longer.

"Much as I should like to oblige you," Jared replied at last, sarcasm cutting through his words, "I have not yet fulfilled my purpose here. I intend to find Lucien Valmont and reunite him with his daughter."

"And I tell you again, monsieur—Valmont is dead."

"If the man who hired me is not who he purports to be, then I still must find him—for Dellie's safety."

"Dellie will be safe enough in our care," Grimaud said, smiling. "You may rely upon it."

The waiter arrived then and set Jared's plate before him. Before the young man could withdraw, Grimaud motioned him closer and whispered something to him behind his hand. He disappeared, returning only a few seconds later with a tall bottle and one glass, which he set down beside the plate.

Jared turned to Grimaud, his brow raised cautiously.

"With my compliments," came the reply. "I know you have a fondness for whiskey."

This Frenchman had an annoying knack for pointing up his weaknesses, but Jared was determined not to let it unsettle him.

"I am surprised that you've taken such an interest in me," he said but did not move to touch the bottle.

"Ah, but you are an immensely interesting character, Monsieur Durant. Dellie has told me that she believes you've come to St. Gervais after pirate's treasure," Grimaud continued. "An amusing theory, but I, myself, do not take you for such a fool."

Jared was surprised to hear of Dellie's suspicions, but he put his own feelings aside for now as he faced off against Grimaud. The man's sharp eyes were fixed on him, awaiting a reply. Jared sensed a change in him. The Frenchman was far too anxious. Could it be that, despite what he'd said, Grimaud half believed in the existence of the treasure himself?

"Who would not be intrigued by such a legend?" Jared said then, baiting him. "A pirate's cache—the most fabulous of the treasures of the Spanish Main—gold and jewels—a priceless emerald. If I had come after such treasure, Monsieur Grimaud, I'd stand to gain a lot more than you could offer me."

At this Grimaud got to his feet and said in a voice that was too quiet to alarm the other patrons, but deadly in its tone nonetheless. "Then you *are* a fool, monsieur, and you will fail, as have all those who've come before you."

Jared leaned back in his chair, unable to stifle the broad grin that spread across his face as he watched Grimaud storm off. The facade had cracked. Beneath that polished manner Aristede Grimaud wasn't so sure of himself after all. Calling for the waiter, Jared sent the bottle of whiskey back—unopened.

The Valmont family cemetery was only a few minutes' walk from the stone cottage in the shade of a sheltering tropical grove, surrounded by a decorative wrought-iron fence. Here, on a ridge overlooking the sea, Dellie's mother had been laid to rest, alongside all the other Valmonts—dating back to Lucien, the French pirate. The headstones were barely visible now amid the tangle of vines and tall grasses, and Dellie promised herself each time she passed by that soon she would take the time to clear away the encroaching vegetation.

Lately, though, all her hours were taken up by her work. Under the direction of Dr. LeClerc, Dellie had nursed Amelie's little son for a week, and as the child regained his vigor, so the mother's confidence in Dellie grew. Ere long the boy was healthy once more: his brown eyes round and bright as he clutched at Dellie's earrings, his lungs powerful as ever as he squalled to be fed. Following this success, more and more of the former slaves came to her for her medicines. She continued to help Dr. LeClerc, too, and soon the days were so full that she had little time to think on her own troubles. But this afternoon she decided to keep her promise to clear the cemetery land.

With an apron tied over her gray cotton skirt and her gold curls tucked beneath her tignon, Dellie climbed the path from the cottage to the ridge. There was a brief struggle with the rusty hinges on the gate before she finally forced her way in. Armed with a machete, she began to hack away at the thick-stemmed lianas and the clumps of fibrous grasses, stopping only occasionally to throw back her head and catch the fresh breeze that blew in off the water.

She grew more pleased with her efforts as each marble marker was uncovered, as if somehow by her actions she were restoring what had been lost that night so many years ago. The Valmonts were a part of this island; and with one hand resting on the weathered stone of Lucien, the first of their line, Dellie vowed they always would be.

The afternoon sun was waning, casting the last rays of golden light out on the waters, when she finally finished her task. She bent to retrieve the dipper from the pail she'd brought along and took a long drink of water. It was only tepid now, but it soothed her parched throat nonetheless. Next she soaked her handkerchief, wrung it out, and mopped the perspiration from her brow before at last shutting the rusty gate behind her and starting home.

She'd not gone far when she became aware of a rustling in the thick foliage nearby. It might have been only a gust of wind that had blown up suddenly or an animal foraging, but as she continued on her way along the path, the movements, augmented now by the sharp snapping of twigs and what sounded like the whisper of a human voice, followed her as she went. With fear rising in her, Dellie dropped her water pail, tightened her grip on the machete, and turned back in the direction from which she'd come.

"Who's there?" she called out. "Why are you following me?"

Suddenly it was very still, and after several anxious moments had passed, Dellie wondered if she'd only been imagining the sounds. Perhaps spending the afternoon in a graveyard had unsettled her more than she'd realized. The trees were casting long, deep shadows across the clearing now. She was still in sight of the headstones and the wrought-iron fence that hemmed them in. Could it have been whispers of the past she'd been hearing?

Not daring to draw breath, she took another step toward the dense thicket, where she'd heard the last bit of rustling. A scream cut the air.

CHAPTER
19

After tying off his horse's reins on a low-hanging branch, Jared crossed the field to the point at the land's end and focused his attention downward to where the ocean was breaking on the rocks. He'd done a lot of thinking after Grimaud left him at the inn, and he'd reached a decision. It was pointless to go on searching for Valmont. It really didn't matter what had become of the man; what did matter was Dellie. Maybe he'd lost sight of that for a time, but now Jared had to admit the truth. He was in love with Dellie Valmont.

It wasn't a selfish emotion. All along he'd wanted only what was best for her, even if it meant cutting himself out of her life. If her father had been alive, reuniting them would have been best, but now he had to accept the possibility that that might not happen. What was he to do, then? Go back to St. Louis? Forget her and leave her in the care of her friends?

That might be for the best. Reaching into his pocket, Jared drew out Kirby's medal, still hanging on its tattered bit of ribbon. The last time Jared Durant had tried to care for someone, it had cost them their lives. But no, he admitted finally, that was too harsh a judgment. For all these years he'd held himself accountable for his brother's death . . . and his mother's. He saw now that he wasn't to blame, though. Kirby Durant had always been willful. Even if Jared had argued against his joining the army, the boy would likely have run off to enlist, and Fate would have played out its hand. Jared clutched the medal tightly in his fist for a long moment, and then, coiling his arm, he cast it into the sea.

Then he drew himself up determinedly. No, he'd not go back. He'd make up for the wrong he'd done Dellie and make her love him—even if he couldn't offer her what a gentleman could. She didn't seem to care about such things anyway, he told himself, and yet his mouth twisted into a wry smile as a thought came to him. He wondered if she'd think any better of him if he could manage to find that legendary pirate's treasure that Grimaud had accused him of being after.

From this vantage point Jared could see the old overseer's cottage where Dellie was living. The afternoon sun had disappeared beyond the trees, which were casting ragged shadows across the quaint, little house. Around its foundation a profusion of exotic flowers blossomed, and vines of scarlet-trumpeted flowers had attached themselves to the sturdy fieldstone walls. Wherever Dellie chose to live, it seemed, a lush garden sprang up around her. Perhaps she was happy living here all alone. It was an improvement over her rooms at Madame Celestine's, at least.

All at once he heard a shrill cry carried on the wind. It sounded like a child's voice—or perhaps a woman's. "Dellie!"

He sprinted across the field to the cottage and drew up suddenly. Standing on the flagstone stoop, he listened again. There was only silence. He reached out toward the door. It creaked open at his touch.

"Dellie?" he called out.

There was no answer. Apprehension rose in him as he crossed the threshold into an empty parlor. Nothing seemed amiss until he reached the kitchen. There, jars and bottles had been tossed out of the pantry and lay shattered, their contents seeping out onto the tile floor. Crocks were overturned, and bunches of dried plants that had been hanging from the ceiling rafters were torn down and strewn about. Someone had sought to destroy Dellie's entire stock of medicines. And then he saw the blood . . . trailed across the floor, splashed on the wall, and dabbed, as if it were paint, into a picture of a coiled serpent.

"Dellie!"

Jared felt his chest constrict until he could barely draw breath. He never should have left her on her own, he told himself, remembering now the look of terror he'd seen on Mama Tess's face as she lay dying, pleading with her final breath for him to protect Dellie.

Jared searched the house again and the grounds outside, but there was no trace of Dellie at all. He went back into the kitchen, closing his eyes against the bloody scene to consider his next move, but in the end he could only stand there numbed, not knowing if Dellie was alive or dead.

Like a covey of birds flushed from their hiding place, half a dozen children fled the thicket as soon as Dellie drew near. They were village children: freckled boys in knee pants and little girls in ribbons and ruffled frocks, and they squealed and screamed as they ran. "It's the witch! Run, run away and hide!"

A lopsided smile formed on Dellie's lips. All this while she'd been afraid that someone was stalking her, and it had been only children, out for an afternoon's excitement.

Her desire to live alone on her family's land, to use her skills to help the poor islanders, her success in gaining their trust—all of this had had a price after all. The villagers, those proud citizens of France who lived comfortable lives in their tidy, little homes, had made up their minds about her: She was a witch.

But surprisingly, this didn't upset her. All those years in New Orleans she'd dreamed of coming home so that she might become what she was meant to be—a young lady of refinement. Now, though, she realized that that sort of life was not what she wanted, not at all. Here she had a purpose in her life; she was useful and needed. With that thought she remembered what Mama Tess had told her: "Where you're needed, that's where your home ought to be." Let them call her a witch.

She had already turned to go when she heard the whimpering from behind a dense hedge of nightsage. Turning back, she went to the spot and found a little girl, who couldn't have been more than five years old, crouched there. The child's pinafore was smudged with dirt, and she'd lost one of the ribbons from her plaited brown hair.

"Hello there," Dellie said softly, trying not to alarm her further. "Have your friends run off and left you?"

The child's eyes were wide with fear. She did not move nor speak. Dellie noticed then that the girl was staring at the machete she still held in her hand. She dropped it at once. "I won't hurt you. I promise. I was cutting the tall grass in the graveyard, that's all."

"Are you a witch?" the little girl asked her in French.

"Do you think I am?" Dellie said, returning the question in kind.

"Witches are old and ugly and eat children for their supper. Pierre told me so. He's my brother, and he knows everything. But you're not old . . . or ugly."

"And I'd much prefer a nice piece of fish for my supper,

or a roasted chicken," Dellie said with a grin. "You can go, if you're still frightened. I won't stop you."

With a mournful wail the child clutched at her skirts, and her tears flooded over. "I don't know the way," she admitted, between choked sobs.

"What's your name, little one?" Dellie asked then.

"Annette."

"Pleased to make your acquaintance, Annette. My name is Dellie, and I'd be happy to show you the way back to the road, if you'd let me. Can you find your way from there?"

Dellie held out her hand, and after a long moment of hesitation, the child took it up and nodded. Retrieving her belongings, and with Annette's small hand in hers, Dellie started up the path once more.

"It will be dark in an hour or so," she warned. "You be sure and go right home."

Annette bobbed her head in reply, and a shiver shook her tiny frame.

"Are you still frightened?"

"Only a little."

"When I was a little girl, I was often afraid to go to bed at night. My papa would sing me a special lullaby, about a child who was lost. It always made me feel better. Maybe if I sing it for you—"

"Oh, please do!"

And so Dellie began to softly hum the melody while they walked along. She was surprised that the words came so easily. After all these years, she'd not forgotten. . . .

"Ere you reach the mountains blue, tarry on the windward shore. There beneath the golden hill, I shall wait, my little one.

"Do not fear the dark-as-night, nor the garden made of stone. I shall light you on your way. There you'll find me, little one."

"That's a funny little song," Annette told her, "but it sounds pretty when you sing it to me."

"You've never heard it before?" Dellie replied, surprised to hear it. "I guess I heard it so often, I thought everyone knew of it."

"Whose house is that?" the child asked as they drew near the stone cottage.

"That's my home. I used to live in a big white house, but it burned down long ago, so now I'm living in the cottage. Do you like it?"

Annette nodded. "It looks like a fairy-tale house with the pretty flowers all around. Don't you get lonesome, though, out here all by yourself?"

"Sometimes I do, but I have friends who come to see me. Maybe you'll come and visit one day."

"I'd like that."

"Now let's sing my lullaby once more, together this time. Maybe if you know the words, you can sing it to yourself on the way home, so you'll not be afraid."

And so Dellie taught her new friend the "lost child" lullaby as she walked her down to the road. Annette squealed as they reached the clearing, for she could see her companions spread out along the road in the distance. They were calling her name.

"So they've finally come looking for you, have they? It seems you won't be going home on your own after all. Best run along now," Dellie said and waved after her as she sent her on her way.

It was only a short walk back to the cottage, but Dellie loitered the whole of the way, staring in the twilight at the path beneath her feet and musing. She'd enjoyed the company of the little girl, Annette, and she wondered now if it would be half so pleasant to have children of her own to raise.

As Dellie stepped onto the flagstone walk that led to

the kitchen door, she was drawn into a possessive embrace. The feel of familiar arms around her made her instinctively drop her head onto his broad shoulder as he whispered into her ear.

"I should never have left you alone. I thought that— that you—"

Dellie looked up into a pair of warm golden eyes, and in spite of all the words of warning that came rushing to her thoughts, her heart leaped with joy as Jared Durant bent to press a kiss on her half-parted lips.

"Come away with me now, Dellie, tonight! I'll protect you. I'll see that no one hurts you ever again."

Dellie thought she was dreaming. She studied him for a long while, realizing now how many times she'd lain awake at night and tried to conjure those beloved features in her mind: those eyes that could pierce her heart with only a glance, the rugged lines that time and experience had etched upon his face, the threads of gold in his tousled brown hair. . . . He was dressed for riding now, his dun-colored trousers tucked into tall leather boots, a double-breasted linen shirt unbuttoned at the throat for comfort's sake.

Dellie choked back a sob. God, how she wanted to believe him! But she remembered too well how he'd lied to her before. What was he after this time?

"I don't need protection," she insisted as she dragged herself out of his arms. "From anything or anyone—but you."

Turning on her heel, she went inside and shut the door, pressing her back against it to shut him out.

CHAPTER
20

It was dark within the cottage. Dellie gasped in surprise when her foot struck a glass jar that was lying on the floor, and it clattered across the tiles. She stepped cautiously through the kitchen, certain that something was amiss. When at last she reached the table, she struck a match to the candle that she kept there, and her heart sank.

The soft circle of light illuminated a portion of the scene at once. Carrying the candle in her trembling hand, Dellie began to examine the rest of the room. Jars had been smashed, crocks overturned, and contents strewn about. Everything had been destroyed . . . all her bottles, the medicines, the herbs she'd collected. Who would have done such a thing? Mischievous children, perhaps?

But then she spotted the bloody drawing of a serpent that had been painted on her wall and the headless carcass of yet another fowl lying in a corner. Now she understood why Jared had been so unnerved, why he'd taken her at once into his arms, stammering and promising to protect her. He'd come in here and seen the blood. He'd called to her, perhaps, and when she did not reply—what must he have imagined then?

A warmth of rekindled affection was rising in her, but she sought to quash it. It could only bring her more pain. As her gaze swept the destruction in the room once more, anger welled up, shutting out all else. "How much more poultry must be sacrificed before this mambo . . . this voodoo priestess realizes that I will not be frightened off?" Dellie shouted as she tried to rub the blood off of the wall with one corner of her apron.

She was not aware that Jared had followed her in until she heard him speak. "What's all this about, Dellie?"

"I came to help the people here with my medicines," she began to explain but without turning to face him, "only to find them in the grip of a terrible evil, their lives ruled by a person they believe to be the embodiment of this serpent."

Jared came up behind her, settling his hands on her shoulders. "It's a part of their beliefs, their religion. You can't fight that."

"I have no quarrel with their religion, but when I learned that children were dying, that this voodoo doctor of theirs had caused more than one death through sheer ignorance, I knew I had to do something . . . and I have."

"By convincing them that you're a witch?"

Dellie pulled free of him. After setting the candle back on the table, she knelt down on the floor and began to gather up those items that could be salvaged. "Let them believe what they will. These past few weeks more and more people have been coming to me with their ailments. Dr. LeClerc comes here in secret to help with those things beyond my skills, and the people do not seem so afraid as they once were."

"So the voodoo doctor has retaliated with all of this,"

Jared said, waving his arm, "hoping that it will scare you off."

"Such tricks won't work on me," she replied. "I'm not the sort to be frightened by a little chicken blood."

Jared found himself smiling at her. He was reminded of the young woman who'd drawn a knife on a drunken sailor in the French Market. Her spirit was one of the things he loved best about her. But he could not forget how he'd been accosted and beaten when he'd loitered outside the home of Marie LaVeau in New Orleans. These voodoo folk were not people to be trifled with.

"This was only a warning," he told her. "When this voodoo doctor sees you'll not be scared off, you could be in real danger. I can't let you stay out here all alone."

Dellie looked up from her place on the floor, blue eyes flashing. "I'll not leave this house," she insisted.

Dellie glared at him, but she could see that he was adamant . . . and she was being stubborn. She had to admit that his suggestions were practical, and so she put her anger aside and accepted his help.

Together they washed down the walls, mopped up the congealing medicines that had spread across the tiles, and swept away the broken glass. Barely a word passed between them as they worked, each afraid a careless comment might bring an end to their uneasy peace.

In the end it was Jared who took the risk. "It will take more than your medicines, you know, to cure the ills of the freed slaves on this island," he noted. "The men need jobs that pay decent wages so they can provide for their families. The land hereabouts is fertile enough, and if it were managed properly, I don't doubt that everyone could benefit."

Dellie turned a skeptical eye on him. "You sound more like a farmer than a gambler."

"I haven't always been a gambler, Dellie," he said,

sounding hurt. "I was born on a Virginia tobacco plantation. Whitehill was my family's home for three generations, and if Fate hadn't intervened, I'd be managing it
now."

Dellie regarded him, surprise plain upon her face. She
was struck by how little she really knew of this man. How
could she think to understand him at all when his entire
history was blank?

"Tell me about your life, Jared," she said, to prompt
him further.

And so he did. Without offering excuses or trying to
gain her sympathy, he related to her the events that had
shaped his life before they'd met: of his family's plantation
and his days as a cadet at West Point before his father's
debacle, of his years as a soldier, his brother's death, and
his work for Allan Pinkerton in Chicago.

Dellie sat back on her heels and listened intently, having
lost all interest in scrubbing the floor. "You must have
hated your father for what he'd done," she said.

Jared nodded but would not meet her eyes. "I'd had my
heart set on a career in the military," he told her, "but
when he died, all my dreams died, too. I had to come
home to take care of my mother and brother."

"Quite a responsibility for a boy of seventeen."

"Far more than I could handle, I'm afraid. I managed
for a time, but in the end, I proved no better a man than
my father."

Dellie knew then that she'd misjudged him. Jared Durant was much more than a riverboat gambler and certainly too complex a man to be solely motivated by greed.
Perhaps her heart had been right about him all along.

"You did all that you could," she said, defending him
since he would not defend himself. "You cannot go on
blaming yourself."

Jared came to her with his hands outstretched. She gave

him hers, and he pulled her to her feet. "I know that now. That's why I came here to see you tonight. You have to listen to me, Dellie. Nothing else is important now, only you and me."

Could it be true? Did he care for her? Dellie's hopes were buoyed by what she read in the depths of his golden eyes. As his one arm coiled about her waist to draw her against him, a light breath caught in her throat. "Jared," she began, "I'm sorry if I—"

Dellie's appeal was cut off by a heavy pounding on the door. Her eyes widened. Had whoever had done this damage to the cottage come back?

Jared's arm tightened across her back. "Who's there?" he called out.

Dellie could barely hear the breathless voice above the pounding. "Help me . . . please."

Pulling herself free, Dellie ran to the door with Jared close on her heels. She knew that voice. She pulled open the door, and Solange Grimaud collapsed into Jared's arms.

CHAPTER
21

"Solange!" Dellie cried. "What is it? What's happened?"

"She's done it!" the girl cried, gasping for breath. "She's put a fix on me. I know she has, Dellie, and now I'm going to die."

Jared carried Solange into the parlor, settled her in the rocking chair, and then brought the lamp from the kitchen and put it up on the fireplace mantel. Dellie stood over her friend, her uneasiness building as the lamplight illuminated Solange's condition. The girl was ghastly white, her breathing was shallow, and she was shivering, even though her brow was damp with perspiration.

"What are you saying?" Dellie asked her.

"Madame Dominique," the girl replied, her eyes wild. "She's evil, Dellie. She hates me and wants to see me dead."

"Calm yourself, *chère amie,* and tell me how you got here," Dellie said, putting two fingers to the girl's throat to feel her pulse.

"I took a horse from the stables. I had to get away from that house. She's doing this to me, with her voodoo powers. You saw that awful charm she put in my bed. You know it's true."

"Have you told your husband about this?" Jared wondered.

"He only defends her," Solange told him, her voice weakening. "She is his mother. Oh, I'm cold. I'm so cold, Dellie."

Dellie turned to touch Jared's arm. "Please fetch a blanket from the bedroom to wrap her in. My medicines have all been destroyed. We've got to get her to Dr. LeClerc at once."

"What does this mean?" Jared asked her. "How could she think that voodoo is responsible for what's happening to her?"

"Someone's been trying to frighten her. She thinks it's Dominique. But this isn't voodoo; it's poison."

There was no time to waste. Jared placed the barely conscious Solange over the front of his saddle, Dellie took Solange's mount for herself, and they rode hard, hoping to reach Marigot and the doctor before it was too late.

When they arrived at LeClerc's house, Jared lifted Solange in his arms to carry her while Dellie ran to the door and pounded until Madame Rousseau let them in. She directed them to a guest bedroom and explained that the doctor was having his dinner, but she'd fetch him at once.

Jared settled Solange onto the bed and stepped back while Dellie brought the basin from the washstand to the bedside table and poured a little water into it. Sitting on the edge of the bed, she began to bathe Solange's face with a cloth she'd dipped in the basin. The girl's thrashing had increased now, and her color had taken on a sallow tone that was frightening to look upon.

Dr. LeClerc joined them shortly, and his face was grave as he examined his patient. "Where did you find her?" he asked.

"She rode out to the cottage after Dellie," Jared explained. Knowing there was nothing he could do, he went to stand at the far end of the room.

The doctor picked up the water glass from the night table, filled it with water, and stirred in a powder he'd drawn from his bag. "In her condition it's a wonder she could ride at all. Has anyone told her husband of this?"

"No!" Solange cried out suddenly, gathering enough strength to reach up and cling to Dellie's arm. "Don't tell them; don't tell anyone where I am. She'll find me then. I know she will. Oh, please, Dellie, please. I'm so frightened. I don't want to die."

"Hush, now," the doctor ordered. "You're not going to die." He gave her the glass he'd been holding, helped her to drink the draft, and then looked to Dellie for an explanation. "What's going on here?"

"She claims it's voodoo—" Dellie replied.

LeClerc's eyes narrowed, and he motioned her away from the bedside.

"We both know better than that, don't we?" he said to her. "You see the odd color of her skin, the dilated pupils. Her breathing is labored, and there is a scarlet rash erupting on her face and arms. Surely you've seen such symptoms before, or at least heard them described. What would you call it?"

Dellie regarded the doctor, surprised that he should consult her at all. Looking back to the place where her friend lay, she hesitated and then told him in a whisper: "Poison."

He nodded. "Exactly so. A highly toxic vegetable poison. I've given her a compound that has been known to counteract the effects, but I cannot say if she'll be strong enough to overcome the shock that's been done to her system."

Jared, who'd been listening all along, approached the

pair now. "How could this happen?" he wanted to know. "Was it tainted food? Could she have unknowingly ingested some poisonous substance? What I'm asking you, Doctor, is: Could this be an accident, or did someone mean to do harm to the girl?"

LeClerc seemed flustered when faced with such a possibility. "Why, I— How can I answer such a question?"

"Solange has the notion that her mother-in-law wishes her ill," Dellie put in cautiously.

"Dominique Grimaud?" the doctor replied, incredulous. "I'd not think so. She's a very sick woman, hardly capable of such an act."

Though Dellie was not convinced of Dominique's guilt herself, her suspicions were growing. This was no accident; someone clearly meant to kill her friend. "You heard Solange just now," Dellie protested. "The last time she came to see me, she voiced these same fears, but I didn't take her seriously; she's always been excitable. But as I think on it, Doctor, she showed signs of illness even then."

LeClerc pulled at his chin, considering this. "If death were to result from a poison administered in small doses over several weeks, the signs would be less apparent, the cause more difficult to ascertain, but I cannot credit that such a diabolical mind is at work here."

"Well, I can," Jared said to this. "If there's somewhere we could talk, Dr. LeClerc, I have something of importance I'd like to discuss with you."

Jared and the doctor went out to have their discussion, and Dellie stayed with Solange throughout the evening, while the girl writhed beneath the bedclothes, held fast in the grip of her delirium. Calming her with words of comfort, Dellie bathed Solange's tortured body with cool water and stroked her fevered brow with a gentle hand. After a time she grew very still, barely drawing breath, and Dellie feared the girl would not have the strength to endure.

Dr. LeClerc was in and out of the room, but it was after midnight when he returned to examine Solange and finally told Dellie that the crisis had passed. Solange had proved more tenacious than anyone could have guessed.

"You're certain that there's no more danger?" Dellie asked him.

"She needs only to rest now," LeClerc explained. "And so do you, Dellie. Monsieur Durant will take you home. There's nothing more you can do for her tonight."

"But if she wakes . . . She trusts me, Doctor."

"She won't wake for hours. Go on, now. Come back in the morning, if you like, after you've gotten a good night's sleep."

At length Dellie agreed. She and Jared left LeClerc's house and headed toward the livery, where Jared had left the horses. "It's too late to ride back to the cottage," he said, slipping his arm through hers, "and besides, your house has been made a shambles. You wouldn't be comfortable there. I'll get you a room at the inn for tonight."

Dellie thought this a practical solution. They changed direction and made their way in and out of the soft circles of light cast by the streetlamps, through the deserted streets of Marigot toward the inn.

"It's been a hectic evening," Jared said to her. "Are you still worried about your friend?"

"Dr. LeClerc has assured me that there's no reason to worry. Solange is safe—for the present."

He laid a hand over her arm. "You believe that there is still danger, though."

"I didn't mention it before," Dellie began, "but Solange found a voodoo doll in her bed a few weeks ago. Someone in that house was trying to frighten her. You didn't see her face when she spoke of Dominique. She was terrified.

Even tonight in the midst of her delirium she cried out in fear of the woman. I'll even admit that I thought there was something odd about Dominique myself, after I'd spent that night nursing her after she'd burned her hands. She has a penchant for voodoo, Jared. I saw some amulets in among her things."

"Do you think Aristede Grimaud is aware of his mother's . . . peculiarities?"

"I don't know," Dellie said, frowning, "but if he doesn't know, I intend to tell him, first thing tomorrow."

When they reached the inn, Jared roused the desk clerk, but he returned to the chair in the lobby where Dellie was waiting for him, wearing a solemn expression. "There are no rooms available for this evening," he told her. "If you like I could walk you back to LeClerc's."

"No," she replied, rather too quickly. What she wanted now was to spend more time with Jared, to acquaint herself with this man she was seeing clearly for the first time.

"Have you any other friends in Marigot?" he asked.

"None that I could wake at this hour," she told him.

"Well, that leaves my room," Jared said. "Now, if I were any sort of gentleman, I'd give it to you and find other accommodations for myself, but quite frankly, I don't relish the thought of spending the night at the livery, bedded down with the horses."

The next move belonged to Dellie. "I'd not think of putting you out," she told him plainly. "I'll make myself comfortable enough in an armchair, so long as you've a blanket to spare. I'm certain we'll manage. We are friends, after all, aren't we?" She met him with an arched brow.

"Yes," Jared replied, grumbling. This was not at all the arrangement he'd had in mind. ". . . Friends."

How long would this game they were playing continue? Jared gave off looking out the window, paced the floor from door to windows and back again, until at last he dropped down into the armchair that Dellie had claimed for herself, pulling off his boots and leaning back to cross his arms over his chest.

When he'd brought Dellie here, he'd wondered aloud if there was anything she needed, and she'd asked him to send down for hot water to wash with. Then, as soon as it arrived, she'd disappeared behind the folding screen and proceeded to undress.

Jared had watched, mesmerized, as she'd tossed her garments over the screen, one by one. He'd tried to turn his attentions out the window, but the the sound of water splashing into the basin drew him back again, and now, installed in the chair, he found he could not look away.

The room was dark but for the chamberstick that Dellie had carried with her to wash by, and standing near it, she was casting a shadow upon the fabric of the screen. It was an enticing silhouette, mirroring each lush curve of that perfect body, beckoning to Jared with each sinuous movement.

As she bent over the washstand, she poured a stream of water over her hair and let it trickle back into the basin. She continued with the ritual, taking each step with aching slowness, as if she knew he was watching her, caressing the cake of soap between her two hands, spreading lather across her skin in ever-widening circles, propping one long leg up on the stand as she washed it and then the next, inching the slender curve of one arm upward so that it just came into sight above the screen, before slipping down again. To Jared, it was exquisite torture.

The heady scent of jessamine and carnations wafted across the room, triggering powerful memories in him of that night on Gallatin Street, when he'd made love to Dellie for the first time, and then he could stand it no more.

Jared sprang from the chair with all the agile grace of

a cat, crossed the room in two long strides, and pushed aside the screen. Dellie looked up, with only a hint of surprise on her face.

"I don't want to be just your friend, Dellie," he said, his voice fading as his gaze drifted downward.

He was distracted for a moment by the brilliant droplets of water scattered like jewels across her breasts. His need of her was a compelling force, there was no doubt of that, but he was determined that she should know that his desires were not purely physical ones. Squeezing his eyes shut, he summoned as much patience as he could muster.

"I've told you about myself, about the kind of life I lead, and while it cannot compare with what some might offer you, I want you for my wife. If you'll have me, I swear that somehow I'll find a way to make for you the sort of life you deserve."

He looked at her again, and there was a long silence as he tried to read her thoughts in the depths of her sapphire eyes.

"I know that you believe I've betrayed you somehow," he went on, growing uneasy at her silence, "but all that I've told you . . . about your father—"

Dellie pressed her fingertips over his lips to silence him. She did not want to hear any explanations, not tonight. He'd said all that she needed to hear, and she wouldn't risk spoiling things now. Edging closer, she molded her slick body against him, dampening his linen shirt.

"Will you?" Jared repeated, pulling in a ragged breath as he sought to maintain his composure. "Marry me, I mean?"

She wound her arms about his neck, drawing him down to her. "Yes," she whispered.

Before another moment could pass, Jared kissed her to seal the bargain. She'd agreed to be his wife when she surely could have had a better man. He could scarcely believe it.

Dellie had almost forgotten how easily she could lose herself in his arms. It would be a pale and lonely life for her without Jared Durant, she knew now. Every fiber of her being told her that they belonged together. "We're a pair, you and I," he'd said to her once, in his gambler's parlance, and it was true. Her fingers fluttered downward, and she began to undo the buttons on his shirt slowly, one at a time, then slipped her hands inside to knead the hard, muscled plane of his chest. With anticipation rising in him, Jared shrugged off the tangled shirt. Threading his fingers through the dampened strands of her hair to cup her head, he lowered his mouth across hers and relished once more the ripe sweetness of her lips.

His kiss was more potent than any wine. With her head spinning, Dellie reveled in the feel of his body, the lean, hard limbs pressed against hers. Her hands lay still for only a moment, though, before she eagerly sought to unfasten the buttons of his trousers. Soon these, too, had fallen to the floor. Jared kicked them aside and caught her hands up in his.

An anguished sigh escaped her then as if she'd suddenly decided that all this might be only a dream, and if she did not act, she might lose him in an instant.

"Easy, my sweet," he entreated, his voice deepened with desire. "We've all the time in the world."

Despite his calming words, the blood pounded against his temples, and a film of sweat shone on his brow. Even the cadence of his breathing quickened as he fought to curtail his own desires, just a while longer, that he might see to hers.

Bent on pleasuring Dellie now, his hands edged down to the small of her back, fingertips trailing in the rivulets of water dripping from her unbound hair, curving lower still to probe the soft inner flesh of her thighs. A cry broke from Dellie's lips as his open mouth slid down across the column of her throat to the soft swell of her breasts, where he captured the peak of one pink nipple and teased it with his tongue.

All at once her knees buckled, and catching her under the arms, Jared lifted her up, pressing her back flat against the wall as he stepped closer. In response, Dellie wrapped her long legs around him, drawing him in, sheathing him in velvet softness. He groaned in reply and began to move deep within her, carefully controlling the rhythm of his thrusts as he watched the fires consuming her, wanting to make certain that her needs, too, were satisfied. It was not long, though, before the driving urgency of his body finally took over, casting them both over the edge and into the fiery blaze. Held fast in one another's arms, they sank down onto the carpet, and the stillness of the tiny room gave way to the rasp of their labored breathing.

Late that same night Dellie and Jared sat cross-legged on his bed. A bowl of fruit, which had been left in the room by the management, lay between them, and they were attacking it with hedonistic abandon.

"What must you have thought when you came into the cottage this afternoon?" Dellie asked thoughtfully, reaching to brush a shock of hair out of his eyes.

He cut a sliver of papaya with his clasp knife and offered it to her, and his brow creased. "I imagined the worst, of course, and I blamed myself."

"You needn't have worried. This isn't the first such warning I've received, and I'm certain it won't be the last, so long as the people keep coming to me with their ills. It's some old voodoo woman, probably white-haired and toothless, who's either lost her skills or never had any to begin with. Of course, she resents my intrusion and would like me to run off, but I won't go, and I intend to find her and tell her so myself."

With that, Dellie popped the fruit into her mouth. Licking the juice from her fingers, she reached next for a banana, peeled it, and broke off a piece to share with Jared.

He watched her in amazement. Her eyes were alight with excitement; her full lips still reddened from his kisses. As she leaned across the bed, the sheet she'd been wearing slipped perilously low, revealing the swell of her breasts to him, and he felt his desires stirring to life once more.

No other woman had ever had this kind of power over him. She was, indeed, a witch, and he was just the man who could vouch for it. But it was this one amazing woman who had proved his salvation, in the end. For the love of Dellie Valmont, he'd dragged himself from the gutter and healed the wounds he'd been inflicting upon himself for years.

"I'm still worried for you, Dellie," he said. "You can't know what went through my mind when I saw that bloody serpent on the wall."

"Theatrics, that's all it was, you know."

"I thought you were dead until I heard you coming up the path—singing, no less."

"I met a little girl in the jungle. She was afraid of me, at first, but we made friends soon enough. I showed her the way home and taught her that little song to sing so she wouldn't be frightened on the way."

Pulling the bedsheet closer around her, Dellie leaned back and proceeded to sing, in French, the lullaby just as she'd sung it to Annette.

"A pretty little tune," Jared commented, "but I can't quite understand the words."

"It's about a lost child. My father sang it to me often when I was a girl."

She began to translate for him, line by line. "Ere you reach the mountains blue . . ."

With each new line the creases in Jared's brow furrowed deeper. "Is something wrong?" she asked him.

"No. It's just so . . . unusual, don't you think?"

"I've never thought about it that way. One of the few clear memories I have of my father is him sitting by my bedside, singing me that song. It's silly, I know, but I feel comforted when I hear it."

"Sing it for me once more, will you—in English?"

And so she did, though not quite understanding what his interest was. Perhaps it was only the sound of her voice, for when she'd finished, he smiled and leaned over to kiss her.

"Oh!" he exclaimed then, as if he'd suddenly remembered something important.

Unfolding his legs, he rose and went to the bureau, where he drew something out of the drawer. Padding back, he settled himself back on the bed and put her silver card case in her hands.

"You left this behind in Celestine's cabin. One of the cards was . . . damaged," he told her, a wry smile twisting on his mouth, "but I've mended it for you."

"Thank you," Dellie replied, staring hard at the chased initials on the lid. Regardless of how she'd felt when she threw it away, it was good to have back this heirloom, her only tangible reminder of her mother.

"You asked me once if you could read the cards for me," Jared said next. "Now that we've decided on our own future, I don't think I'd mind so much to hear what your tarot has to say."

Dellie met his eyes, brimming now with golden warmth. She prayed that he could not see the uneasiness that lurked just behind her thin smile. Was their future really so certain? As much as she would like to believe it, and in spite of all they'd shared tonight, Dellie had yet to learn why Jared had lied to her about her father and the true reason why he'd come searching for her in New Orleans in the first place. She was almost afraid to hear his answers, and she was certainly afraid of what the cards might tell her. "Tomorrow, perhaps," she said.

She put the tarot cards aside and did not touch them until much later, after Jared had fallen asleep. Rising from the bed, she picked them up and went to sit before the table by the windows, where moonlight flooded in through the open shutters. She shuffled the tarot deck, reacquainting herself with the feel of it, closing her eyes in deep concentration. The very first card she turned made her heart drop. It was just as she'd feared. On the table lay the Eight of Swords—a card of betrayal.

CHAPTER
22

Dellie was not at all surprised when she awakened the next morning to find herself alone. Jared Durant had taken what he wanted and left without a word, but this time Dellie only sighed; she had no one to blame but herself.

She rose and dressed quickly, hoping to leave before the memories of the night before, so fresh in this room, could inundate her. She gathered up her cards, and on the table beside them she noticed a pad of paper and a pencil upon which several lines had been scribbled. It was not any sort of message, though, only the notes one might make when deep in thought. There were drawings, too, intersecting lines and boundaries that formed what might have been a map. Dellie read the words he'd penned there and was left more confused than ever.

"Mountains . . . northwest shore . . . hills of gold . . . graveyard . . ."

As she stared again upon the map he'd drawn, the realization came, and all her doubts returned in a rush. He'd been using her. She saw now that he'd only been after that damned pirate's treasure. All the rest of it had been lies.

*   *   *

There was no time for Dellie to feel sorry for herself; she had a score of her own to settle. She had to see that Aristede Grimaud understood what a dangerous woman his mother was. And so she rented a horse from the livery and rode out to see Aristede.

When she arrived, Henriette, the maid, informed her that Monsieur Grimaud was out riding in his fields. Dellie asked then if she might see Madame Dominique, deciding to face her directly with her accusations. The girl took her upstairs, then scurried off, leaving her standing before the closed door. Dellie knocked. "It's Mademoiselle Valmont," she called out. "May I come in?"

There was no reply. Perhaps Dominique was resting. Dellie opened the door and peeked in. The shutters were closed against the bright morning light, and the room within was cloaked in shadow. Dellie could see no trace of damage from the disastrous fire. Furniture had been replaced, walls repainted; all was good as new.

At last she spotted Dominique, sitting in a chair beside her bed. She wore a long wrapper decorated with a Chinese floral pattern of vivid reds and golds. Her long black hair was wild and unkempt, her complexion sallow. The age lines seemed to be etched deeper in her face today, and perspiration was beading her brow. She was staring straight on, seemingly unaware of Dellie's intrusion—her eyes wide and vacant.

"How are you feeling today, madame?" Dellie asked cautiously as she advanced into the room. "Are your hands nearly healed?"

"Nearly so, but I am ever plagued by these headaches," Dominique replied, sounding quite lucid. "They grow worse by the day. If not for my medicine, I don't know what I should do."

Standing near the woman's chair now, Dellie could see

a spoon and a water glass on the table beside her, and the open bottle of morphine powders. Her brow arched in surprise. "Where is the nurse Dr. LeClerc sent for you?"

Dominique frowned. "I made Aristede send her away. She was doltish and ill-bred and slow as molasses."

Dellie doubted whether any of those accusations were true. More than likely the girl had been following Dr. LeClerc's orders to wean his patient from her dependence on the "medicine" and had thus earned Dominique's displeasure.

"I can't believe that Aristede would ignore the doctor's orders," Dellie said, almost to herself, but she put a smile on as she addressed Madame Grimaud. "I imagine your Sophie must be pleased with this turn of events. Where is she this morning?" She half-expected to see the old woman lurking in a corner somewhere, spying.

"She's gone to the village, I expect," Dominique said. "Poor dear! She has so much to do." Shaking her head, she became more agitated. "There's so much to do."

Dellie reached out a hand to Dominique's arm, intending to calm her, and was startled by a hissing sound. Looking down she saw, coiled in the woman's lap, a large brown snake. She gasped and drew back her arm at once.

"No need to fear, mademoiselle," Dominique said, and her dark eyes glittered with an unnatural excitement as she stroked the snake's smooth head. "He's a pet. A gift from my Sophie. He's quite harmless, I assure you."

Nevertheless, Dellie could not help the shudder that ran through her as the creature rose up and began to entwine itself around Dominique's arm.

"You can't be afraid of snakes, you know, if you plan to live on this island," she went on, her smile seeming to taunt. "They're everywhere. Why, you never know when you'll wake to find one sunning himself on your front steps."

Dellie regarded her in disbelief. Could this be a reference to the drawing she'd found on her flagstones? But how could Dominique know about that? Had she a closer connection to the voodoo priestess than Dellie had imagined? Or was it only a coincidence?

"Who made those voodoo charms of yours, madame?" Dellie asked, deciding to confront her before she was distracted again. "Were you responsible for leaving one in Solange's bed?"

"*Moi? Non,* mademoiselle. But you'll know soon enough. I can promise you that."

With this the woman tossed back her head and began to laugh. The sound was wild and unearthly, and her exotic looks were charged now with a deep malevolence. Dellie decided that she was seeing Dominique Grimaud's true nature for the first time. It frightened her. The woman sitting here before her was no gracious plantation mistress, no helpless invalid. She was evil and calculating . . . and fully capable of poisoning her son's wife or mounting a campaign of hatred designed to drive Dellie off the island.

Dominique Grimaud, a voodoo priestess? The possibility sent a chill through Dellie. But if it was true, it would explain so much. No wonder the people feared her wrath; the Grimauds wielded great power on this island. No wonder she could no longer cure the ills of her people; the drugs she was taking had begun to affect her mind.

And if all this were true, was Aristede aware of his mother's dual personality? Dellie thought on the affection he'd shown for Solange, on all the kindness he'd shown her, and decided that he could not have known. Perhaps, she surmised, Sophie had been helping to keep the secret all the while, to protect her mistress. But now Dominique's addiction to the morphine was slowly revealing the dark side of her personality.

Aristede must be told of this at once, Dellie decided,

and turning on her heel, she quit the room, with Dominique's laughter still ringing in her ears.

She had scarcely reached the bottom of the landing when Aristede Grimaud strode through the front door, tossing his riding crop onto the table in the foyer. He looked shaken and went at once to take up Dellie's hands.

"I've just come from Dr. LeClerc's," he told her. "I must thank you, Dellie, for all that you've done for my wife."

"I need to speak with you at once, Aristede," Dellie replied.

He led her into the parlor and settled her on the sofa. Despite the early hour, he poured himself a glass of sherry, drank it down, and then came to sit beside her.

"My poor Solange," he said, wringing his trembling hands. "My poor sweet child! I wanted to take her home at once, but the doctor would not let me. He said she could not be moved yet. How could such a thing happen?"

"It had to be someone here in the house," Dellie said.

"No. I cannot believe it. That one of my own people—"

"Worse than that, I think, monsieur."

From out of her pocket Dellie drew the voodoo doll Solange had given her. As she laid it in Aristede's hands, she carefully explained about the poison, though he had likely heard that story from LeClerc. She went on to relate Solange's fear of Dominique, and each of the incidents at the stone cottage, and finally her meeting this morning with his mother. When she began to draw her conclusions, though, and all but accused Dominique of being the voodoo priestess, Aristede got to his feet and started pacing.

"I assure you that my mother's interest in this 'voodoo' is harmless," he said. "The headaches she suffers from have made her desperate for a cure. Surely you can understand that. I myself have purchased all manner of useless potions at her request, afraid to deny her any chance for relief. But believe me when I tell you that she has not the stamina to carry out the destructive attacks you've described. And my mother has never expressed anything but affection for Solange."

Dellie was touched by his devotion to his mother, but he had to understand. "Yet Solange *is* afraid of her," she reiterated.

Aristede had come to stand beside the mantel now, beneath the portrait of Dominique. Dellie could see that, despite what he'd said earlier, he was digesting her words. She went to lay a hand on his arm. "I'm telling you all of this so that you can help her," she told him. "Some of the drugs she is taking have begun to affect her mind. Dr. LeClerc saw it happening. Surely he warned you after the fire in her bedchamber."

"She seemed reasonable enough when I talked to her afterward, and she's been so quiet lately. I suppose I thought that the old doctor was exaggerating the dangers."

"Go up and see her now, Aristede. Speak to her, and then we'll talk again. If you find her well, then I shall apologize and take back all that I've said."

Aristede headed for the door, shaking his head. "I still cannot believe that she could manage this, all on her own."

When he left her, Dellie paced the length of the room twice with his words still ringing in her ears, before she realized what was bothering her. All on her own? Of course Dominique had not acted all on her own; she'd had Sophie's help.

And then suddenly Dellie remembered the snake. Dominique had told her that it was a gift—from Sophie . . . Sophie, the wizened old servant who had disliked Dellie from the start. Perhaps it was not Dominique, after all, who was the voodoo queen. Could Sophie be the one who'd left those warnings for her at the stone cottage? If so, then poor, sick Dominique had been no more than a pawn, and Dellie had done her a great injustice.

She had to know for certain, before she could face Aristede again, and so she left the house to ride back to the village, where she hoped to find Sophie and learn the truth.

It took several hours of combing the streets of Marigot before Dellie located the old woman. She caught sight of her at last, coming out of one of the small shops near the waterfront, carrying a market basket, brimming with goods. Rather than confront her in the midst of the busy street, though, Dellie pulled a shawl up over her head and, keeping her distance, began to follow her. Once they were out of the village and on the road to Aristede's, she reasoned, they could have a good, long talk.

When Sophie reached the crossroads, however, instead of heading home, she turned northward, away from the Grimaud lands. Dellie had no choice but to follow, and before she'd realized it, Sophie had veered off the road, heading for the ruins of the old Valmont sugar mill. Once there she disappeared inside.

Dellie approached the ruin cautiously. The circular stone tower was still standing, but the roof and the giant wood and sailcloth vanes, which had once served to catch the ocean winds and turn the rollers to grind the cane stalks, were gone now. They'd been burned in the fires set on the night of the slave uprising.

Dellie's heart was pounding as she edged nearer to put a hand on the wall, made up of smooth fieldstones chinked with mortar. It was in this very building that her father had lost his life. What could be here now that would interest Sophie?

The sun was sinking behind the trees; it would be dark

soon. Dellie thought she heard the whinny of a horse somewhere nearby, but after several minutes the sound was not repeated, and so cautiously she peered in the wide entrance.

Through arched windows set high in the walls, streams of sunlight filtered down to the floor of the tower, illuminating those fallen sections of charred timber that had not yet rotted away. Dellie stepped inside to get a better view, reluctant to draw breath lest she be discovered. At the sound of movement within she quickly secreted herself behind a stand of debris and pulled her skirts closer around her, trying to ignore the occasional skittering sound of vermin crossing the flagstones beneath her feet.

From this hiding place Dellie could see Sophie quite well. The old woman was bent over a crate, where she had just spread a cloth. Drawing items from her basket now, she set them on the makeshift table: a flagon of water, a loaf of bread, and a thin wedge of cheese. This was certainly a dismal setting for a picnic.

"That's all for you today," Sophie said, and only then did Dellie realize that there was someone else in the tower.

Craning her neck, she spied the figure of a man sitting on the floor. He was shackled by the legs to an iron post that had once supported the mill machinery. He wore a gentleman's dark waistcoat and trousers, but his linen shirt was torn and grimy.

Dellie's heart began to beat faster. Who was this man, and why was he locked up here in this ruin with a half-crazed old black woman for a jailer?

"How much longer am I to be kept here?" she heard the man say.

Sophie did not reply, only gathered up her things and turned to walk away. Dellie stepped back into the shadows as the old woman passed her by, but instead of following her out, she kept her eye on the chained man, determined to learn his secret.

Expelling a long sigh, he got to his feet, and dragging his length of chain, he limped awkwardly toward the wall, where a lantern was hanging from a peg. He struck a match to light it, and as he turned around, Dellie saw his face.

She would have sworn her heart stopped beating for an instant as a tingling started at the roots of her hair and then spread through her entire body. She knew this man.

"Papa?"

He shaded his eyes and strained to see across the room. "Louise? Is it you, Louise?"

Heedless of the danger, Dellie ran to throw herself into his arms. "Papa, it is you! You *are* alive! But what have they done to you?"

Dellie pressed a hand to his cheek, gently touching the long scar which ran down the right side of his face. He looked older, to be sure; his black hair was threaded with silver and his features softened with lines, but he was alive!

"Ma chère! Ma Chandelle!" he said, choking back a sob as he folded his arms about her, but then promptly released her. Wiping the tears from his eyes, he said: "You must leave here immediately. Do you understand?"

Dellie would not listen. "We must free you from these chains," she replied. "Is there a key hereabouts? Have you seen one? If not, we'll have to break them somehow."

Lucien Valmont grasped his daughter by the shoulders and made her look into his eyes. "Listen to me. You must go. There is great danger here."

"What? From a crazy old voodoo woman, you mean? I'm not afraid of her, and I'll see that she's punished for what she's done."

"She is not alone in this," Valmont replied just as Dellie turned to see Aristede's tall form looming in the doorway.

She felt the relief spread over her at once. He must have been following her all afternoon. Yes, that was it, and now he was here to help. She ran to take up his hands. "Oh, Aristede, thank heaven you've come. It's my father. He's here. He's alive!"

Aristede's hands closed tightly over hers. He was still dressed for riding, with his shirtsleeves rolled to the elbow, and as Dellie looked down, she saw, for the first time, that there was a tattoo on his forearm. It was a coiled serpent.

"How good of you to come, *ma chère,*" he said. "This will be a very important night for us all. And you've saved me the trouble of going to fetch you."

CHAPTER
23

A full moon rose high over the Blue Mountains that night, lighting up the landscape bright as day. The steady beat of the Rada drums echoed in the deep valleys and carried far across the isle of St. Gervais. Not far from the old Valmont mill the people had gathered for the evening's celebration. A bonfire illuminated the sleek, black bodies of the dancers in the clearing and the trio of drummers, intent on their rhythms. Each reveler took a generous swallow from the bottle of tafia liquor as it was handed around and joined in the chants to their voodoo gods. Dominique Grimaud was nowhere to be seen, but there beside the drummers old Sophie stood watching, with arms folded over her bosom.

It was Aristede, though, who was clearly the central figure of this group. So there was no voodoo priestess, after all—but a priest. He addressed his followers now with arms akimbo, wearing an amulet made up of bones, the firelight gleaming on the bared planes of his chest.

Dellie stood before him, golden hair tumbling over her shoulders, in the thin, white shift she had been made to wear, her arms outstretched, a white candle burning in each upturned palm.

"You will join our circle tonight, *ma chère,*" he said to her. "The people will know that there is but one master to serve on this island, and you will kneel before him now."

He looked like the devil himself, standing there with sparks flashing in his dark eyes. Dellie raised her chin and met those eyes with a defiant stare. As if he'd anticipated her reaction, Aristede pointed to the place where her father stood nearby, bound to the trunk of a tree, to remind her that his fate lay in her hands.

"Aristede, why?" she asked him then, her expression softening, her voice only a whisper. Perhaps he could still be reasoned with, perhaps a part of the man she'd called her friend still remained somewhere within.

"Why?" he repeated, his voice rising up. Harsh laughter rumbled deep in his chest, and then he turned back on her. "You ask why I should desire vengeance? You have seen for yourself the pitiful woman that my mother has become. But do you know that she, like so many others on this isle, was destroyed solely by the greed of the Valmont family?"

Dellie was silent as she waited for his explanation. It came soon enough. "When she was only sixteen, my mother was seduced by your grandfather, Philippe Valmont. He told her that he was tied to an invalid wife, whom he did not love. He told her that she was beautiful, and he promised her many things. He was dashing and handsome, the most powerful man on the island, and she was young and naive. She believed."

Hot candle wax was dripping onto the palms of Dellie's hands, but she dared not move. Aristede took a step closer to her and continued. "He used her, and then when he'd tired of her, he tossed her aside—*comme bagasse, comme ordure!* Using his power, he banished her to the other side of the island. The shame has been eating away at her all these years. Even after she married my father, even after I was born, she was haunted by her past. When I was old enough, she told me the story. I vowed that very day to exact retribution from the Valmonts somehow."

The rhythm of the drums pounded in Dellie's brain as the heat of the great bonfire sapped her strength, and so she was not surprised when she began to hallucinate. She saw now, repeated quite clearly before her eyes, another voodoo ceremony—the one she'd witnessed as a child on the night of the revolt. She saw an exotic woman, wearing her brown snake like a shawl and a young man with dark hypnotic eyes, inciting the revelers. Shaking off the vision, Dellie looked up into that same pair of eyes.

"You!" she spat. "You started the fires and instigated the slave uprising."

"Exactly thirteen years ago—to the day," Aristede replied, lifting his head proudly. "We gather here tonight to celebrate."

"You use these people and their voodoo religion for your own evil ambitions," she accused.

"There is nothing I would not do to destroy the cursed Valmont name."

"And what of me?" Dellie said boldly. "Will you slit my throat as you would one of your goats or chickens and convince these people that it was a necessary sacrifice to satisfy their voodoo gods?"

"Nothing quite so bloody," he said in a low voice that was no less threatening. "You're far too lovely for such a fate. You'll bring me at least as much pleasure as my mother brought Philippe Valmont."

Standing very close now, he began to caress her outstretched arms, pressing them down to her sides and causing the candles she'd been holding to roll off into the dust, where they were extinguished with a hiss. Dellie dared not meet his eyes for fear she'd be caught up once more in his hypnotic spell.

Feeling the leather cord hanging like a magic charm about her neck gave her courage, though. When she'd been given this shift to put on, no one had watched her dress. They had not seen her take the sheathed knife she always wore tied at her waist on a leather thong and slip it around her neck beneath the shift. It hung there, her last resort, if only she could find a way to use it.

Aristede's hands were exploring in intimate fashion now, and Dellie feared that soon he'd discover her secret. She pushed herself back from him, and as he grasped the shoulder of her garment, the fabric began to tear.

"No!" she heard her father cry out, writhing against his bonds.

"Don't worry, old man," Aristede told him. "I won't shame your daughter. Once my little Creole wife has been dealt with—and properly this time—I intend to marry Dellie Valmont. Don't you see the humor in that? She will be my wife, and then all your lands—everything the Valmonts have on this island—will rightfully belong to me."

"So it was you who poisoned Solange," Dellie said, not bothering to hide her disgust. "You never cared for her at all."

"I was grateful for the handsome dowry her father offered, and she was a pleasant creature at times, but she's long since outlived her usefulness. I'm done with her. Now I intend to have you."

Taking hold of Dellie's hair, he snapped her head backward, and his mouth closed ruthlessly over hers as if to affirm his possession.

"No!" Lucien Valmont shouted. "You cannot do this. She is your own blood, for God's sake!"

Suddenly the drumming stopped, and silence spread

over all. The revelers' attention had been drawn to Valmont now, and their whispers and looks of astonishment confirmed that they recognized this man; they'd all thought him to be dead. Aristede released Dellie, and she stumbled backward, gasping for air.

All eyes were on Lucien Valmont. He straightened himself up as best he could, and though still bound, he began to tell his story. "It's true that your mother was my father's mistress," he said, "but the rest of what you've been told is a lie. My father did not send Dominique away because he'd lost interest, but because he wanted to spare her shame. Your mother was carrying a child, *his* child. Do you understand what I'm telling you? You are my half-brother, with as much Valmont blood running in your veins as any of us."

Aristede shook his head. "You're lying, old man. You're only trying to save your child."

"Ask your mother's maidservant," Valmont responded, tossing his head at Sophie. "She was there; she knows I speak the truth."

Aristede turned on her. "Sophie? He's lying, isn't he? Tell me, Sophie. I want the truth now!"

The old woman would not meet his eyes. "As a child, your mama had heard stories about the Valmonts' pirate treasure and the power of the Eye of the Serpent," she admitted. "She believed in it, every word, and wanted that stone for herself, and so she took Philippe Valmont to her bed, hoping to get it from him."

Sophie shook her gray head. "After she'd given him everything, she still could not make him tell, and she grew to hate him for it. The hatred poisoned her mind. And later she came to believe her own stories, I think."

Valmont picked up the story. "My father built her a home, and even after she'd married an itinerant artist to give her son a name, he continued to support them. On his deathbed he told me this and made me promise that I would see that Dominique and his child lacked for nothing, and until the day that Fate swept me from this island, I did as he'd asked me to."

Aristede's face was drawn and washed of color. "My whole life, all of it, has been built on lies. I would have done anything—" he stammered. "It was for my mother, can't you understand?—for the wrong that had been done her."

All the while Dellie had been putting together the pieces. It was Aristede who'd been after her in New Orleans, Aristede who'd come up to her room on the day of the hurricane and left his man there, the man who'd beaten her and murdered her beloved Tess.

"Murderer!"

In one quick move Dellie unsheathed her knife and lunged for him, intending to bury it, to the hilt, in his heart. He would pay for what he'd done. Aristede stepped backward, amazed by her reaction, and the tip of the slender blade only grazed his face as he sought to escape her. Blood began oozing from the long, jagged cut, and he swiped at it before he reached out and caught her arm, trying to wrest the knife from her.

Desperate now, Aristede struck her with the flat of his hand, and she fell backward in the dust, losing her grip on the knife. As he knelt over her to retrieve the weapon, a shot rang out.

Into the circle of firelight stepped Jared Durant. "Touch her again, friend, and I'll kill you before she gets the chance."

With his revolver pointed at Grimaud, Jared came forward. Grimaud's eyes shifted beneath his heavy brows as he assessed the situation. He was still on his knees, but his body was tensed, his hands clenched in two tight fists, as if he were anticipating another move toward the knife.

Jared seemed to sense his intentions. "Don't bet your life against mine," he warned. "I've the damnedest luck you'll ever see."

At this he retrieved the knife, which he carried to Valmont and used to cut the man loose. "I knew you were somewhere on this island," he told him. "But I didn't guess where until I heard the drums."

"I've been Grimaud's unwilling guest now for more days than I care to recall," Valmont explained. "I am surprised to see you, monsieur. Come all this way after me and my daughter, have you?"

"When I take on a job, I like to see it through to the end," Jared said, handing him Dellie's knife. "Oh, and I believe this belongs to you as well."

Reaching into his pocket, he drew out a length of heavy gold chain. Suspended from it was a medallion of wrought gold and at its center, an enormous emerald.

"The Eye of the Serpent," Valmont said in disbelief, as he held it up and green shards of light spilled from it in kaleidoscopic fashion. The crowd was awed.

"So it does exist," Aristede said. "Mama was right."

Dellie, having finally recovered from the blow she'd been delivered, clambered to her feet to rush into her father's arms. He fastened the emerald necklace around her throat, and she turned to glare at Aristede Grimaud. "She'll never have it; it belongs to the Valmonts, do you hear?"

Her breath was drawn in ragged sobs. "A curse on you and your wicked mother!" she spat. "May you perish in flames as you would have had us do."

Dellie's words hung on the air for a long while, and then slowly the people who'd gathered here to worship their voodoo gods began to disperse. They all seemed to freeze in their steps, though, as Sophie pointed to a red glow on the horizon. "Look there!" she cried.

Aristede knew at once what it was. "Mama! She's set the house afire again! We must hurry!"

He went to the place where his horse was tethered and when he'd mounted, he looked back to his people. Not one of them made a move to follow. He rode off into the night . . . alone.

Safe in the circle of her father's arms now, Dellie could see that Jared Durant had been telling her the truth all along. She'd run from him more than once, afraid of being hurt, but no more. She turned to tell him so, but he had disappeared.

CHAPTER
24

Leaning on the rail of her father's steamship, Dellie plucked a flower from the bouquet she'd found on her breakfast tray and watched a gray curl of smoke edge upward from the island into the dawn sky. Word had just reached them. The Grimaud estate lay in ruins, burned to the ground by Dominique's hand. Those who'd been there said that Aristede had rushed headlong into the burning structure, heedless of the warnings his men had shouted after him, bent on rescuing his mother. But in the end both of them had perished in the flames.

Dellie shivered at the sound of those words. How could it be that those hateful words she'd cursed them with had come so swiftly to pass? Was there some power, after all, in the stone the ancient Indians had called the Eye of the Serpent? Or was it only coincidence?

"If you can drag yourself away from that rail, my dear," her father said as he drew up behind her, "I'll take you ashore. It's a beautiful morning."

"I can't help thinking that it's my fault, all of what's happened, because of what I said."

"Nonsense," he chided. "These events were set into motion long before you were ever born. Such a tragedy was bound to happen."

Dellie scattered a handful of petals into the water, admitting to herself that the tragedy wasn't all that weighed on her mind. More than anything, she wanted to know what had become of Jared Durant. Had he saved their lives last night and given her father the emerald only to assuage his guilt so he might make off with the rest of the treasure? She couldn't believe that, not now. Yet he was gone, just the same, and it was quite possible she'd never know the truth.

With a wistful sigh Dellie smoothed the skirt of the familiar blue linen dress that she'd come by secondhand and turned from the rail, intending to take her father's arm.

"I'd be happy to escort Mamzelle Valmont."

At the sound of the deep, familiar drawl, Dellie looked up in surprise. There before her stood Jared Durant. His sandy brown hair was swept back from his brow, his face clean-shaven. He looked unusually respectable in his gray frock coat and silk cravat and with a waistcoat of sober hue. Dellie was so pleased to see him that she nearly threw herself into his arms at once, but caution made her hesitate.

"Monsieur Durant," her father acknowledged, "I believe you have already met my daughter, Louise. *Ah, pardon,* I have forgotten again. She wishes to be called Dellie now."

"Dellie and I are . . . acquainted," Jared replied, but only she noticed the glimmer in his eye as he emphasized the word.

"Mr. Durant and I have been discussing his fee for services rendered," her father explained. "He is interested in acquiring some of our property and settling here on the island."

Dellie's brow went up in surprise.

"It is a paradise," Jared replied, his gaze settling on her. "Don't you agree, mamzelle?"

"*Mais oui,* monsieur, a paradise," she told him, rolling the word slowly over her tongue.

Jared had hired an open carriage, and so he and Dellie went out to look over the property. For most of the drive Dellie only listened while he spoke of fields that ought to be planted in cane and those which should be reserved for tenant farming, of the agricultural techniques he planned to study in order to increase yields, and of sites which could provide adequate housing for workers. She had to admit that she was impressed with his knowledge . . . and his enthusiasm. But he was so polite, so formal, almost as if they were strangers. Did he simply wish to forget all that had passed between them?

Suddenly Jared pulled up on the reins, and the carriage rocked to a halt. "You know I didn't bring you out here just to see the land, Dellie," he said, almost as if he'd been reading her thoughts. "I spoke to your father at length this morning, but it wasn't all business. I told him that you and I plan to be married, and he's given us his blessing. If you've changed your mind, though, you've only to tell me now."

With those words all her fears melted away. Capturing his rough face in her two hands, Dellie made him look into her eyes and then silenced him with a kiss. Drawing back, she smiled. "What? And give up a chance to be the wife of the one honest gambler in all of New Orleans?"

"When your father first sought me out," Jared began, a serious expression overtaking him now, "I was certain he'd put far more trust in me than I deserved. He said that I was a man who understood honor, a man of skill and determination, a man like him—but, in truth, I was none of those things. I was foundering; I'd lost sight of my own future, until I saw it—here in your eyes."

"I do love you, Jared," Dellie replied. "You are all of those things Papa said you are . . . and more."

Jared reached up to smooth the pale tendrils of her hair that the wind had ruffled. "And now I have something special to show you," he said with a gleam in his eye.

They left the carriage and walked arm in arm until they neared the wrought-iron fence and marble stones of the Valmont graveyard. "I discovered it purely by accident," he explained. "After your father disappeared, I began to search the island for him, but without success. And then one day I heard you singing that lullaby. The words struck me immediately as odd. I wondered if perhaps your father hadn't made them up to point to some secret hiding place of his, but when I followed the letter of the words, I found something else entirely."

"Old Lucien's treasure?" Dellie guessed. She could not help but be pleased to hear that it was her father that Jared had been searching for and not the pirate's treasure. "Well?" she prompted. "Do you propose to show me exactly how you managed to discover what has eluded generations of Valmonts?"

Jared pretended to think on it a while, and she scowled at him. Then taking her arm, he led her out to the edge of the ridge, where together they looked down on the ocean.

"It's been there all along, you know, in the words of that lullaby. You told me that your father taught it to you when you were a child, as I'll wager he learned it from his father and he from his. Old Lucien the pirate was a sly one. Rather than commit his secret to paper, he put it in the words of a song, a harmless little child's tune. Somewhere along the line, the true meaning of the words got lost—even though they continued to be handed down through the generations."

"Look now," he directed her. "It's exactly as the song says: 'Ere you reach the mountains blue, tarry on the windward shore.' "

He pointed out the curve of beach below them. " 'There beneath the golden hill'— Do you see it? That outcropping of limestone—the way the sun glints off of it? Stand anywhere you like along this ridge, and it looks the same. Now if you want to go on, we'll have to climb down."

"*If* I want to go on?" Dellie echoed. "I'd not miss this for anything."

Jared kept a firm hold on her arm as they descended by the precarious path, but she could not deny the excitement building in her as she scrambled over the rocky outcroppings with brambles tugging at her skirts.

Once they'd reached the shore, they sat down on the rocks to remove their shoes and stockings. Jared shed his elegant jacket and rolled up his trouser legs, and advised Dellie to tuck her skirts up into her waistband to keep the hems from dragging in the wet sand.

When they had prepared themselves, they padded barefoot along the shore, just out of reach of the lapping tide, until finally they reached a spot where the beach curved away. They were faced on the one side with a wall of sharp, black rock and only water before them.

"Now where?" Dellie wondered as the brisk sea wind blew in a salty spray that took her breath away. But she found that the discomforts of treasure-hunting did not affect her in the least; she was truly caught up in this adventure.

"Just follow me," Jared instructed.

Taking her by the hand, he led her out into the surf, keeping close to the shore. Once around the line of jagged rocks, Dellie saw that they were standing directly beneath the limestone bluff. Here, the sunlight reflecting off the water was blinding. Shading her eyes with her hand, she cried out when at last she saw where Jared was headed.

"I see it now!"

There was a tidal pool, sheltered by the rocks, and just beyond it a cave that had been cut into the base of the cliff by the advancing tides.

" 'Do not fear the dark-as-night,' " Jared said now, his voice echoing as he led her into the wide mouth of the cave. It took a moment for Dellie's eyes to adjust to the sudden darkness.

Above their heads she noticed the leaflike projections that hung down, formed by the action of sediment and water over hundreds of years. Here and there on the floor of the cave, too, these odd stone formations rose up. " 'Nor the garden made of stone,' " Dellie chimed in.

" 'I shall light you on your way,' " she continued, looking about for the next clue.

Jared drew her on, pointing upward where a small hole near the top of the cave let in a shaft of light. Following the path of that shaft through the darkness, they came at last to a massive chamber. Sunlight streamed in from somewhere above and along one wall, a waterfall tumbled down into a deep, clear pool in the center of the floor.

Dellie drew an astonished breath. "Oh, Jared. It's beautiful!"

He led her on to the far end of the chamber and showed her the remnants of a rock wall that had been built to conceal a niche in the limestone. Behind it lay an old sea chest, and when Jared lifted the lid, Dellie's jaw dropped open.

Inside, just as the old legend had promised, were what must have been the most spectacular objects of the pirate's booty: a service of golden plates, stacked one upon the next, goblets encrusted with gemstones, a vase wrought of silver and inlaid with colored glass, dozens of pieces of jewelry and lengths of solid gold chain.

Jared was no less awed as he looked upon the treasure a second time. Lifting one of the goblets, he was surprised at its weight and turned it in his hand, admiring the workmanship. Each of these objects was a work of art. No wonder old Lucien had set them apart.

Behind him Jared heard a splash, above the sound of the cascading waters. He turned to see that Dellie had shed all of her clothes and dived into the pool. Now she was engaged in swimming its length. A smile twisted on his lips. What sort of woman was this he'd chosen for his wife, who found more interest in a spring-fed pool than a chest full of pirate's treasure?

Reaching the shallows, she came to stand beneath the waterfall, stretching like a cat as she let the water rush over her.

"Can we keep this place our secret?" she called to him. "And come here together, again and again, just you and I?"

Jared threw back his head and laughed aloud. "Have I told you today that I love you, Dellie Valmont?"

In reply Dellie dived back into the water and crossed the pool to the place where he was standing. He held out a hand to her, and when she took it, he caught her up in his arms.

"What will you do with all your riches, my love?" she asked.

"I may have been the first to stumble on this pirate's cache," he replied, "but I've brought you here to claim it for your father. By right, the treasure belongs to the Valmonts." He reached to brush the droplets of water from her face as he lowered his mouth onto hers. "I've already found mine."